CW00591940

U-BOA'
ATTACK ON AMERICA

Ian T Gwilliams

First published in 2023 by Blossom Spring Publishing
U-BOAT 931 ATTACK ON AMERICA Copyright ©
2023 Ian T Gwilliams
ISBN 978-1-7392955-3-0
E: admin@blossomspringpublishing.com
W: www.blossomspringpublishing.com

For Jane, Craig, and Kayleigh

Many thanks to Dave, without his encouragement and cajoling I would never have completed this novel.

AUTHOR'S NOTE

This novel is a work of fiction, yet all the weapons, technology, science, and timelines are factual.

The line that exists between fact and fiction can be tenuous, and sometimes blurred.

If the actions depicted in the story had actually taken place, the course of the war may have turned out differently, and the world as we know it today might be a different one.

CHAPTERS

	PROLOGUE
1	FRANCE
2	ORDERS
3	BERLIN
4	REICHSTAG
5	SURTR
6	BARRACKS
7	FLOWER
8	PEENEMÜNDE
9	PHOTO
10	MOSQUITO
11	DEPARTURE
12	CHANNEL
13	TORPEDO
14	MESSAGE
15	ATLANTIC

16   CROSSING

17   SEARCH

18   DRIVE

19   VIRGINIA

20   RICHMOND

21   DELAWARE

22   WASHINGTON

23   CAPITAL

24   MARBLES

25   LAUNCH

26   ESCAPE

27   FJORD

28   DISPOSAL

        EPILOGUE

PROLOGUE

The basement room of the science block felt like a furnace, but it wasn't the ambient temperature that was making Professor Klein sweat as he worked. It was the unwanted presence of the three men standing in the far reaches of the room. It was the unannounced arrival of the unwelcome guests, a complication he could have done without. The preceding three weeks for Klein and his team had been so stressful, he could count the hours of sleep he'd managed to grab on one hand. This wasn't the way to work; mistakes could be made at this late stage, consequently delaying the project, and that just couldn't happen. Any set back now would not be tolerated; he had been told that more than once in a very uncompromising way.

He could hear the three of them talking quietly amongst themselves but couldn't catch anything that he could distinguish. They had walked in ten minutes ago, a superior arrogance surrounding them. Now, they were standing at the back of the laboratory not saying anything to him or the other two of his associates. His colleagues dared to take surreptitious glances at the men, who were all dressed in pitch-black uniforms, lurking back in the shadows.

The scrutiny of the men present was an undesired burden. What they hoped to achieve by coming here today wasn't clear. The task should be completed on time, as requested.

He may have felt a little easier if it had just been the two SS officers standing there. He'd met them before when the project was first discussed with himself and his superior, Professor Steiner. But the appearance of the diminutive figure with them took the significance of the situation to another level – one that went right off the scale.

Unconsciously, he mopped the sweat from his brow again with his handkerchief, replacing it in the top pocket of his white lab coat. His levels of anxiety were now reaching critical levels. Looking directly at the third visitor as he worked was not an option. Of that, he was sure.

He concentrated on the task, his hands working autonomously as he carefully placed the foot-long steel canister in its place on the left of the device and fitted the two clamps which would hold it in place, before connecting the set of four thin copper pipes leading from the canister to a steel manifold block situated to the left. A set of a dozen multi-coloured wires ran from the top of the canister and spiralled on to the main control panel. These would receive the signal from the master switch, which was located inside a wooden box about the size of a small suitcase, all designed to be as compact as possible, yet able to perform the intricate task asked of it.

His colleagues were putting the final touches to the larger wiring harness for the main control systems on another table to his left. Both usually chatty men were as quiet as mice, probably not daring to breathe, never mind say something in the tense atmosphere that permeated the room.

He jumped as one of the officers spoke.

"All good and on time, Professor?" It was more of a command than a question. He summoned up some courage quickly and turned to face them, beads of sweat still trickling down from his bald head. His glasses were misting slightly, so he removed them before replying, absentmindedly rubbing the lenses on the cuff of his white lab coat.

"Yes. I can say with confidence we will be finished by

the end of the week."

It was then that he inadvertently caught the eye of the man who stood in the middle of the two SS officers. He looked directly back this time. Klein was transfixed but didn't say a word or acknowledge the man looking back at him. The second or so of the stare seemed an age to Klein, a cold chill running down his spine as their eyes locked in that moment. Then, suddenly, the central figure broke his gaze and walked directly out through the open doorway, quickly followed by his two sycophants.

The lab technicians and the professor looked at each other, all breathing an audible sigh of relief as they heard the click of jackboots on the tiled floor slowly fading as they retreated off down the corridor and away.

CHAPTER 1 – FRANCE

The submarine was gliding effortlessly on the surface at a speed of fifteen knots, cruising through the cold, unusually calm, dark waters of the North Atlantic as it sped east towards its home port on the French coast on March 8th, 1944. The captain of U-931, Ahron Roth, looked up to the stars in the cloudless sky. He could find some solace from the enormity of the heavens above no matter where he found himself, on land or sea. Towards the stern from his position on the bridge, the phosphorus green glow that trailed out from behind the sub's wake was being highlighted by the light of the full moon and was giving away the sub's position to any eagle-eyed air crew searching the waves for them. The white crested bow waves, with their silvery troughs, lapped around the front of the boat and then fed down along the sides. The sound of splashes against the hull was the only noise he was aware of right now.

He was reflecting on a poor hunt during the six weeks since they had left the relative safety of Saint-Nazaire and their fortified submarine pens. Only two hits on merchant ships, an estimated twelve-thousand tons of allied shipping either sunk or severely damaged. They had received the signal telling them to cut short their mission and return home a few days ago. Why they had been told to go back so early, he had no idea. It was no use speculating; it could be one of many reasons. He'd learned a long time ago not to question the bureaucracy of the Kreigsmarine and its admirals. He sighed long and deep, his heart heavy. At this late stage of the war with the allies surely about to launch a second front in Western Europe at any moment, Nazi Germany's defeat was only a matter of time. And yet, he and his experienced crew had sent more merchant seamen to a watery grave over the last sixty-five days. It didn't sit right with the young veteran from Hamburg.

It had seemed so very different back in those heady days of '38 when he received his commission. As he now stared out into the gloom, he fingered the Iron Cross that hung around his neck, given to him in October '39 by Admiral Doenitz for his service aboard U-47, at a ceremony on the quayside at Brest. The oak leaves that also adorned the medal were awarded eighteen months later when his own achievements as a U-boat commander warranted them. The Knight's Cross with diamonds that he once coveted seemed a very distant goal now, though.

The North Atlantic battle ground had been like a feeding frenzy for the German navy in the early years of the conflict. When Roth had enlisted back then, he started out as a naive young man in the wolf packs of the Kreigsmarine. How times, and indeed he, had changed. Gone now was the self-assured, proud German whose strongest quality was his unnerving knack of doing the right thing when it mattered the most, ultimately keeping his crew safe over the years. He now questioned the path that Nazi Germany had taken during the last five years and how far down that path Hitler was prepared to go – possibly the destruction of the fatherland?

He wasn't the tallest commander in the service at one-hundred-and-seventy-three centimetres, or indeed at twenty-seven the oldest around, but what he lacked in height and age he more than made up for with his commanding presence and stature. His thick red hair and matching beard, now both tinged with an early onset of grey, together with his ice-cold blue eyes gave him a Nordic appearance. His peers admired and respected him for his achievements, especially for one so young, but also his strength of character when dealing with his superiors, many of whom were watching his progress in the service with a critical eye, as was the case for all young captains; they were just waiting for him to make an error of judgement for which they could bring him to task. He knew only too well that one wrong move on his part either at sea or on shore could well mean being dead in his 'iron coffin' at the bottom of the Atlantic, or him being put in front of a firing squad. It would be a swift end to someone who didn't toe the line or speak out in front of a superior who wasn't going to stand for his impertinence. Many fine officers had been shot for the slightest of infractions; you may be put in front of a firing squad because you were deemed a threat, or perhaps for the simple fact you had dared to question a superior officer's order. Now was a time to obey without question or suffer the consequences.

His mind drifted again. This time it was to Ginette, a nineteen-year-old French girl he knew back in port; a girl he'd become attached to. The thought of their liaison filled him with dread and desire at the same time. Their association was dangerous, especially for her. In his mind's eye he could see her long brown hair and hazel eyes, her figure so slim, her stature so tiny and frail, yet a character so strong at the same time.

Over the years he'd frequented brothels with his crew in many ports across Europe; it had become a distraction, a brief interlude from the horrors of war, he'd told himself. He'd even visited the one in town, the 'Blue Watch' bar with its French girls who did not concern themselves with whom they slept. He had grown tired of listening to women who didn't care about him or his troubles so long as they got paid. Now he would only get drunk when he went to town with his comrades. Recently he had begun to despair more and more about his future and the war's end, but then he had the chance encounter with Ginette.

He'd walked past the fruit and flower stall so many times before as he'd strolled through the town but hadn't even registered its presence, barely looking at the two-wheeled wooden cart with its striped green and white canopy. It was difficult to miss, what with the two contrasting, large, bright, yellow-painted spoked wheels with red handles. But, one day, he'd noticed this young woman standing to the side of the cart and had stopped to stare at the Gallic beauty. She'd stared back, but only briefly, which had taken courage on her part. Here was a French girl having the audacity to look at a German officer. That first look drew her to his heart in an instant! He walked away that first day, glancing back like a lovesick teenager as he did so, but he returned the next day. He strode up to the stall and bought a bunch of flowers, which he immediately presented to her; she blushed, and their romance started.

Because of his duties, and the long patrols out to sea, they'd had to meet in secret, only six times so far, but each encounter had eclipsed the previous one. They had yet to make love; a few gentle kisses and holding hands was the furthest they had been so far, but that was enough for him. He loved her. His French was passable at best, but words didn't need to be a barrier to their passion; that was something that could be overcome in time. He was beginning to think he had to get her back to Hamburg somehow, so their love could endure and last after the war, yet he could not find any way where that would be possible. They'd met in secret up the coast, away from the town and a few miles from the nearest houses, too. Ginette would get there by using her bicycle. Roth would take a car from the motor pool, telling anyone who asked that he was just going for a drive to get away from the daily stresses of the day-to-day running of the sub.

They'd meet up at an isolated, abandoned, and run-down cottage. The whitewash on the walls had faded and was peeling, the odd stone from the walls was missing here and there, and pigeons were beginning to make nests in what remained of the roof beams. It was a hundred yards or so back from the shoreline, and Roth would park behind it so that the car could not be seen from the road. Ginette would lean her bike against the wall at the rear, also. They would arrange it so that she arrived first. That way he never passed her on the road, meaning no one would ever see them near the cottage at the same time. He left first for the same reason, Ginette leaving at least twenty minutes after him. When he could get away from his duties, he'd go to the flower stall, buy an apple or a similar pretence, and let her know when they could meet.

As he stood now on the bridge of the sub, he imagined them both lying there on the blanket he would bring, the dew from the grass seeping through and making it damp. She would giggle at his schoolboy French, correcting him and repeating the phrase back and forth. He would sweep back her long hair as it would fall across her eyes with a gentle touch of his hand. He had even thought of going back to that place after the war, renovating the cottage for them both. Its thatched roof had long since gone, as had the glass from the windows, but structurally it looked sound enough. He knew that living in a ravaged Germany was not going to be easy for him post conflict, never mind for a young girl from France. No, it would be easier to settle here, he envisaged.

But now was not the time to think of the future. He looked down at the luminous dial on his watch; it showed the time as 0430 hours, five hours from the safety of port and the escort vessel that would guide them past the minefields. The boat was now entering the Bay of Biscay that had once been a haven for the countless U-boats that had sailed out toward the unforgiving North Atlantic and onto numerous victories, but now it had become known as the 'valley of death' because of the high toll of boats lost here since 1943. Many U-boats sustained damage or destruction here. Death was awaiting the careless submarine and its crew, either on the way out or as they came back in.

The charcoal black of the night sky was beginning to recede, slivers of light appearing on the horizon as they headed east, but this, in turn, would magnify the dangers to the boat and crew. Somewhere in southern England, RAF and USAAF flight crews were gearing up, readying their planes to come and search for any U-boats or German ships that were off the coast of France. The likes of Bristol Beau fighters, Sunderland flying boats, Liberators, Catalinas, and many more all taking off just before first light with just one goal: to find and destroy. The truth was now they no longer waited for daybreak – the advent of efficient radar systems that the allied planes possessed meant that they could patrol twenty-four hours a day. Another submarine captain had relayed to him how in the dead of night a plane had attacked them while on the surface. It had appeared from nowhere, not picked up by the sub's radar, a mere five hundred metres behind them when they heard it. Suddenly, a light like he had never seen before lit up the sub. It was like a thousand candles were turned on together, blinding him and the lookouts. The attacking plane was fitted with a new type of powerful searchlight, illuminating the scene below. Then the aircraft's machine guns strafed the sub, multiple strikes hitting home all around, two men next to him were killed instantly. They crash dived, lucky to escape. The allies' ingenuity knows no bounds; they seem to come up with new ways of killing U-boats every time they put out to sea.

It had become the most dangerous of times, the home stretch. If spotted, they could face an onslaught ranging from depth charges, torpedoes, heavy machine guns, and anything else the air crews could throw at them as they tried to sink him and the forty-four men under his command. He also had to worry about the Royal Navy, whose patrols were becoming more frequent, mostly because the Luftwaffe had become so ineffectual as their own numbers had declined each day with the allied air superiority becoming overwhelming. That, and the fact that surface vessels of the Kreigsmarine were like hens' teeth, a very rare commodity.

Roth, usually the consummate professional, allowed his mind to wander yet again for a moment to thoughts of his father in Hamburg. Letters from him used to be frequent, vibrant, full of patriotic news from home; that is until his mother, Inge, was killed during an air raid back in September '42 as she came home from the market with a bag of meagre pickings for them both. His father, himself a soldier in the Great War, was now a shell of a man as he came to terms with the loss of his wife of thirty-three years. Now his letters, when they did arrive, were short and terse. It had been two years since Roth had been home. He'd even been denied leave to go to his mother's funeral, for 'operational reasons', he was told.

He was brought back to the present by the sound of talking from two of the lookouts on the bridge with him, something about what they were going to do once back on shore. He spun around.

"Concentrate on the here and now!" he scolded. "Or we'll all be bloody fish food!" The two lookouts became silent and immediately returned their gaze to the sector of sky they'd been told to watch. Both were thinking the same thought: how much the captain had changed on this last tour. Gone was the humour that he used to use together with a firm hand, if needed. It had been replaced with scowls and short bursts of temper when he barked out his orders. There was an atmosphere on the boat now, one that didn't exist a few short weeks ago. The respect that they all had for him was waning in a few of the crew. This long war was starting to eat at all of them and grind them down. Even the best, like Roth were affected. "I'm going down below, all of you keep your eyes on those skies and the horizon. A moment's glance away could cost us all!"

He walked over to the hatch and stepped onto the top rung of the aluminium ladder. He climbed down quickly and, upon reaching the bottom of the ladder and the control room, removed his white service cap, now more a dirty grey than white if truth be told. He glanced across to where Schmitt, the boat's chief, was watching him with a concerned look. He too, like the crew, had observed a change over the last tense weeks and months. After discussing the matter with the captain, he had concluded that it was an overwhelming concern for the safety of the crew as the war drew to a close that bothered him. He didn't want them all to die now, so fruitlessly. A curt nod to each other was passed between the two officers, and then Roth proceeded to his cabin.

It wasn't really a cabin in the true sense, just the captain's personal space with a curtain separating it off from the boat. He stepped inside, turning and drawing the thin cotton curtain across before sitting on the edge of his bunk, twirling his cap in his hands as he did so. This space was his sanctuary, but even here he felt the claustrophobic confines of the sub closing in on him with each passing day. To think, he'd volunteered for this! He felt a lump in his throat, a cold sweat starting to envelop him. It was as if a giant clammy hand was slowly squeezing the very life from him. These panic attacks had started shortly before they'd left port this last time. All the previous years of a strong self-confidence had gone in an instant, replaced with doubt and worry, attributes he'd never even contemplated as a successful U-boat captain. He mentally swept aside such thoughts from his mind – for the moment, at least. He took in deep breaths and calmed himself.

His gaze wandered up to his few books lined up on the small shelf above. All were held back with a single length of wooden dowelling to stop them falling off as the boat crashed through the swells of the ocean. Each book had its own significance for him, a microcosm of his early life. First, there was a red leather-bound copy of *Mein Kampf*. Hitler's own words! Roth remembered buying it from a stall whilst shopping with his mother in Hamburg's Gänsemarkt, back in June 1938. Originally it had been a birthday present for his father. He had read it and passed it on to Roth who, at the time, was intrigued and had leafed through the tome during any spare time he had while doing his training at the naval academy. Perhaps he'd subconsciously bought it for himself?

Truth be known, it was no page turner. It was a long, boring rant, written by a small, insignificant man, who, at the time of writing, was on the bottom rung of the National Socialist political ladder. What it was, and more to the point what it became, was a description of the Führer's vision for a greater Germany, and it had made many a common man of the disillusioned working classes turn and begin to listen to the propaganda that was being propagated. It sowed seeds of hatred towards communists, the Jewish and non-Aryan people of Europe. The book listed all the wrongs that had been perpetrated on the German people after the end of the war in 1918. Reading it hadn't made Roth into a Nazi, nor had it his father, although he understood why his father had urged him to read it; it had made them both understand how it might make other Germans think along those socialist lines.

Germany had paid the price for starting, and ultimately losing, the Great War. Blockades and restrictions, ordered by the League of Nations – which was made up mostly of the United States, France, and Britain – using the Treaty of Versailles as its baton to beat them with. Ultimately leading to the starvation and death of tens of thousands of Germans in the early twenties. Then there was the loss of lands and territories, plus the reparations. The German people and nation were humiliated as they were brought to task. It had kindled a spark in Roth's belly that had been burning like a roaring winter's log fire – one which had now become a flickering candle, threatening to be snuffed out by the slightest of breezes.

The burden of being a U-boat commander, and the responsibility of the lives of his crew, was now starting to crush him under a mountain of ever-increasing mortal danger. What had begun as a just and honourable undertaking, a truly heroic adventure, was now starting to leave a bitter taste in the mouth. One of his greatest fears now came when they were attacked with drop charges. He didn't show any emotion to the crew at the time of an attack, but as they waited for each one to be dropped, he likened it to looking at an open wound on your arm and the dread of someone touching it; you know it's coming, but you still jump when they do. As he sat and contemplated the reasons behind why he personally entered the 'great adventure', as it was called, he looked at the next book along: *A Christmas Carol* by the English author Dickens. There was no underlying or thought-provoking reason for having this, it was just a great read, a simple tale of one man coming to terms with his own morality and the feel-good factor when everything ends up right: a happy ending.

The third and final book was a dog-eared copy entitled *Boat Attacks Again*. He'd owned it for ages, read it repeatedly. It had been written by one of his heroes, a U-boat legend; Wolfgang Lüth. It told of the thoughts and exploits of possibly one of the U-Bootwaffe's greatest captains, a fascinating insight into the mind of a devout Nazi and natural leader of men. Roth had never met him but had heard from others who had served with and under him that, whilst being the brash and arrogant type, he was very formal and disciplined in his views, especially those concerning morality, for example. He wouldn't stand for impropriety but would look after his men like no other. Where one commander may bark orders at his men and be hated, Lüth could do no wrong in the eyes of his subordinates.

Another thing he'd gleaned from the writings was that the crew were like a mirror to the actions of their captain. For instance, when the sub was under attack the captain was forbidden to show panic or fear as this would then be transmitted to the crew. If they saw their captain as vulnerable, then they too would crumble and start to fail in the very tasks that might ensure the ultimate survival of the boat. He'd also learnt from the book about the struggle with the endless hours of boredom, the monotony when there was no action. This, too, could lead to mistakes when concentration was everything when under attack. Lüth would organise quizzes, chess tournaments, and singing contests; Roth had introduced similar activities on board his boat in the hope it would have the same result, which he thought, over the years, it had.

Roth lifted his feet up and swung them over the edge of the bunk. He laid his head down on the pillow, ignoring the smells of stale sweat and diesel which permeated everything, and the multitude of noises that circulated around the sub. He closed his eyes while trying to ignore the constant drumming of the diesels only a few feet away. He wouldn't sleep, just rest for now. He hadn't slept for more than two hours at a stretch for months, if not years.

CHAPTER 2 - ORDERS

It had been a short, restless sleep for Roth under the thin blanket of his cramped bunk, – it was more a quick nap, really, – and when he awoke the previous tensions had not diminished. It was clear to Roth how brief his nap had been; the dark of night must still be visible outside, evident below by the fact that the control room was still bathed in the eerie glow of the red bulbs that were on to help with the crew's night vision if they ventured up top. He stood and pulled back the curtain. Without saying a word, he entered the control room, striding the short distance across to the phonograph player where he cranked the handle a few turns before placing the needle down onto the record which lay on the turntable. He turned around and began to climb back up the ladder to the conning tower to resume his place at the front of the bridge as the first bars of 'Little Blue Boat Take Me Home Again' started to play.

A few of the crew began singing down below, their voices filtering up through the opening below Roth's feet. He knew that he was letting his emotions get the better of him and he had to put a stop to it, and soon. He'd chastised the lookouts for not doing their job; well, he wasn't doing his job now, was he? If there were any enemy ships close by, they could pick up the sounds emanating from the boat from miles away with their sonars; sound waves travelled far easier through water than air. He climbed back up to the bridge and once there began to peer towards the distant horizon, a smile slowly breaking out across his face as he listened to the music below.

The next few hours passed by without incident, and

the boat sailed into the Bay of Biscay and towards the port of Saint-Nazaire on the west coast of France. At around 1000 hours they had spotted their escort boat on the sub's sonar. It was disguised as a fishing trawler and would guide them past the mine fields and then on through the anti-submarine nets that stretched across the harbour's entrance. It was a comforting sight to those who stood in the conning tower when first the dotted roofs and then the patchwork of different coloured houses came into view along the distant coastline. There was a low cloud base today, and now a good steady drizzle which was helping keep any allied planes from seeing the orchestrated docking of the seventy-metre-long Type VIIC submarine as they entered the harbour. Roth and the first and second officers, Berger and Fischer, plus two other sailors were standing on the thin hardwood slats that made up the floor of the conning tower. They were all kicking their heels together and rubbing their hands to try to keep warm, the damp and frigid morning air gnawing at their exposed skin. Their eyes glanced towards the concrete sides of the approaching dock whilst also looking back to the skies, searching the heavens with their binoculars and listening with vigour, just in case any allied planes broke through the murk and attacked the German submarine while it was at its most vulnerable.

In the past, their return would have been welcomed with a brass band and crowds on the dock, followed by a huge feast of lobster, crab, fine French wines, and good German beer. Perhaps a medal or two, also. Not now, though. It reflected how the war had turned, how times had changed. In just a few short months the allies had gained the upper hand in the battle of the Atlantic. Oh, how he wished for the days of '41 to '42 and the 'Happy Time', as it was known; the period in the war when U-boats had sunk the most merchant shipping.

Once they had passed through the fortified lock at the entrance to the submarine basin he could see the towering concrete submarine pens ahead, fourteen in all. The thickness and strength of the steel-reinforced concrete had been tested time and time again over the last two years by American bombers in the daytime, and by the British at night. But still they were standing, battered and bruised like a heavyweight-boxer, but ready for the next round. The boat glided into the cavernous expanse of the pen. A large number nine was stencilled in flaking blue paint on the interior wall. The wall itself soared up high to the ceiling on his left, and to the right another U-boat was already docked in bay ten; it was U-355. There was a small group of French workers standing on the edge of the dock as the boat slowed to a crawl as it came alongside, waiting for the boat to stop so they could moor it up, their voices echoing off the walls like in some huge cave. There were also some officers of the Kreigsmarine waiting there, standing off to one side of the dock workers, but it was his crew's commanding officer who stood staring at the approaching boat that caught the captain's attention. It was unusual for him to greet their return in these times, and Commodore Hoffman looked more haggard than usual.

He first met Hoffman back in April 1940 during Operation Weserübung – the invasion of Norway. It had only been a brief encounter back then on the docksides of Hamburg, as they'd both been preparing their respective U-boats for the offensive. As it turned out, neither had seen any action as any skirmishes had not happened near their sectors off the Norwegian coastline. When they had spoken back then they'd enjoyed a mutual understanding and respect for each other from the outset and had expressed the feeling of déjà vu when they had compared Weserübung to Operation Sea Lion, the invasion of

England. It struck a chord with both, the two of them sharing a cigarette and staring out at the hundreds of barges and converted ferries tied up in front of them, a testament to the sheer endeavour and resourcefulness of the German soldier and sailor, but, at the same time, a great waste of time and resources.

Back then, Roth's sub had been tasked to lay mines in the English Channel in what might have been a vain attempt to stop any Royal Navy ships attacking the invasion armada. But laying mines was a task which every submariner detested for many reasons, but the one that struck a chord with most was that a mine might not destroy a ship for months. It's a weapon of stealth and deceit, whereas a torpedo was instantaneous and satisfying; a weapon worthy of the terror it inflicted. It was still a fact that Operation Sea Lion had never officially been cancelled. Hitler, it was rumoured, said of it: "the threat was real, even if the invasion never was."

The last time Roth had seen Hoffman was shortly before they'd departed for this latest patrol, and he was a shadow of his former self even then. Now, as Roth looked at him, it seemed that his long, woollen, black coat wasn't enough to keep out the early morning chill. He was shivering and his face had a drawn, hollow appearance. Hoffman stood on the upper level of the two-tiered dock, his arms clasped behind his back and staring down at the conning tower of the sub. Roth felt he was staring directly at him.

"Stop all engines," Roth ordered.

"Stop all engines!" shouted Berger, the first officer, relaying the captain's orders down through the open hatch of the conning tower where, in turn, these were repeated back to him from below. The steady, unremitting drum beat of the diesel engines stopped almost immediately.

"Cast the forward and aft lines," barked out Roth. A

sailor on each side of the bow and stern threw a rope to a waiting dock worker on the quayside as the boat glided up to the edge of the dock and came to a dead stop. Roth was busy with the docking of his submarine but, at the same time, couldn't take his eyes off Hoffman. The commanding officer's gaze hadn't left him for a moment; surely it wasn't a good sign that he was the focus of his attention?

The gang plank, a three-foot wide by twenty-foot-long wooden board with two low sides, was passed down from the concrete quayside and placed on the deck of the boat at an angle of thirty degrees or so to allow the crew members to disembark. Seven crew members, who had been standing to attention on the aft deck of the boat as it had sailed in, now moved towards the ramp after a nod of the head from Berger had allowed them to move. They walked slowly and a little unsteadily at first. One after the other they went up the board, slowly getting their land legs back but at the same time keen to get back on dry land and away from the confines of their 'iron coffin', as it was known throughout the naval service. The officers climbed down from the conning tower and stepped over to the edge of the boat. Roth turned to the chief of the boat, Schmitt, who walked over from the aft deck as the captain prepared to step off.

"Make sure the repairs are taken care of, Jonas. Get those spares we need and don't forget to get laid in the next day or two, okay?" he said with a grin, glancing back up to commander Hoffman who hadn't moved an inch since Roth had first seen him on the dock. "I have a feeling our mire is about to get deeper, my friend." Schmitt looked up to where Roth was looking to see Hoffman looking back down at them. A hint of concern appeared on Schmitt's face as he did so.

"He looks worse every time I see him. Find out what

he wants and come back to us soon. I'll stay on the boat until I hear from you," he said, "and remember, don't volunteer us for anything unless it's polishing Adolf's medals back in Berlin."

Roth shook his head and smiled at Schmitt's comment. After shaking hands and returning Schmitt's naval salute, Roth stepped off the boat and onto the gangplank, sailors on the quayside standing to attention and giving a salute to him as he did so.

Roth strode purposely over to the stone steps that would take him up to the higher level of the dock and the waiting officer. As he did so, one of the waiting French dockers, a man of around forty dressed in the typical scruffy trousers and blouse favoured by the French, approached him and barred his way, forcing Roth to stop dead in his tracks.

"Captain Roth, may I have a moment please?" he said in French, a look of concern on his unshaven face. Roth glanced up towards Hoffman who was waiting patiently on the quayside for him.

"What is it?" urged Roth in his best French; he was impatient to see his friend.

"My name is Claude Villiers," the dock worker said. "Ginette is my daughter. I know of your, shall I say, tryst? I'm here to tell you, Captain, that she has gone away."

Roth concentrated on the words, translating and understanding at the same moment.

"Gone away! Where? What do you mean, *gone away*?" demanded Roth.

"I will not tell you where, Captain, only that she is safe, safe from the hands of the resistance." His voice was tinged with emotion now and he fought back tears. He continued, "What were you thinking? She is nineteen! They will kill her just for the idea that she may like you!

If they find out you have been meeting, she's as good as dead! She told me that nothing has happened between you and her and I believe that is so, but it must end, and this is the only way. She has left Saint-Nazaire for good. She is our only child, all we have. She is with friends, far from here, gone. Gone away, safe in the countryside. Goodbye, Captain Roth. I wish you good luck." And, with that said, he turned to leave, but Roth grabbed him by the arm and pulled him back, a burning rage quickly enveloping him. With Ginette's departure, Roth could see his world spiralling further down into a dark place he never wanted to see.

"I can look after her, send her to Germany, she'll be safe, I promise!"

"No! That's not possible. Germany? You're mad. She's gone, safe, as I said. Please leave it alone, forget you ever met her. She told me she loves you, but that can't be. In such a short time, it's infatuation. She's young, impressionable. You should've known better, an officer of your standing. If you do love her, let it rest, and maybe after all this madness is over you can come back to France and find her here. Good day."

Roth still had a firm grip of the Frenchman's arm. Ginette's father looked Roth in the eye and then looked down pointedly at Roth's hand. He released his arm, realising that any further talk was useless. The Frenchman nodded, turned, and walked away, leaving Roth standing alone, contemplating what had just transpired. Ginette was the only bright light in all of this. Their future had been something that he could use as an escape when his duties and combat were crushing him into the ground. After a moment or two he came to his senses and turned his head to look back up to his commanding officer, who was still waiting patiently on the quayside above. He walked slowly to the stone steps and, with a heavy heart, climbed up.

Hoffman came towards Roth as he approached and they saluted each other, even though they were of a similar rank. Hoffman was clearly looking at the back of the departing French dock worker who Roth had been in an animated conversation with.

"Is there a problem?" he asked.

"Problem?" replied Roth, understanding Hoffman's meaning as he turned to look at Ginette's father retreating in the distance. "No, just a small matter of no consequence." He quickly changed the subject. "I'm not so sure your presence at our arrival is a good thing, Karl. Do we have a problem, being recalled so early?"

"I'm not sure myself, Ahron. You have a visitor in my office, a Captain Weber from the Wehrmacht. Your orders to return here came through from the highest level, a special delivery. Then, this Wehrmacht officer turned up about an hour ago, hasn't said a word except to inquire when you'd be docking. I tried to quiz him about why the army has an interest in one of our submarines, but he kept saying he had strict orders to speak to you, and you alone."

The two seasoned veterans turned on their heels and walked towards the grey painted buildings at the edge of the dock that housed the offices. They were of brick construction, but most of the windows had no glass or frames; having been bombed out so many times, there was no glass left to replace them and so were mostly covered over with sheets of plywood or left open to the elements. From behind the two men came a cacophony of shouted orders as the officers of the sub began to organise the crew and dock workers in the repairs and resupply of the sub. From somewhere, a hint of cooked bratwurst wafted across the bay causing Roth to instinctively lick his lips, his stomach groaning in sympathy. A flock of seagulls circled overhead, the screeching calls to each other piercing the early morning air of the French dockside. As they walked on, Roth looked at Hoffman and thought to himself that his commanding officer really did seem like a shell of the former imposing man he'd known. He'd lost a lot of weight, had large, dark bags under his eyes, and his complexion had paled. It was only a few weeks ago since they'd last met, but it seemed as if his friend had become a phantom of his past self. Roth came to a halt and Hoffman did too as he realised his compatriot had stopped walking.

"How are you, Karl?" Roth asked his friend.

"Me? I'm fine. Well, as fine as I can be. Did you know that when this whole mess started back in '39 we only had fifty-seven boats? Now there are over two hundred lying on the bottom of the sea, thousands of our comrades and friends lost. Two more boats gone this week. No contact with U-329 or U-724 for a week now. Even the Black Pit isn't safe anymore! That haven in the mid-Atlantic that was once free of allied aircraft is no longer, they have planes there now, also."

Roth thought briefly of his friend Peter Vogt, whom he had begun his training with at the naval academy in Flensburg back in 1938. He was a serving lieutenant on U-329.

"This war, which was supposed to last months, is taking its toll. To be brutally honest, I'm sick of sending young men to die in what seems a hopeless cause which doesn't have any chance of improving. I'm tired, too. I don't sleep much and if I do the nightmares make me wake up in a cold sweat."

"I'm hearing that the ranks are being backfilled with children and old men. Is this what it's come to?"

"It would seem so, my friend. It's not a case of if, but *when* the Americans and the British will come knocking on our door here, and then we're truly screwed! I'm not convinced that all that concrete, steel, and guns which make up the Atlantic wall will be enough to stop the inevitable. Perhaps you have a way out of this insane madness with this officer of the Wehrmacht?"

"I suspect whatever it is he wants, it won't be easy. A cushy desk job in Berlin with a pretty secretary would be nice, though." The two of them smiled and Hoffman slapped Roth gently on the shoulder and then gripped it firmly with his hand. He looked at Roth and smiled again, his eyes welling up slightly as he did so. Here was a man on the very edge, both mentally and physically. Roth was about to continue over to the offices, but Hoffman had now gripped his arm near the elbow, preventing him from continuing. He moved closer and began to talk in whispered tones, glancing around to check that no one had come up on them from behind and could overhear their conversation.

"I'm hearing rumours, my friend."

"What rumours?" Roth was intrigued and yet at the same time concerned with how his friend was acting.

"There are some amongst us that believe the time has come to put a stop to this madness. If we act now, we can stop the allied invasion. Countless lives will be saved; Germany will not be razed to the ground." Roth looked gravely at his friend and commanding officer, unsure what to say. "There is a group of generals, one of them an old friend. There is a plan." Roth didn't like where this conversation was heading and tried to step away a little, but he was held firm by Hoffman's tightening grip. "He must be stopped and now, before the British and Americans land. Then we may have a chance, we may be able to argue for agreeable terms of peace." Roth was filled with paranoia himself and began looking all around, checking they were still alone. It was a moment or two before he spoke.

"If I believe my ears and what you are saying, then you are mad. Whatever you believe is planned, you can't go through with it, and-"

"We must go through with it, do something. He can't be persuaded that all is lost, he's mad, it's got to stop!" Hoffman's tone was rising now so Roth urged him to lower his voice by gesturing with his free hand, then looked around once more.

"This is suicide. If you're found out they'll string you all up. Your friends and family, too. It's been tried and failed before, it's crazy to even think about it."

"It's in motion – the plan, that is. Once he is gone there will be a grab for power by Göring, Himmler, Goebbels, and the like. We must be strong and stand firm with those who have undertaken this course of action. I need to know that you are with us when we strike. You are respected by those above and beneath you. They will need your guidance. Tell me you are with us, my friend?"

Roth slowly shook his head. "I'm not saying you're wrong," Roth said, "but you need to be careful, keep your distance. If it happens, then will be the time to act. Just wait."

Hoffman released his grip and stepped back.

"No. We wait for our comrades to return from the sea every day and fewer do. We can't afford to wait any longer." Hoffman turned and made his way over to his office. Roth swallowed hard and then followed his friend.

They quickly reached the office door. Hoffman grabbed the handle then stopped, turned back to look at Roth, and gave him a reassuring smile before opening the door, gesturing for Roth to go through. As they entered, they heard the distinctive sound of heels being clipped together coming from the room. In front of them stood an immaculately dressed young officer in the field grey of the Wehrmacht who threw them both a firm Nazi salute. He introduced himself to Roth.

"Good morning, Captain. My name is Weber," said the baby-faced officer, who then addressed Hoffman. "If possible, I would like to speak to Captain Roth in private?" It was more of an order than a request.

"By all means," he replied. "If you have time, come and see me before you leave Ahron, okay?"

"I will," replied Roth and, with that, Hoffman walked out of the office.

Weber watched Hoffman through the dirty cracked panes of the office window as he walked back across the dockside before he continued.

"I have orders to escort you to Berlin, Captain. A car is waiting to take us to the airfield at Montoir. There we will fly to Berlin, and then on to the Reichstag for a meeting, sir."

"And what is the purpose of this meeting, Weber?" replied Roth, a note of anxiety in his question.

"I have told you everything I know, Captain. My orders are to get you to Berlin safely and quickly. Your boat is to be prepared for a return to the sea while you are away, and I will give orders to that effect to the naval authorities here, to Captain Hoffman. Now, if you would please follow me, we must be on our way. The car and driver are just a short walk away." He pointed to his left and the way back out. Roth wanted to know more and continued to quiz Weber.

"Do you have any idea at all as to the nature of my orders, Captain Weber? To be called back early from our mission and then summoned to Berlin in this manner is unusual in the extreme!"

"As I said, Captain Roth, my orders are to get you to Berlin where you will be told everything. My apologies. Here, these are your orders, sir." Weber handed over an envelope stamped with the imperial eagle that he withdrew from the inside of his breast pocket in his leather great coat. Roth opened it up and read the document it contained. It was, as Weber had described, simple orders ordering him to Berlin with immediate effect, signed by some general that Roth had never heard of.

"Can I have a few moments with Hoffman, take a shower, get a hot drink, even?"

"I'm afraid not, we have to be on our way immediately." There was a moment's silence as Roth became resigned to the fact that, for whatever reason, there was no way he could delay his departure.

"We'd better get going, then. Lead the way."

The two of them left the office and walked outside. The sun was still trying to break through the low grey cloud, but Roth hoped that it wouldn't succeed as he feared for the safety of his men if the flying conditions improved. He looked across to his boat and could see a flurry of activity all around and was going to demand of Weber that he speak with his boat's chief, but decided it would be a futile request. But one man amongst the melee by the U-boat stood out; it was the lonely figure of Captain Hoffman. He was staring back at Roth and Weber as they made their way across the cobbles of the dock, his eyes never leaving them. Roth wasn't sure, but it appeared Hoffman was crying.

CHAPTER 3 - BERLIN

The airfield was only a short drive from the base, but the journey was conducted in silence by the two officers sitting in the back of the open topped Kübelwagen car. The corporal who was driving never even turned to look at Roth, the only acknowledgement given was a salute as he opened the car's door back at Saint-Nazaire. Roth was pondering his fate. Did a trip to the Reichstag imply something sinister? Surely not. If his superiors wanted rid of him, he wouldn't be heading to an airfield; a luger pistol to the back of the head in a nearby field would be a more likely scenario. So, what did the future hold for him? Weber had told him the sub was being prepped for sea again, so he surmised that he'd be in command again on some special mission? All sorts of possibilities raced through his mind. It did no good to think too far ahead. Experience told him not to expect anything, as you'd be let down hard when you found out the reality of the matter.

The ride to Montoir was accentuated by too many bumps to count along the twelve-kilometre route, but finally, after around thirty minutes, the car turned onto a country dirt road and then pulled up to the sentry box at the edge of the airfield. Weber showed his credentials to one of the two blue-uniformed Luftwaffe sentries guarding the entrance. Roth thought he looked about seventeen years old! Perhaps the rumour about children being recruited was true. The guard studied the airfield security pass and verified the photo matched Weber before returning the document.

"Sieg Heil," said the guard, clicking his heels together and at the same time giving a Nazi salute. Weber returned the salute and told the driver to carry on.

The two-tone, dark green camouflaged Fieseler Storch spotter plane started up its engine as the car approached. Weber could see by the look on Roth's face that he wasn't impressed by the plane's appearance. It could only carry three people in its cramped cabin, as its main role was observation, and its wing was over the fuselage to give the observers a clear view from the cockpit. It looked outdated, a remnant from the end of the first war instead of something from this era. *A flying 'crate' would be a good name for it,* he mused.

"That's all we could get, Captain. The Luftwaffe isn't as grand as it once was, but I assure you that these things are sturdy, and although we aren't travelling in style, we will get to Berlin," stated Weber. Roth stayed silent for the moment, still wondering what this trip held in store for him. The car came to a halt just to the side of the plane. Roth grabbed his 'Cooper' peaked captain's hat from his head as he stepped out of the Kübelwagen, the prop wash from the single engine blowing him back as he neared the plane. The door was open, and the pilot beckoned them to get on board with a gesture of his hand. Roth climbed in, squeezing past the pilot's seat. Weber quickly joined them and shut the door behind him. The engine roared louder as he did so, the plane fishtailing slightly as the pilot fought to balance the two-hundred-and-forty horsepower Argos V8 engine as the Storch lurched forward on the damp grass of the airfield. It was only a relatively short distance before the plane left the ground, the pilot immediately pulling back on the stick as far as he dared to get as much altitude as quickly as possible to gain height, which would hopefully make it difficult for anyone on the ground to take a pot shot at them. Weber turned in his seat to try and engage with Roth once again, but the captain was already asleep, his cap pulled down over his eyes and his breathing heavy as he lay to one side of his seat. The inside of the plane was very spartan. The metal-tubed seats with thin fabric coverings offered little comfort. It was also extremely cold inside the cramped cabin, colder still as they climbed higher, plus the noise from the engine was deafening. Weber folded his arms across his chest to try to keep warm. He studied the slumbering Roth and wondered what lay ahead for this hero of the Reich. He, too, then drifted asleep.

Twenty minutes later, a sudden lurch to the left and an increase in revs by the plane woke Roth from his deep sleep. He lifted the peak of his cap to look at Weber through half-closed eyes, but the captain was slumped in his seat, fast asleep. As Roth looked down at the lush green fields slowly rolling past a thousand feet below, his thoughts turned to his early days aboard U-47 as an ensign under the command of Gunther Prien.

What an exhilarating time it had been! He'd been lucky enough to be stationed on U-47 back in June '39 as a young, inexperienced junior officer, the prospect of war becoming more of a reality as events across Europe transpired. It was only a matter of time before the might of the Wehrmacht was unleashed across Europe. An invasion of Poland, perhaps? Months of bluff and counter bluff by the politicians, meanwhile tanks, artillery pieces, and soldiers were being moved across Europe like pawns, bishops, and knights in a gigantic game of military chess.

He could still picture that cold, moonless night in late October when they had slipped into the bay of Scapa Flow in the Orkney Islands. His heart beat a little faster even now, just as it did back then as he had stood next to his commanding officer in the conning tower. The captain's hands were gripped tightly on the handles of the periscope, eyes pressed onto the rubber cup of the viewfinder. He was quietly issuing ranges, depths, and orders to the crew as the boat crept forward as slowly and silently as they could, further into enemy waters, picking their way around the 'block ships' (the merchant ships that were deliberately sunk in harbour entrance channels to block access), and then on through the anti-submarine nets. The red running light of the submarine's interior cast an eerie glow across the crew's faces and mixed with the grave like silence of the sub, it had given a surreal tone to the proceedings.

This was Roth's first mission since leaving the naval academy at Flensburg, and when Prien whispered to the crew on that fateful night that he could see a battleship at anchor dead ahead, he could hardly believe his ears.

He remembered the sweat dripping in rivulets down his forehead as he stood there, his clothes bathed in perspiration, and he was greatly aware that at any moment they could be discovered and his first mission would surely be his last. The atmosphere on board the submarine that night was palpable, the tension and heat near unbearable. Year after year, month after month of training and preparation had led to this very moment. The looks on the faces of the crew around him were vivid in his mind's eye even now; fear, anticipation, and, yes, excitement, too.

The illusion that the great Royal Navy was invincible was about to become a myth, for the time being, at least; sinking a ship in the safety of its home port would surely be a moral victory for the Kreigsmarine and the German people.

Prien had stepped back from the scope and beckoned Roth over to look for himself. He positioned himself in front of the tube that extended down from the ceiling and peered into the rubber eyepiece. As he looked at the black and white image before him, he could see the outline of the considerable superstructure of the battleship moored up along the quayside. The outline of the ship was visible against the darkened skyline, and surprisingly there were a few lights coming from the ship itself – unforgivable in a time of war.

Roth backed away to let his captain continue the attack procedure. After a moment or two, and a final range setting, Prien gave the order to fire four torpedoes. One failed to launch but three left the sub bound for the target: the *Royal Oak*. Unsurprisingly to everyone on the sub, because of the torpedoes' known unreliability, only one of them hit the target, the other two missing completely, but the expected return of fire from the ship failed to materialise and so Prien quickly ordered another attack. This time three torpedoes were fired from the bow tubes and hit the out-dated ironclad amidships. Three huge explosions ripped through the still night air, instantly causing colossal damage and loss of life. The ship listed almost immediately, and she started sinking within moments of the attack. The submarine quickly turned around, sank into the depths as close to the bottom as they dared, and quickly slipped away before the inevitable hunt for them began. The boat had returned home to a tumultuous reception, the likes of which had never been seen before. The greatest of heroes returning to the Reich!

Back in the Storch, Roth subconsciously slipped his hand into his coat pocket and felt the small medal in there that he kept pinned to the lining. It was the Iron Cross, second class, that all the crew received for the attack. His second one with the oak leaves hung around his neck.

Roth had been transferred back to shore in January '41 for further officer and weapons training, and was scheduled to return to Prien and U-47 when it was announced in March that the boat had failed to return from patrol after engaging a convoy off the coast of Ireland. There were no more details. It was still a mystery as to what had happened to one of Germany's greatest heroes, but now, so late in the war, Roth reflected on how many comrades and friends he had lost, buried at the bottom of the Atlantic in their metal tomb, every one of them a hero to him.

Roth could now see that they were approaching the airfield at Tempelhof in the heart of Berlin, so he sat up, pushing back his cap on his head as he did so, the plane on its final approach. Weber too sat up. The sun was breaking through the clouds now on what appeared to be a pleasant looking day, but he stared in disbelief at what he could see as the sunlight lit up the scene below him. The destruction of the German capital spread out below was shocking. Instead of the uniformity of buildings with their straight lines, edges, and roof tops stretching out into the distance, and instead of people going about their daily business in crowds, shopping, talking, laughing, all he could see were the sides or corners of buildings, piles of rubble, and fingers of blackened stone pointing accusingly into the sky, interspersed with columns of smoke rising from countless fires below.

With the roofs of most of the buildings missing, it reminded him of a honeycomb in a beehive. He'd seen bombed buildings before of course, but never from the air or for as far as he could see now. What had happened to Germany? They were invincible, the masters of Europe, taking on the world, all powerful, crushing all who stood against them. He now realised, as he stared at the destruction below, just how short a time they had left. What had Hitler said back in 1940? "If the RAF drops three-thousand bombs, we will drop one-hundred-and-fifty-thousand bombs!" Well, it looked like the allies had paid him back, with interest. Surely there was no way

Germany could go on to win this war, especially against the industrial giant that is America as Britain's ally.

The plane touched down lightly onto the tarmac runway, the pilot throttling back on the engine as it did so. They taxied up to a large hangar were five or so fighter planes – Messerschmitt Bf 109s and Focke Wulf 190s, plus a Junkers Ju 52 transport plane – were parked up outside. The Storch came to a stop, the engine quickly switched off by the pilot. Roth touched the peak of his cap with a finger and said, "Danke," to the pilot who just nodded back in way of a reply, and then Roth clambered out of his seat as Weber unlocked the door and climbed out first. Twenty metres or so away a corporal of the Wehrmacht stood at attention alongside a Mercedes 170v staff car, staring at the two officers as they walked towards him.

"Captains Weber and Roth," stated Weber to the pale faced young soldier. "Are you our driver?"

"Yes, sir. I am to take you directly to the Reichstag building," he replied. He turned and opened the door of the car. Roth didn't get in immediately. Instead, he stood there for a moment. Something was not right, but he couldn't place it. And then, he realised; there was no bird song, none. In France he had enjoyed hearing the early morning chatter of hedge sparrows and the like as he strolled through the streets on his way to breakfast from his lodgings, but here there was nothing. Was it a sign that even mother nature had abandoned Germany?

The short, six-kilometre journey took nearly an hour as the driver had to pick his way through streets filled with traffic consisting of horses and carts, some trams that were still amazingly running and others that were only burnt-out shells, their wire framed carcasses pushed to the side, off the tracks. Army trucks and civilian cars were all trying to weave around the masses of bricks, masonry, glass, and timber that were strewn across the roads and pavements. There were also civilians going about their business or helping clear up from the previous night's bombing. Lines of ordinary people were passing debris along a human chain into organised piles. They were helping clear the roads to let the traffic flow, but as they did so they would stop abruptly when they discovered the remains of someone buried amongst the debris. He also watched the scrawny dogs that were sniffing around the streets, looking out for any meagre scraps they might find – perhaps even body parts. What Roth didn't know was that the dogs were in competition with the hungry populace of the city, and may even end up as food for a hungry Berliner themselves.

Roth was astounded even more now by the destruction before him as they drove along Tempelhofer Damm in the Bergmannkiez district of the city. It was brought home quite more horrifically by the numerous bodies lying along the street edge, covered by blankets and sheets. The bodies of men, women, and children. Twenty or more were laid out in front of one pile of rubble alone. Twenty pairs of feet – some shoeless, some with torn stockings, all with legs covered in blood – poking out from beneath the debris. And the smell of death was all around, too. It was a combination of cordite, burning wood, faeces, and human flesh that seemed to permeate right into your soul. The carnage was extensive. It was everywhere.

But the next sight he saw made his eyes widen with disbelief. Hanging from one of the few streetlamps still left standing was the figure of a young man, a thick rope around his neck, his hands bound behind him. The car was crawling along now with the slow-moving traffic and was creeping past the gruesome scene to Roth's right. He could study this hideous spectacle in more detail.

Immediately Roth had recognised the US air force leather jacket with its distinctive fur collar, which was still on the body even though it was slashed in multiple places. The trousers too were torn, and blood stained. One of the airman's legs was grotesquely bent in an unnatural way. The corpse was twisting around in the breeze, as if doing a macabre dance. The head was at an angle to the shoulders, the face bloated and badly beaten. One of the eyes was missing.

Weber had been studying Roth looking out of the window and began to explain.

"American airman, beaten to death by a civilian mob. When they parachute out of their stricken bomber, they are now praying to land safely and fall into the hands of the military. They might be beaten and tortured, but they'll probably live and get thrown into a Stalag Luft. But if the locals get them first it's a different story. So many civilians have been killed as the RAF and Americans continue to attack cities that they are turning on the 'Terror flyers', as they're called. They attack them like a pack of dogs. They will beat, bludgeon, stone, stab, kick, and punch them to death. Goebbels wrote in the papers that defenceless women and children were being murdered in these air attacks and that, as Germans, we should not protect the airmen from the wrath of the people. An eye for an eye, a tooth for a tooth. 'A policy of non-interference must be adopted,' he has said."

Roth averted his gaze. The hanging figure, perhaps in his early twenties at best, was now receding away behind them as the car gathered a little speed.

Straight ahead, the Reichstag building now appeared in the distance. It was flanked to one side by a tall, newly built building that stood out from its surroundings due to its height; it towered over its neighbours. But this was no ordinary building, this was one of the flak towers that had sprung up all around the larger cities of Germany. They were in response to the visits of the allied bombers. Each building had a radar station which was in turn linked to a series of anti-aircraft guns which adorned the top, mostly manned by teenage members of the Luftwaffe. Too young to fly, but old enough to fire these deadly weapons. Roth was amazed at the lengths that man could go to in its efforts to kill one another. He turned to his left and spoke.

"Are you from Berlin, Weber?" Roth asked. He was trying to change the subject and erase the scene of the airman from his mind's eye, if only for a moment.

"No, thank God," he replied. "I'm from the countryside, just outside Munich. This bombing of civilians doesn't sit well with me. Military targets, yes, but this is modern warfare, I guess. Bomb your enemy into submission, no matter what the human price may be. I've been here in the city when the bombers have struck, and I'm not afraid to say how terrifying it was. I'm a career soldier, ten years, but I'm a clerk, not a fighter. I've never seen any action and I've no wish to, but I'm also prepared to die for my country and if it means I must pick up a rifle, so be it, but not this!"

"We may all have to pick up a rifle in the end if that's what it takes. I too have trouble with this matter of warfare. My mother was killed in a raid over Hamburg, and too many civilians are dying. Soldiers are meant to fight and die in war, not women and children."

The imposing Reichstag building now loomed in front of the car.

"Well, we are here at our destination, Captain Roth. Perhaps your next mission will help change our fortunes, with God's help?"

"Perhaps?"

CHAPTER 4 - REICHSTAG

The car slowed down as it approached the sentry box and barrier that blocked the entrance to the eastern side of the imposing Reichstag building. A towering wrought iron fence, newly painted gloss black and adorned with gold spear-like tips, ran along the sides of the building and around the corners. As they passed the main entrance of the 'Neo-Baroque' building, Roth was impressed by the six Roman 'Doric' columns that held up the pediment roof, and by the size and grandeur of the tall windows that stretched from floor to roof along the front. He was a little perplexed, though, as he had believed that after the fire in 1933 that the building wasn't in use anymore. Roth noticed that there seemed to be SS guards everywhere he looked, all immaculately dressed in their black uniforms and highly polished jack boots, machine pistols in their hands. One of them, a tall soldier who appeared to Roth to be easily over two metres tall, raised his hand to make sure the driver of the car stopped, staring him down as he did so. Another guard to the left raised his Schmeisser pistol and pointed it in the direction of the car. They seemed on edge to Roth – or was it just their normal everyday demeanour? He couldn't quite gauge it.

The first guard approached the right side of the car and, in a strong authoritative tone, spoke through the open window.

"Papers!"

Weber handed his identity card together with Roth's over to the guard who studied them as Weber spoke.

"We have an appointment with Hauptsturmführer Felix Haas."

The guard said nothing but turned away and gestured to another soldier to raise the barrier. He handed back the cards and told the driver to park by the two other staff cars just over to his right, and then marched over to the sentry box and picked up a phone. There were now six SS guards staring at them, machine pistols at the ready, as Weber and Roth got out the back of the car.

The click of steel-tipped boots on the cobbled courtyard drew their attention to the arrival of a middle-aged officer coming out of the building to the left. He marched over to them, came to a halt, clicked his heels together, and threw a Nazi salute before introducing himself.

"SS Hauptsturmführer Haas, can I see your identity papers, please, and orders?" Once again, the two captains did as they were told, Roth thinking that security here was at a level he'd never witnessed before. The SS officer read the orders, looked at the cards, and compared the photos on them to Weber and Roth before speaking once again. "Follow me, Hauptman Roth. Hauptman Weber, stay here with the car." Roth stole a glance at Weber as he moved away and saw him give a slight nod of acknowledgement.

The two of them went through the same door Haas had previously come through and into a high-ceilinged corridor leading to a wide staircase that they started to ascend. The building inside was undergoing a serious renovation; there was evidence of fire damage here and there on the walls and ceiling still, but workmen of all descriptions seemed to be everywhere, busy working away. Ladders, pots of paint, and scaffolding were also evident. At the top of the stairs, the first floor opened into a wide expanse with approximately ten or so oak-panelled doors on either side, each four metres high. The floor was covered in a lush, bright red carpet. The whole expanse was bathed in sunlight, streaming through the huge windows that Roth had seen on the front of the building earlier. At the far end, where the two of them were heading, was a set of double doors and above those was a three by two metre red, black, and white swastika flag. A beam from a floor mounted spotlight was enhancing the colours. The flag was striking in its appearance, a statement on its own. Two SS guards were standing to attention on either side of the doors, once again their Schmeisser pistols at the ready. This time, though, these guards were both immaculately dressed in ceremonial black uniforms. A brightly polished leather lanyard was slung across their chests, and their highly polished jack boots and Stahlhelm helmets caught the sun's rays coming through the windows. Both had a piercing gaze and appeared to have an air of confidence, menace, and arrogance about them. Haas stopped at the foot of the door and knocked twice on the highly polished oak.

"Enter," a voice barked loudly from inside, and Haas turned the brass handle on the right door and walked into the room followed by the submarine captain.

They entered an outer office in which there was a female secretary who was, presumably, the owner of the voice who had spoken. She was busy typing away furiously; she didn't even look up as they came into the room. Haas now strode over to a second set of doors. Again, he knocked. This time a clear, loud male voice could be heard from the next room.

"Come!"

Roth stepped into a huge office as Haas led the way, but as he got out of his field of view, he couldn't hide his amazement as he saw the Reichsführer, Heinrich Himmler himself, seated behind a grand, leather-topped walnut desk with two more SS officers standing to one side of the room. Haas clicked his heels together once again, introduced Roth to the innocuous bespectacled man sat behind the desk, threw a Nazi salute, and, with authority in his voice, he spoke.

"Heil Hitler!" He spun on his heels and marched out quickly through the double set of doors, closing the open one as he did so.

Roth now noticed two other people in the room. The first he recognized as Admiral Karl Witzell of the Kreigsmarine, and the other was a small, bald man in a navy-blue suit and tie who was sitting in the green, high backed leather chair over in the corner of the room when Haas and himself had walked in. As Roth tried to comprehend just what was happening here, one of the SS officers approached him.

"Hauptman Roth, let me introduce those present here today. I am SS Sturmbannführer Emil Fuchs of the 22nd Panzer Grenadiers, and this is SS Obersturmführer Leon Vogel, also of the Grenadiers," he pronounced. The second SS officer gave Roth a nod of the head as an acknowledgement to his introduction. "I'm sure you recognize Admiral Witzell?" Fuchs then turned to introduce the bald man in the chair, who rose as his name was mentioned and strode over to shake Roth's hand. "This is Professor Peter Klein who works directly with renowned Professor Paul Steiner, our top scientist in the field of physics in Germany." Roth was waiting for the Reichsführer's introduction, but it never came, a fact that became clearer to him later. What the hell had Roth been summoned here for? He glanced towards Himmler who remained silent as he sat behind his desk, peering over his metal framed glasses at them all. Himmler not speaking filled Roth with a fear the like of which he'd never experienced before.

The five of them were now gathered on the magnificent Persian rug which lay just in front of Himmler's desk. Fuchs, a man who looked everything like a poster boy for the Aryan race with his blond hair and blue eyes, continued to speak: "You have been ordered here today, Hauptmann Roth, for a very special mission, one that will have a great impact on when the Reich will win this war, and its importance to the outcome cannot be stressed enough. You, your crew, and submarine are most fortunate to bear this great responsibility. I will now let Professor Klein explain more and with some detail."

The middle-aged professor, a small man with a drinker's nose and stomach to match, began to speak to Roth.

"Captain, have you ever heard of nuclear fission?"

"No," replied Roth.

"Well, in simple terms, Captain, everything we see all around us is made up of atoms, immensely tiny particles of matter. If you split certain atoms in a special chamber called a fission reactor, they create huge amounts of heat and power, and if you do this in a certain manner you can create a super bomb – a bomb so powerful it could raze a city like Berlin to the ground in seconds, killing hundreds of thousands instantly. The release of energy is unimaginable. We think the Americans are only months away from developing such a weapon, perhaps to use on us when they launch a second front in the West. We are perhaps a year behind them in our efforts to have a weapon of our own, but we have managed to create this nuclear fission and there is a biproduct of this technology. It's called Plutonium 237, and it's a radioactive material. Have you heard of Marie Curie, Captain?"

"I seem to remember from my school days that she discovered radium or something and that it killed her, is that the same as these 237 materials?"

"In a way it is, Captain. This radioactive material is lethal; it kills indiscriminately, it's odourless, you can't see it or touch it, but it taints everything it encounters. You wouldn't even know that you'd been near it until you started feeling sick, and by then it would be too late. You'd be dead within weeks, if not days."

"What does all this have to do with me? Why am I here?"

"Let me explain further, Hauptmann Roth." It was Vogel who now spoke. "We haven't developed a bomb to drop on the Americans, and even if we did, we haven't got a bomber with the range to get it there. Some of our other scientists have developed rockets that can reach England, but they can carry conventional explosives only and we are years away from a rocket that can cross the Atlantic. We need to take the war to the Americans now, to stop them from launching a second front in Europe.

"Our plan is to get a device on American soil and detonate it, to then tell them that we have more similar devices and that if they start a second front in the West we will attack them with these weapons, stopping them in their tracks. With our help, you and your submarine will take the bomb to America!"

CHAPTER 5 - SURTR

"I'm not sure I understand," said Roth. "You said you don't have a bomb, but you do have this weapon? So, what do you plan to do? What's my involvement?"

It was now Witzell's turn to speak.

"As you are aware, we have been successful earlier in the war when we deployed U-boats off the American coast to sink allied shipping. Indeed, you yourself took part in that operation, and we believe we can get a sub through their defences again."

What Witzell had said was true. Roth had been deployed on one of the submarines under the command of Reinhard Hardegen during Operation Drumbeat in the spring of '41. Five U-boats had sunk thousands of tons of shipping just off the American coast; the Americans' arrogance had prevented them from learning from the mistakes made by the British earlier in the war. Rumour had it that the crew of U-123, captained by Hardegen, had even been able to see the lights of the Manhattan skyline – they'd been that close.

Fuchs continued where Vogel had left off previously.

"We don't have this super – or atom – bomb, as they call it, just as the professor has said. What we do have is the radioactive material, and the experts have told us we can make what they are calling a 'Black Bomb'. We take the Plutonium 237, surround it with conventional explosives, and, when detonated, it blows up like a normal bomb, but it spreads the Plutonium into the atmosphere, and, wherever it lands buildings, cars, ships, and people will be contaminated for years and years. People near the explosion will die very quickly, as in a conventional detonation. Anyone who survives the blast but are in the immediate area will be contaminated by the

Plutonium as it spreads in the air. They will also die eventually, after a long and painful passage of time. Material things are tarnished with a radioactive coating, and if you go near them, you will get the sickness, and eventually you will die and effectively this will render that area inhabitable for years. The medical services will be overwhelmed with the sick and dying. Another effect that this bomb will have, though, is the psychological damage to the civilian population. Just think what the great American public will say when we detonate a bomb like this right in their heartland!

"There is another phase to this operation, too. Let me explain further. The time of detonation in Washington will coincide exactly with three further explosions of a similar force in the capital, but they will be of a conventional type. These secondary explosions will be delivered by three V1 rockets!"

Roth interrupted once more.

"I don't understand. V1 rockets? What are they? The professor said rockets can't reach America?"

"Quite right. I'll elaborate. V stands for Vengeance! Our Führer has demanded we retaliate on England for the heavy civilian loss of life in our cities, inflicted on us by the murderer Bomber Harris of the RAF, and the Americans. We have manufactured such a weapon in our hidden secret laboratories, but we don't intend to launch the rockets that are targeted on London. No, that time will come very soon. Our V1s in this operation will be launched offshore, near the coast of Delaware."

Roth looked really confused now and looked around the room for someone to further clarify just what he was being told. Admiral Witzell spoke once more.

"We have modified three of the new Type XXI U-boats to facilitate the launching of a modified V1 rocket. These 'electro-boats' have the capability to travel far greater distances under water, at greater depths and for longer periods of time, and therefore enabling them to avoid detection.

"Each boat has a launch ramp fitted to the forward superstructure from which to fire the rocket. These V1s are smaller in size so that we can launch them off the submarine – about a third smaller than the ones we will be launching on England. And so that they still have sufficient range, the bomb load will be reduced. They will be able to reach Washington from over one hundred miles offshore, from a place called Cape May Point in the Delaware Bay. Each rocket will be disassembled and stored in the forward torpedo room of the boat before they leave port and then will be reassembled directly before launch. There will be technicians on board to assemble and launch the rockets. The scientists at Peenemünde on the Baltic Coast, and at another secret facility, have been working on this U-boat-capable system since 1943.

"The rockets will detonate in the heart of Washington, close to where the black bomb will be placed. The U-boats will submerge immediately after the launch and then slip away unnoticed, which is crucial for any future attacks. We don't want the US navy knowing how to intercept our boats," Fuchs continued.

"The idea is that there will be four explosions in the city, which should be in the same general area, giving the illusion that all four were sea launched. We will then inform the US government that the rockets were carrying radioactive warheads, thus giving the illusion that we have launched an atomic strike and that there are more submarines stationed off the coast ready to launch more. They will be forced to listen to our demands! Plus, we will tell them that these atomic weapons will be used against any attacking forces on mainland Europe!"

It was beginning to dawn on Roth now how the plan was designed to work. His involvement and that of his sub was now clear. He was to ferry the device over to America. The thought of having this atomic material on his boat with his crew filled him with a sudden foreboding. He looked across to Himmler who was just sitting there and not saying anything. Roth thought he understood why. In the event this all went wrong, and Germany lost the war, Himmler would deny his involvement at any subsequent war trial.

"The Delaware Bay is, if memory serves me right, in the heart of busy shipping lanes for the US navy. It'll be a miracle if they get through, never mind surface and launch these rockets of yours. They really need to be further out to sea to have a chance of not being detected. Can't you put the bomb on one of the V1s, anyway?" enquired Roth.

"No, it's too heavy and would greatly reduce the range of the rocket even further, thus making the plan worthless. We have every confidence in these new submarines getting through undetected, plus the accuracy of the rocket cannot be guaranteed the further they are from the intended target. The device must be detonated on the ground in the capital. The whole concept is that America is vulnerable to an atomic attack and would sue for peace, hopefully on our terms."

"Why don't we use this weapon on the Russians? We need to stop their advance on Germany now, I'd have thought?"

"This is a weapon of terror, Captain. It has no destructive power. If we had the capability of the full bomb, we could win this war tomorrow, on all fronts. But we can't deliver the bomb as we would wish. Like I said, perhaps in a year or two we will have the capability. The upside, as far as the Russians are concerned, is that once we hit Washington and our deception has worked it may well stop them in their tracks."

"Indeed! No one will dare to attack the might of the Third Reich again!" It was Vogel who had interrupted, clear venom and menace in his tone. "If we don't do this and then lose the war, the aftermath and humiliation we suffered with the betrayal of Versailles in 1918 will pale into insignificance!" This last statement struck home with Roth. There was a moment's silence before Roth spoke again.

"So, I'm to transport this 'Black Bomb' in the submarine to the coast of America?"

"Yes, Hauptmann. From there Fuchs and I will be met by members of the Nazi party, or fifth columnists, as they are known, who will assist us in getting the bomb to its destination where it will be detonated in an open area close to where the V1s will land. Our bomb will be fitted with a timer, to coincide with the V1's arrival."

Witzell now spoke again.

"Your crew has been ordered to put to sea from Saint-Nazaire as soon as they are refuelled and re-stocked, and they will make for Peenemünde where you will rendezvous with them in three days' time. The device will be placed on board there. It weighs around twenty kilograms, plus the two-hundred-and-twenty kilos of RDX explosive for the detonation. From there you will sail directly to the East Coast of America. You will only know the destination once you have been at sea for thirty-six hours through the sealed orders you will be given as you disembark. There will be only one radio transmission from your boat. That will be when you have safely traversed the coast of France and out into the Atlantic. Then you will send the code word, and only then. This will signal the operation is under way and we can inform the rest of the group to proceed. "We have called this

'Operation Surtr,' after the God of Fire, Lord of the Blackened and Burning Earth. Very apt, I think."

"Just one transmission?" enquired Roth.

"We believe that the allies are intercepting our radio broadcasts, they may have even cracked our enigma codes, that's what we're hearing from Abwer. Once you have delivered the bomb along with Fuchs and Vogel, you shall take the boat on a course that takes you near Chesapeake Bay. You will have a cover story for the sub that you intended to lay mines in there, just in case your presence is discovered, and you are captured. We do not want the real reason for your presence in US coastal waters revealed to the enemy. You shall rendezvous with a 'Milchkuh,' the modified type VII submarine designed to resupply and refuel U-boats, to refuel in the Atlantic at a point off the west coast of Africa, and then resume normal operations attacking convoys until your return to Saint-Nazaire. It goes without saying that you are not to divulge details of this operation with anyone, including your crew, until you open those orders at sea. Understood?"

Again, Roth stole a glance towards Himmler, careful not to catch his eye, but the Reichsführer had not stirred since they had all entered the room. He just sat there staring impassively at the assembled group standing around him. Roth had grave reservations about this plan but knew that there was no way he could get out of obeying his orders.

He could see that the operation was fraught with dangers and so much could go wrong, especially when he handed the package to the SS officers in America. He'd have to sail into an inlet of some kind and unload onto a jetty with a crane; he was presuming all this had been already worked out, but he was worried for himself and his crew. This could go wrong in so many ways.

Fuchs interrupted Roth's thoughts.

"Right, Hauptman Roth, if you'll follow me. I think we should have some lunch and you can tell me all about life on a submarine. Vogel and I are seasoned soldiers and have never been to sea before, so we would appreciate an insight into your world."

Witzell put his hand out and Roth took it, shaking it with his normal firm grip.

"Good luck," said Witzell. "I'm sure we have chosen a worthy submarine, crew, and captain for what could be Germany's finest hour. I bid you farewell and good sailing. Heil Hitler!" With that said, he turned and left the room. Fuchs watched him depart before he turned to Himmler and, along with Vogel, barked, "Heil Hitler!" Both clicked their heels in unison and turned around to leave. Roth gave his own salute to the Reichsführer, whose cold hard stare had sent a shiver down his spine and was about to leave the room with the two SS officers plus Klein when, suddenly, Himmler spoke.

"Fuchs, Vogel; a word." Such a simple phrase, but commanding, nevertheless. The four of them stopped dead in their tracks upon hearing his voice and as one they all turned back to look at the leader of the SS who was still seated behind the desk.

"Of course, Reichsführer," replied Fuchs before speaking to Roth. "Wait outside, Captain." With that, the two SS men walked back into the room as Roth and Klein continued to walk out into the hallway. The two SS guards stationed there were still at attention on either side of the doors, staring impassively ahead.

Fuchs and Vogel had returned to stand in front of Himmler, closing the door as they'd entered back into the office. Meanwhile, back in the corridor, Roth turned to his right as he watched three other SS soldiers approach him and Klein.

"Professor, would you come with us, please, we have transport waiting for you," said the first one. The hairs on the back of Roth's neck stood up as the SS corporal spoke. It appeared to be an innocent request, but it also seemed to him that it had sinister overtones. The professor looked nervous, apprehensive, but bade Roth farewell and good luck and then walked off with the three soldiers. Roth couldn't help but think that Klein was about to become another victim of the Reich. A loyal servant one moment, and then a bullet in the back of the head and a shallow grave the next. *Dead men and all that,* he mused. Could that be a fate that awaited him and his crew if things went wrong? It was clear he couldn't trust these swines.

*

Back inside the office, Fuchs and Vogel stood in front of Himmler at attention. The room was suddenly bathed in sunlight as the sun broke through the clouds and past the Prussian blue velvet curtains that adorned the floor-to-ceiling window in the grand office. Strangely, though, the room remained cold. The Reichsführer, still seated, spoke in his calm yet unnerving manner.

"Failure of this mission is not an option. No one outside a small circle of trusted people know of its existence. Roth and his crew are just a delivery method; no more, no less. Upon their return they shall not meet with the supply sub as expected. No such rendezvous will take place. You will leave a bomb on board which has a twenty-four-hour timer fitted that you will activate as you leave the boat. You will obtain the bomb from one of my aides at the quayside at Peenemünde. You will hide the bomb and timer in the torpedo room of the sub.

"If we fail in this task, we do not want any witnesses to report on the failure of the mission or our involvement. The Reich is depending on you to do your duty and show the allies that we are still the master race. Germany is standing at a crossroad, and it is our task to go forward and not deviate from our chosen path. It is our destiny to rule the world and with this weapon we will achieve all that our Führer has predicted for the German people. The scientists who have worked on the device will shortly disappear, together with any others who are of no consequence; they are of no further use and may be a security risk. Admiral Witzell will unfortunately commit suicide a few days after you have sailed. Professor Klein is being dealt with as we speak.

"I have chosen you two because you are my most loyal officers and I know you will ensure that all goes well – even if it takes your lives to achieve our goals. After you have detonated the bomb in Washington you will find a second car awaiting you, the details of which will be told to you by your contacts upon your arrival in America. You will use this transport to make your way down to the border, and from there into South America and onto a village called La Cumbrecita in Argentina, which is a German enclave. There you will be welcomed by some fellow SS men loyal to me, and then, after a short while, if things have gone to plan, you shall return home to a hero's welcome and all the military riches I can bestow upon you.

"This undertaking will be our finest hour and will ensure that the start of the thousand-year Reich will go down in history. We will all be propelled to the highest peaks of power within Nazi Germany and will be forever in the gratitude of its people. Do I make myself clear?"

Both SS officers gave the Nazi salute and said with gusto, "Heil Hitler." They turned as one and left the room once more.

As Fuchs and Vogel left the room, closing the door behind them, Himmler pressed a buzzer located to his right on the desk. As he did so he took out a slim manila folder from a drawer and placed it on the desk in front of him. Within a moment or two a door behind him opened and a frail, insignificant figure of a man walked in. He was in his early seventies, his slight limp was aided by the walking stick he used, and he looked all of his age. Cataracts were also beginning to diminish his eyesight now as he peered through his thick bottomed glasses. There was also, of course, the matter of his facial features and his heredity that made him stand out like so many of his compatriots. Factors of birth and genetics that ensured he stood out in the racially intolerant society that was Nazi Germany

Here was a proud man, a proud Jew, but at the same time a subjugated one. He had been spared the ignominy of not having the star of David sewn onto his coat, but make no mistake, here was a man like all the rest who was under the control of the jackboots of the Nazis. Like so many before him, he had only been allowed to live because of his expertise and knowledge. His close family had been spared a trip to the death camps run by the SS, and it was clearly an incentive to carry on his work. He stood in front of Himmler's desk and waited to be spoken to.

"Professor Steiner. I believe you have an update on your progress?"

"Yes, sir. I'm sorry – Reichsführer," he corrected. "I do."

"Continue, then."

"As you are aware from our last meeting, we have made great strides in all three rocket projects. The guidance problem with the V1s is behind us and the work that was carried out on the U-boats has been completed. We shall be able to start launching the land-based rockets destined for London by the beginning of May. Von Braun is continuing his work on the V2s and has told me to inform you that the latest tests have shown much progress after the earlier setbacks we encountered. He is estimating an attack by September first."

"And what of your project?"

"Major General Dornberger, the new head of all projects at Peenemünde, has told me to pass on his apologies for not being here today as ordered, and asked me to inform you that he shall be here personally tomorrow with a full update from all the V projects. As for myself, once Professor von Braun has completed his final tests and problem solving with the V2, he will switch his attention and time over to our project. I estimate a test launch within the week. We have encountered similar troubles with the other rockets guidance issues, but we believe we now have an answer. One other item of note is that due to the larger fuel and payload the launch vehicle has had to have major alterations to be able to carry the load, but those are also on time."

"The payload, it is still of a conventional type?"

"Yes, Reichsführer. I regrettably inform you that no progress has been made in that area and the date of a possible completion for the project is still February next year at the earliest."

Himmler stared directly at Steiner with cold, piercing black eyes for a moment and then spoke again.

"Do we have an estimate for a possible launch on the target with the nine hundred kilo warhead?"

"The end of the year, at the latest."

"And what of the Washington bomb, have you done the modifications I ordered?"

"We have. As requested, the bomb will detonate immediately when the green timer button is pressed. The delay function of the bomb has been deactivated."

"Good. That is all, you are dismissed." Steiner turned and slowly walked back out through the door from which he had come, leaning a little heavier on his stick as he did so, the weight of the meeting bearing down upon him. How he hated being summoned here. But he gleaned some comfort in the knowledge that what he had told Himmler was only partly true. The final rocket was on programme as far as the Reich was concerned, but with the help of his like-minded fellow scientists it would never be finished. The Nazis would never have their wish granted for that weapon. So long as the allies made it to Berlin by early next year, that was. For that was as long as they dare hold back on any progress without being found out.

Back inside the office, Himmler opened the file he had taken out earlier, wrote a few notes on the first page with his fountain pen, and closed it again. He also made a mental note to have Steiner's family moved from their family home where he'd deliberately left them to install a degree of control over the professor; the time had come to exert some pressure on the man.

He opened the top drawer in the desk, took one last look at the title on the file, 'New York Rocket', and then put it back.

CHAPTER 6 - BARRACKS

Lunch for Roth and the SS officers was at the SS Leibstandarte barracks, once a former Prussian cadet training school located in the southwest of the city. Roth couldn't help but be impressed by the facility. The main entrance gates had a stone statue on either side, each standing over nine feet tall. These sentinels were replicas of a German soldier and were complete with rifle and helmet. They then drove across an immense parade ground before reaching the two-story brick building that was to be their home for the night. It was adorned with a huge bronze eagle holding a swastika in its talons and was also complemented by two large swastika flags draped either side of it.

The meal turned out to be a buffet, one which Roth was suitably impressed by. It was very lavish, he thought, considering the state of the country and how scarce food could be on the front lines and civilian homes. It irked him somewhat to see such a lavish array of food. He had grown accustomed over these last few years to eating less and less, and it had become harder to even find an appetite when you did eventually have something to eat, either when out on patrol or on shore. Especially when he saw all those around him going hungry. Subsequently, his frame reflected his poor eating and he looked thin for his height of one-hundred-and-eighty centimetres, but then you never came across a fat submariner in the Kriegsmarine.

The dining table had been laid with a fine cotton tablecloth – yet more Berlin extravagance. He looked across at the two SS officers seated opposite, his new comrades in arms who were eagerly tucking into their plates of food which were piled high, and he began to study each in turn. Fuchs was the taller of the two and exuded confidence bordering on arrogance, probably a requirement for a major of the SS. Now that he had removed his peaked cap, Roth guessed that he was in his mid to late twenties, his full head of blond hair and his black dress uniform making him stand out as a true Aryan.

Vogel on the other hand didn't strike Roth as such a strong character compared to his senior officer, but as he had only just met them both he couldn't afford to make such an assumption; it could be a dangerous mistake to underestimate either of these two men. Vogel was of a similar height and build to Roth, but the broken nose and scarred left cheek gave him a look of real menace; he'd clearly been in a fight or two. Vogel's head was shaved to being almost bald and he looked the part of a killer who belonged in the SS.

Suddenly, Roth was startled to hear someone speaking English – it was Fuchs. "So, Roth, I understand you are from Hamburg originally?"

Roth was taken aback at being spoken to in English but replied in the same language.

"Yes, Hamburg, but how did you know I spoke English?"

"You were not singled out for this mission by chance, far from it. I have studied your file from cover to cover. We know that your mother was from Munich, your father from Hamburg, and your father met her while he was working as a trawler man, correct?"

"Yes. They met in a bar in Hamburg, my mother was in town to see her cousin."

"What I did find most interesting was what happened to you all after the Great War. Please, tell us the story of your father."

Roth was aware he was being interrogated to a degree

by these thugs and was wary of them. He was determined to only give them a brief outline of his past, he didn't fancy giving them any morsel that they could use against him later. The double S, or 'Schutzstaffel', insignia on their lapels was a stark reminder of just who he was conversing with here.

"My father, Gerard, was a sergeant in the infantry, serving in the trenches. He was wounded on the Somme, August '16, and was invalided out shortly thereafter. He despised the French, hated them, and always did, as he once told me. He saw the Treaty of Versailles as this country's greatest betrayal after all the sacrifices he and his comrades had made. Germany had been humiliated, the country divided into pieces. The people were also divided, and because of the sanctions imposed later by the treaty, people were starving and dying. So, we sailed to America, leaving the great complexity of Europe, as he described the politics there, far behind. It was 1919. I was only two at the time. We settled in Charleston, South Carolina – a large fishing port where he got a job on a trawler.

"I grew up having an American childhood, but as I grew older, I began to suffer more and more abuse and bullying because of where I came from. My parents raised me with German values and taught me both German and English as a language, but they made sure I always spoke to anyone in English; they knew that we may be persecuted as Germans living there. I never advertised my heritage, but the other kids just knew, so I was always getting into fights, defending my past – a past I knew little of.

"Then, in 1936, we came back. My father had read and heard how the Führer was getting Germany's lands and dignity back. He liked what was happening here, how National Socialism was the answer to the rising threat of communism and how the Nazis were controlling the country. Plus, it was becoming evident that Germans in America were even less popular than before. We settled back in Hamburg, my father turning to the fishing trade once more. Shortly after we got back, I joined the naval academy in 1937 at Flensburg on the Jutland peninsula, a couple of hours away by train from Hamburg. I was lucky to serve some time aboard the tall ship the '*Gorch Fock*', a fabulous three mast sailing vessel. I admit I fell in love with the thought of the sea because of my time on board there, but then I signed up for the U-Bootwaffe, mainly enticed by the glamour, and its leader, Doenitz. I then underwent seven months of training at Neustadt Holstein. I was involved in Operation Sea Lion back in '40, if you can call it an operation. We were going to provide a submarine screen to protect the barges that were going to be towed across the channel, but the so-called beaten RAF put up a bit of a fight and the rest is history, as I'm sure you're aware of?"

"I read in your file that your mother was killed in an air raid?"

"Yes. She was coming back from the street market, near our home." Roth changed the subject; he didn't feel comfortable relating anymore. "Your English is excellent, also," he remarked to Fuchs.

"Yes, it's passable. During our time together at sea we will practice our English with you to try to eradicate our Germanic phrases. Vogel was educated at a university in England, the London School of Economics, on an exchange course. I studied English at Bad Tolz, the SS officer training school in Bavaria. I'm not bright enough to attend any university, plus I'm a few years older than Vogel here. I'm told I could pass for an Englander, but it's an American accent I've been working on for the last month or so. We need to pass for plain, local civilians once we land, as part of the plan, nothing out of the ordinary – but more about that when we are at sea. On that subject, what can we expect about our journey?"

"It's no picnic on board, that's for sure. We take fresh produce with us, all strung about overhead in the boat or stuffed under bunks, as there's little room. But the fresh food soon runs out, and then it's tinned food or jars. It's the humidity that's the real problem. Everything is soaked through, the food starts to rot, and the bread goes mouldy within days. Moisture drips from the walls and pipes constantly. Unfortunately, the freshwater is for drinking only, no washing or shaving for the length of the trip; you can imagine that body odour is a problem, but you get used to it, eventually. We wear civilian clothes, for comfort's sake. Sometimes there can be words exchanged between comrades, friends argue. We are pushed to the limit – forty-five men in such a confined space for weeks on end, nerves can be stretched. Most of the crew stays below for the trip, they don't get a chance to go up to get fresh air or see the light of day.

"Of course, then there's being under attack. That is something else, too. Waiting for depth charges to explode is as terrifying as one might imagine. You hear the splash as they enter the water and then you wait. The wait is unnerving. One of my crew compared it to a childhood experience he remembered. He said his neighbour's Alsatian was growling at him, ready to pounce, he thought. He was rooted to the spot. He knew it was going to bark at him or snap, but he still jumped out of his skin when it did. It's the waiting, and there's nothing we can do. Then there's the stench of the diesel fumes. The sweat and urine smell can be overpowering. Plus, the air tastes foul when we are submerged, but we continue to do our duty."

"You said urine. There is, of course, a toilet on

board, yes?"

"Of course. In fact, there are two, but one is used to store food and if there is an enemy ship above us, we can't flush the toilet as the bubbles released from it would give our position away. So, for the duration of any action, we pee in open jars or tins, which can spill over sometimes. We were once submerged for eighteen hours and had over a hundred depth charges dropped down our throat, each explosion chalked up on the small blackboard we keep hanging up in the control room. Not a pleasant time, I can assure you both."

"That may well be, Captain, but like the Spanish conquistadors we intend to leave our mark on America! Our trip in your submarine doesn't sound like a picnic, as you said, but the ends will justify the means, as the British say. Come, enjoy your food, Captain. We will fly to Peenemünde in the morning, where we will await the arrival of your submarine."

After they had eaten, Fuchs and Vogel bade the submarine captain goodnight and then Roth was shown to his overnight quarters on the second floor of the barracks where he took a greatly needed hot shower before collapsing between the sheets and succumbing to a very deep sleep. It had been over thirty-six hours since he'd had a chance to close his eyes. At first, his mind wandered to the day's events and what he had been ordered to undertake, but the weariness he felt overcame any desire he had to process the enormity of the task ahead.

As Roth dropped off to sleep in his quarters, Fuchs and Vogel stood outside in the cobbled courtyard of the SS barracks. They were both smoking. The sun was high now in a crisp clear blue sky as soldiers of many different ranks went about their duties, passing by the two officers.

"They are getting younger, my friend, every time we

see them. Soon they will be wearing nappies and throwing toys at the advancing Russians on our front lines!" said Vogel. Fuchs shook his head slowly as if in agreement and he stared at one of the passing storm troopers, who was seventeen at the most, before he replied.

"It worries me greatly seeing where we are now. This mission of ours could be our only hope to save Germany and the Third Reich. We must succeed and stop the allies from launching a second front. I fear that if we fail it will only be a matter of time before our little corporal and his gang will all be swinging from a rope, with you and I waiting in line to join them. Something else, too. What of the bomb built by Klein, this black bomb? If we can detonate it in Washington, what next? What else does Himmler have planned for the potential of such a bomb? London perhaps, when the V1s are finally launched from the French coast – will they carry such a weapon?"

The two men puffed on their cigarettes simultaneously and there was a slight pause before Vogel continued.

"I'm not sure what he has planned. We can't trust him and must watch our own backs all the time. Trust no one. If we are successful in America, what of our escape? If we manage to pull it off and evade capture, we will be hunted like dogs. Can we even make it to Argentina?"

"We will succeed, have no fear, I am confident of that, but we may have to die doing so. This is the greatest test we have had to face as soldiers in this war, and it's one we must complete. Escaping to Argentina and back home eventually may be just a dream for us, but if we don't look to the future then all is lost. But this attack in America's backyard by this weapon may have far greater consequences than we can imagine. If the Americans do have the atomic bomb as we fear, they will reduce Berlin to ashes in a single moment, and that changes everything, my friend, to a level far beyond us as simple soldiers. It may change the world, one way or the other."

Fuchs now changed the subject as he took one last draw on his cigarette before throwing it on the ground and stamping it out under the heel of his boot.

"What do you make of our captain?"

"His service record is exceptional. He's done well to get this far. Last year I heard that four out of five U-boats didn't come back from patrol, and the chances of outlasting the war on one of those sardine tins isn't great. I'd take my chances on the battlefield any day compared to the chance of slowly suffocating on the bottom of the Atlantic. Can't say I'm looking forward to two weeks stuck in that thing. I've never been on a boat, never mind a sub! The confines, the smells, the dangers, I might as well be in a Munich beer hall!" The two men laughed.

"They've also picked him because of his nerve. He's gotten out of many scrapes, by all accounts. Then, there's his experience, not to mention the tons of merchant shipping to his name. One of our best!"

"One of the only ones left, too!"

"I don't think we have anything to fear from Roth, he will do his duty and get us there safely with our package. Come, old friend, your talk of beer halls has made me thirsty. You can buy me a beer and tell me again about that French widow you slept with in Paris, the one whose husband was killed on the first day of the invasion, back in '40." With that, the two comrades strode off towards the bar.

*

It was a couple of hours later now, but Roth felt like he'd drifted off to sleep only a few minutes ago when he was awoken suddenly by shouting coming from the corridor. Someone was banging violently on his bedroom door.

"ACHTUNG! ACHTUNG! Get to the shelters!" Roth

could hear the air raid sirens now. He rose from the bed and looked out the window, peering into the dark night sky. The long fingers of searchlight beams crisscrossed the view outside. Flashes of flak were coming from behind the buildings in the courtyard. The sound of hundreds of bombers was now ebbing through to Roth; it was yet another air raid.

CHAPTER 7 - FLOWER

The sounds of utensils banging against pots and the appetising smells of cooking were drifting across in the morning breeze to where First Lieutenant Peter Robinson was sitting on a crate located on the side of the naval dockside in Hull, Northeast England. The sounds were coming from the galley aboard his ship, *HMS Zenobia*. It had seemed ages since breakfast, he thought, and his stomach rumbled as if on cue. A glance at his watch told him it had just gone 1030 hours. He knew that it was 'blind scouse' for lunch today; a traditional meal from his hometown of Liverpool. It was normally a vegetable and lamb stew, but there was no meat in it today, hence the name, rationing responsible for the lack of protein. The memories of home had brought a smile to his face when the cook had told him earlier that it was the stew for lunch. He took solace in the fact that meals in port were far better than those out at sea. Because of the lack of storage for fresh food, they would become reliant on potatoes and corned beef once underway. *Not a happy prospect*, he thought.

This wasn't his first time in the port of Hull. He'd passed through there at the very start of the war, back in '39. He didn't have happy memories of his brief visit. The Germans had been quick off the mark once hostilities were announced and had laid anti-shipping mines in the narrow channels that led into the harbour. Some had been laid by boats, but some also from the air and they were of a new design, unlike the contact mines that he knew. These new ones would lie on the seabed and detonate as a ship passed overhead; how they worked he wasn't sure, but what he did know was that they were hard to find and extremely deadly. The merchant ships *Broadmere* and

Pendragon Coast had both fallen victim to these new mines back then and had sunk. The superstructure of one of them could still be seen at low tide out in the harbour.

As he sat here now on the dockside, – wearing his blue overalls over his uniform, his cap perched at an angle on his head – he was having a well-earned cigarette break. He'd just supervised the last of the ammunition for the *Zenobia*'s four-inch gun to go aboard via the dock cranes, and it was now being safely stowed away below deck. There was, of course, no smoking allowed during the loading operation, but as it was now safe to do so he'd told the lads on the dockside to light up if they wanted to. From his perch on the dockside, he looked across at the small ship that was moored there – a large 'K52' was painted in black on its bow. Its original design had been as a whaler, but it had then been redesigned for its current role. He was unsure about the Flower-class corvette as a fighting vessel, and, as it lay there in the waters of the harbour, it was being dwarfed by the imposing J-class destroyer, *HMS Jervis*, moored on its far side. The sea grey coloured superstructure of the destroyer towered above the smaller ship. Most of the lease-lend batch of ships from the Americans were mainly fine, but these corvettes rolled and pitched terribly in rough seas, apparently.

He'd heard an American sailor on the quayside the other day say that these small ships would struggle to stay upright in a saucer of milk, that they were slower than a surfaced U-boat and reputed to sink faster than a brick with an anvil tied to it. Apparently, the ships themselves were so named because Churchill had ordered it. Because, he said, "The Germans wouldn't like being sunk by a vessel named after a flower!" It didn't instil much confidence in Robinson at all.

He'd served on similar destroyers to the *Jervis* earlier

in the conflict and in the much warmer waters of the Mediterranean campaign but had been transferred to this type just three weeks ago, and he was still finding it hard to comprehend why.

His previous captain had informed him that, quote, "His experience was needed on the *Zenobia*, as the crew would benefit from it." Robinson viewed the move as a demotion, even though he still held the same rank as before. What really irked him as he took another long pull on his Woodbine cigarette was the fact that *Zenobia* was to be no more than a bloody glorified mail van. It was unlikely to see any action as they steamed around dropping off mail here and there, or ferrying an admiral or two from port to port, all helping the second front – whenever and wherever that was. There was a need for a ship to help with communications during the build-up to the invasion, but he was irritated over being the one to have to do it.

Having lost his uncle on *HMS Hood* back in '40 to the *Bismarck*, he wanted to get payback, but that was now unlikely as the war ended. He drew long and hard for the last time on the cigarette, threw it to the ground, stood up, and extinguished the butt by stamping it with the ball of his foot. He was thinking of asking his new captain, Prince, about allowing him to take the evening off so he could pop into town. He wanted to continue practicing his charm on the barmaid at the Crown Pub. She wasn't the prettiest girl he'd met during this war, but he mused that she was only a line or two from her falling for his patter. It was at least a month since he'd last had sex, and that was with the wife, so it didn't count. Anyway, if she didn't come across, he'd have a few beers and then go and get a hot bath; the ship's hot water always seemed so tepid to him.

His mind made up, he started to make his way toward

the gang plank which would take him back onto the *Zenobia* and was about to shout to some crew members when he heard the distinctive sound of a motorbike approaching. It was slowly bumping along the cobbled dockside to his left. The dispatch rider slowed down and came to a halt next to the twenty-nine-year-old officer, the rider switching off the engine as he did so.

"Looking for *HMS Zenobia*, sir, and a Captain Prince," said the rider.

"This is *Zenobia* and I'm the exec," replied Robinson. As he did so, he reached into his right-hand breast pocket beneath his overalls and produced his credentials. He passed them over to the young Royal Corps of Signals corporal who sat astride the olive green coloured Norton16H motor bike. The distinctive odour of petrol was wafting up from the hot engine. The rider lifted his goggles and pushed them on to the top of his leather helmet. He took the papers from Robinson, looked at them for a moment, and then passed them back. He then reached into his satchel which, was slung around his neck, and pulled out an envelope which he passed to Robinson together with a small note pad.

"If you could just sign my book to say you've had this, sir, I'll be on my way."

"Of course, no problem." Robinson signed the chitty and gave it back. The rider then saluted him, which Robinson returned.

As the rider kick-started his bike and set off, Robinson shouted over to the crew still grouped together smoking and shouted an order.

"Right, you lot, back to it. Get the last of those spuds on board and then come back and get the rest of those provisions back there in the shed onto the ship, too!"

He then spun towards the ship and strode off to find the captain. As he reached the wooden gangplank, which rose at a steep angle from the dock to the ship above, he contemplated for a moment about his new captain, whom he had only met two weeks previously. He'd heard about him and his previous deployment, but that didn't bother Robinson. No; it was his quiet demeanour that he couldn't come to terms with. The man didn't strike him as a natural leader. His character was, in Robinson's opinion, weak. Robinson had served under two great captains while in the Indian Ocean during the early part of the war, both of whom had shown moral fibre and quick decision making while under enemy fire, which had ultimately led to the ship's survival. Whilst Prince was yet to prove himself, Robinson couldn't help but judge the man on his performance in front of the officers and crew so far. Not very inspiring, he thought.

*

Captain Prince was seated at his desk in his cabin on board *Zenobia*. The radio was on low and tuned into the BBC home service, the music while you work programme. Holst's *The Planets* suite was playing. Prince had been buried under a mountain of paperwork for most of the morning; correspondence of various designs, bills for the ship, routine signals from the admiralty, and so on. He paused for a moment. In his left hand he held a framed photograph of his wife, Jane, and himself on their wedding day. It had only been two days since they had been together last, at home in Margate, Kent, but he missed her so much. She'd be busy back home, working as a ward sister in their local cottage hospital. They'd been lucky to be able to spend their leave together this last time, as most of the time previously they had not been able to meet up, their schedules clashing.

He thought back to his wedding day, back in 1927. He was twenty, Jane was nineteen. They'd met in a pub in Oxford. He was studying for his degree in Geology, a career in teaching – his long-term ambition. At the same time, he'd been in the Royal Navy Volunteer Reserve, – something he'd joined while at the University – but he'd been persuaded by his commander to join the navy instead of going on to become a teacher. "There's a war coming, David," he had said. He'd been married for seventeen years now and had a daughter, an only child called Pauline. She was aged twelve and living with Jane's parents in Wales for safety. God, it had been over a year since he'd seen her. His eyes welled up as he pictured her standing on the station platform by the train before she left for Conway.

The portholes of his cabin were open as it had felt quite warm in the confines of the converted whaler, and he could hear the busy harbour; it was a compromise, keeping cool but having to listen to the noises outside. The banging on metal with hammers, the sawing of wood, and the banshee-like screech of grinding metal was interspersed with shouts and even laughter occasionally from the workmen on the quayside who were busy day and night working on the other ships in the docks. Multiple sounds from within the confines of the ship were drifting through to him as well. He raised his glass of gin and took a sip, still looking at the photo of his wife. There was a knock on the frame of the entrance to the cabin.

"Enter," said the softly spoken commander. His exec, Lieutenant Peter Robinson, pulled back the curtain which served as a privacy screen and came in holding a buff-coloured envelope.

"This has just been delivered by dispatch rider, sir," he said and gave the envelope to his commanding officer.

"Could be our first duty in the invasion build up, Peter. Are we ready?"

"Ships company all back from leave. Most of the

provisions and munitions are stowed, sir, and all but a few of the workmen have gone ashore. Couple of them are working on the armour around the Hedgehog, sir, securing the plates to the deck. How exactly does that work, sir?"

"The Hedgehog? Better than the depth charges, I'm told. Its forward firing, up to twenty-four mortar bombs with contact fuses, so, unlike depth charges which explode at a guessed depth of the submarine, these explode upon hitting the target and should in theory do the job more efficiently. It has a large spread, or field of fire. Just one of those babies hitting the target and down goes 'Jerry'!"

"We just need a quick trip out in the bay to see she's all ship shape and Bristol fashion, sir. As a matter of fact, before we head out, I was wondering if I could slip away for a few hours this evening, sir?"

Prince smiled inwardly at Robinson's Liverpool accent. It had taken him a while to even understand the broad scouse twang of his exec, but these days he embraced its northern warmth; it was a world away from his own southern accent. He didn't offer a reply to the request but turned his attention to the matter at hand.

Prince gestured for Robinson to take a seat as he then slipped a letter opener into the end of the envelope and slid it across before reaching in and pulling out the three sheets of paper inside. It was a moment or two before he spoke again.

"Nothing exciting here, I'm afraid, just routine orders to proceed with sea trials as soon as possible and then report to Portsmouth harbour on the fifteenth, and on then to new duties. We shall receive sealed orders when we arrive at port."

"Anything about taking any action in the invasion itself, sir, or are we to patrol the coast or deliver bloody mail as per our original orders? Could do with something with more of an edge, if you get my drift, sir?"

"I've been pushing the brass for something of more significance in the forthcoming action, but they keep fobbing me off, saying what we'll be doing is vitally important, which I guess it is. Just as dull as dishwater, I'm afraid. The orders are telling us to get out to sea as soon as possible, get these trials under our belt, and be ready for deployment. So, we'll go out on the next tide, which I know is only two hours from now."

"That's cutting it fine, sir. We need that time alone to shake down the crew, half of them don't know the others and some are raw recruits. We need training on the guns, depth charges, these new Hedgehogs, everything! Ideally, we need at least another four to five days before we're halfway ready, sir!"

"You're right, but they won't learn anything sitting here. As soon as we're underway I want a full schedule of practice started on all the essentials. Put together a quick program for me to look at, will you? How quickly can we get underway?"

"At least all those two hours, sir. It'll take a while to get us fired up and the last of the gear stowed."

"Make that an hour and a half, I want to make that tide. Tell the officers I'd like to see them in the wardroom in ten minutes, would you? I'll brief them then, and could you get the chief here now, too?"

Robinson stood, saluted, and went to do as he'd been ordered. Prince sat there for a moment, contemplating the task of the sea trials, thinking deeply about the possibility of forthcoming action and, also, reflecting on the past. He'd been the executive officer on board *HMS Holcombe*, sunk in the Mediterranean by a U-boat only four months ago, in December. The destroyer and so many comrades were lost to the sea whilst on convoy duty near the coast of Algeria. He wasn't sure he'd ever get another chance on board a front-line command. This new commission had come as a surprise, so quickly after *Holcombe*, but he was determined to grasp it with both hands. This ship, one of the latest corvettes, was more than capable of seeing the job through. It was faster than the older types, with newer armament. It carried nearly double the amount of depth charges, and the latest radar and Asdic had been fitted during her refit. He was confident in his and the ship's capabilities. The only doubt in his mind was the inexperience of most of the crew, but they all deserved a chance of some action, not the sort of action they'd been tasked with.

Although the allies hadn't launched the so-called second front, it was only a matter of time before the end of this horror would be in sight. 'Over by Christmas' was a popular perception amongst the masses, but he himself didn't lean towards that way of thinking. There was a glimmer of hope, of course, with the Russians advancing in the East, and the Germans losing in North Africa and now fighting a retreat up through Italy. Maybe another year, eighteen months perhaps, and he'd be home watching his daughter grow up in a peaceful world.

Prince was suddenly aware that someone was coming down the corridor towards his cabin, the heavy sounding footfall distinctive in its own way. He looked at the open door as the ship's chief petty officer, Scott, knocked, saluted, and walked in.

"You wanted to see me, sir?" he asked.

Prince looked at him, smiled, and spoke.

"Yes, chief. Looks like we're back in the war!"

"Depends on your perspective, sir, if you don't mind my saying so," the rugged looking forty-year-old replied.

"I want to leave port in under two hours, so get those boilers stoked up and ready. All your men are old hands, aren't they? No fresh blood to mother, anyway?"

"Yes, sir. I don't mind admitting it's easier with the old salts down there. Except old Charlie. Always been hard work, that one, since I've known him. 'Like a tree from the bollocks up', as my old dad used to say. We'll be ready, sir. Is that all?"

"Yes. Dismissed." Scott saluted and left. Prince smiled to himself again.

In the wardroom, the four officers under Captain Prince had assembled, as requested. They hardly knew each other, having only come together in the last few weeks on board the ship.

"What was it you said you wanted to be, Clarke, before the war?" asked Lieutenant Jones, trying to make conversation with the young officer with whom he'd only snatched one or two brief moments with so far.

"I was going to work as an apprentice carpenter. Always liked working with my hands, and my uncle is in the building trade, so he promised me a slot under him, but then Jerry intervened so that was that. What about you?"

But, as Smith was about to reply, Prince walked into the wardroom and saw Robinson with the three other officers standing in a huddle together. They turned as one, all giving a smart salute to their commanding officer as they did so.

"Please, gentlemen, take a seat," said Prince. They did as they were asked. Prince remained standing and looked to Lieutenant Jordan, a young officer, just like many other officers serving on these corvettes, having been drawn from the naval reserve. "How are we in regard to the Hedgehog and training, Eddy?"

"Well, sir, it's early days, I'm afraid. As you know I'm only recently back from the course on how to use it myself, and although I feel confident in my abilities the men are all new to it. I've got a mixture of experience and raw talent in the squad, but they seem willing to learn. Just need a few days to get them up to speed so its second nature, rather than having to think about it. It's the reloading where we need to practice and drill; that's the key to sinking a sub. Get as many of the projectiles in the water, in the right spot at the right time. Then, of course, I've also got to train the gun crew, all new, I'm afraid. They've had training on shore, but it's another thing to do it on a rolling ship and potentially under fire. I'll have it all done by the time we reach Portsmouth, sir, I'm sure."

"Thank you. Now, what about Asdic and radar operations, Lieutenant Smith? I trust there are no surprises there?"

"No, sir. Fortunately, all the men are experienced sailors and well versed in the use of the equipment. The sets are brand new, the latest specifications, and are working fine. Once we're at sea I have a timetable of drills I want to go over with the operators. No problems there, sir."

"Thank you, Graham." Prince now looked to the youngest and least experienced officer: twenty-year-old midshipman Phillip Clarke, who was responsible for the general running of the boat, paperwork, stores, etc.

"Most of the stores are still being put away, sir, as the deliveries seemed to all come at once. Munitions are safely in place, thankfully. We will probably still be sorting out the stores, unfortunately, as we set sail, but all should be done an hour or so later. I will then attend to my paperwork which I regret to say I have let lapse," replied Clarke. His face blushed ever so, underlying his youthful exuberance, perhaps. The boy looked as though he should be doing a paper round tomorrow morning, not sailing off to fight a hidden enemy in treacherous seas.

"Right then, it seems like we have things under

control. No time for a snorter, I'm sorry to say, so I look forward to a drink and the pleasure of your company later, perhaps this evening. Right, I'm off to the bridge, Peter, can you join me, please? As for the rest of you: dismissed." All three stood to attention, saluted, and filed out of the wardroom behind the captain. Robinson spoke as the captain was about to leave.

"I'm right behind you, sir, just gotta check on an issue with the Boefers gun ammunition that I was told about on my way here, won't be long."

"Right, see you there, X.O."

It only took a few moments for Prince to reach the open bridge located on the forecastle, a high forward vantage-point of the ship – just forward of the mast and behind the four-inch gun located on the main deck. The small open plan design was dominated by a raised central pedestal containing the ship's compass and telegraph, both sitting on the wooden deck. Standing there gave a slightly better view of your surroundings. Several brass voice tubes, which connected the captain to different parts of the ship, lined the front wooden partition of the bridge; the other three sides of the bridge had similar chest-high wooden sections. The front partition screen was topped with glass which was supposed to act as a shield against the wind and waves, but in truth did little to protect the captain and crew from the elements. In fact, any waves that crashed over here washed down through into the bowels of the ship. One drawback of the ship's open design was its tendency to let in water on rough seas as many of the passageways were open, leading to a nickname of the floating colander.

The captain's wooden chair, which could swivel, stood empty and Prince made his way over to it. The area was usually crowded with members of the watch. The two 20mm Oerlikon machine guns covered over with their tarpaulins stood silent also, but now, whilst they were in port, all was empty and quiet. The only sound now to be heard was a distant steam whistle as a train departed the dockside. Before he sat down, he reached into his jacket pocket and produced a pack of Woodbine cigarettes. He took one out, lit it, took a long satisfying pull on the tobacco within and sat down.

He took another pull on the cigarette, blew out a stream of smoke, and then peered out into the distance and the open sea. His head fell back slightly, and his gaze wandered upwards. A few cumulus clouds were drifting aimlessly high above, painted white across a canvas of deep blue, it seemed. A lone gull floated across the scene, gliding on the breeze. He remembered a similar start to the day aboard *HMS Sterling*, a ship he'd served on as a lieutenant back in '41. They had been hunting submarines just west of the Bay of Biscay and he'd been on watch. The difference from that day to this, and what came to mind now, was the shout from one of the lookouts that broke the morning's calm.

"ENEMY AIRCRAFT! Ten degrees off the port bow, heading this way!" and then the klaxon sounded, its alarm piercing and echoing off the steel walls of the destroyer. Prince found himself back on his old ship, when he was Lieutenant of the *Sterling*. All hell broke loose as sailors scrambled to their action stations. The anti-aircraft guns all around the ship were uncovered and quickly manned, the training and experience of the crew coming to the fore. Lieutenant Prince raised his binoculars skyward in the direction of the sighting. At first, he couldn't pick them out, but then he saw them: two Junkers Ju 88 attack bombers, around one-thousand feet high and maybe a quarter of a mile apart – a usual formation for an attack at sea.

The Ju 88 was a formidable opponent. Armed with a

20mm cannon and three 7.92mm machine guns in its nose, plus its array of fifty kilogram or five-hundred kilogram bombs, it was ideally suited to the dive-bombing role that the Luftwaffe had bestowed on it. Only its cousin, the 'Stuka' dive bomber, could outshine it in that role. It was fast, too, and, unlike the 'Stuka' which dived at a near vertical angle, these would make their attack run at a much shallower descent.

The deafening sound of the four 40mm Bofors guns on the port side of *HMS Sterling* opened up simultaneously, their rhythmic *thump, thump, thump* reverberating through the deck beneath Prince's feet. The puffs of black smoke on the skyline were evidence of the flak bursts as they sought to bring down the attacking aircraft. The twin 20mm Oerlikon machine guns began firing, too, as the Junkers drew nearer, continuous short bursts of shots rattled forth from the barrels in their direction. The drone of the twin-engine planes could clearly be heard now, the light sea grey of the underbellies of the plane momentarily merging within the haze of ocean and sky. Prince had dropped his binoculars down onto his chest now, held there by its thin leather strap, and he was sweeping his sight from the two different places that the planes were coming in from, tracer rounds from the machine guns arcing towards them as the sailors manning the guns adjusted their fall of shot. The Junkers were offering little in the way of a target as they came in, low and from the side of the ship.

Prince couldn't hear the guns firing from the attacking planes at this distance, but bursts of smoke exploded from the noses, followed by high columns of spray erupting from the sea in parallel lines as they drew ever closer in an accelerated procession towards the ship. What he *could* hear were the two inline V12 engines on full throttle as they powered the planes ever closer. The sky was full of thousands of rounds of ammunition racing skyward from the decks of the *Sterling*. Empty brass shell cases tinkled as they cascaded free from the guns once spent and hit the deck, scattering all around. The air was filled with the overriding smell of cordite. When it seemed like the Junkers, now only a few hundred yards apart from one another, would crash directly into the ship, they pulled out from their dives and released two bombs each.

The sound of the whistle of the bombs falling towards the ship pierced through the cacophony of a multitude of guns that were firing on board. Three bombs fell short; huge spouts of water shot skyward as they exploded, drenching the gunners on that side of the ship. But then the fourth bomb struck the destroyer amidships, directly between the two funnels and into the engine room itself. A massive explosion ripped through the steel plates and wooden decks of the twenty-five-year-old vessel. The five hundred pounds of TNT within the bomb caused extensive damage, making the crew, who weren't instantly killed, stumble and fall as the ship rocked over to its right momentarily. The planes roared overhead, the engine noise deafening now. Tracer rounds followed their path as they flew over at nearly four-hundred miles an hour, barely a hundred feet high, the draft caused by their passing washing over all who stood on the deck. The guns on the starboard side now took up the fight as they passed overhead and turned to make another pass. Cries of dying sailors could be heard above the chatter of the guns as they traced after the two circling planes that were coming back for a second run. Merciless, savage, bright orange flames could be seen licking up all around the shattered remains that was once the heart of the *Sterling*. A strong smell of fuel oil permeated the air and plumes of smoke began to billow out from the many fires that were raging on deck, the calls for fire crews to quell the inferno immediately rang out as the flames were threatening to engulf the destroyer.

The guns on board fell silent for a moment as the planes were out of range. The gunners used the time to replenish their ammunition and to sweep away with their feet the hundreds of shell casings that littered the deck. Some of the guns on the port side had been destroyed by the explosion, the ship vulnerable now to the second attack that was bearing down on them once again. Prince was transfixed as he looked out to where the planes were lining up for another run, his eyes stinging from the smoke and ash that was sweeping across the bridge from the fires behind him, blown there by the wind.

Remarkably, the crew on the bridge were all still alive, untouched by the attack. The captain was barking an order to come about down the voice tube to an unresponsive and fatally wounded helmsman below him. Prince stood there, the two dots in the distance growing ever larger, the experienced Luftwaffe pilots changing their angles of attack as they raced in for the kill, their prey below seriously wounded. Their forward momentum slowed down, ready for the 'coup de grace.' Once more, the remaining guns on the ship began to fire at the oncoming planes, closer and closer they drew, seemingly untouched by the hail of lead that swept up to meet them. Once more, the planes opened up with their own guns, the bomb bays wide open, the engine noises increasing in volume as they neared the destroyer and helpless crew below. The ship loomed large in the bomb sights of the Junkers as they lined up the stricken ship.

Prince watched as the bombs fell away for a second time from the bellies of the planes, each one emitting that harrowing, screeching whistle that filled all below with a terrible foreboding, four more projectiles arrowing towards them. He could clearly see each bomb hurtling down, even the fins on the back as they twisted through the air, plummeting downward, drawing closer.

Back in the now, Prince quickly sat upright; a sharp sudden pain in his right hand had woken him. He shook loose the burning cigarette that was there and threw it onto the deck of the *Zenobia*, the hot embers stinging his flesh had brought him back from his stupor. He stood and quickly stamped out what remained of the Woodbine he had lit just a few moments earlier. He turned to see Lieutenant Robinson appearing from the rear of the bridge; he composed himself and addressed his officer.

"What do you make of it all, Lieutenant? This ship, the invasion, I mean. An honest opinion, if you may?"

It was a moment or two before Robinson replied.

"Well, sir, to be frank we need more time to train, which I know we can't have. But, then again, if we only end up with escort or patrolling duties we might scrape by, what with all the young and inexperienced officers and crew on board. We can only learn from experience, and to get that you need to see action. We're damned if we do and damned if we don't, sir, if you get my drift?"

"Do you include myself in those thoughts, Robinson?"

"I'm sorry, sir, I'm not sure I understand?"

"I get the feeling you don't want to be on this ship. Perhaps my authority isn't as commanding as you'd like. I realise that you last served on a destroyer and have more experience than myself, but let me assure you that my quiet disposition does not in any way reflect how I operate when the situation calls."

"I'm sorry, sir, if you think I haven't shown you the respect that you and your rank deserve, but I feel that as we are only at the beginning of our working relationship that any misgivings on either of our parts can only dissipate as we come to know each other, and the ship and crew start to become one. As for me coming from a bigger ship, I can see I haven't hidden my displeasure at being assigned to the *Zenobia*, but I can only state that you will have one-hundred percent commitment and loyalty going forward. You will have absolutely no worries about me carrying out my duties to the best of my ability."

"I'm glad to hear that. After reading your service record, I'm in no doubt that I have a fine executive officer to rely on to help me run this ship, but if at any time you feel the need to speak to me about anything in regard to *Zenobia*, I want you and the other officers to approach me. I don't want us to second guess each other or have any regrets, do I make myself clear?"

"Yes, sir. Thank you." Robinson saluted his commanding officer, turned, and left.

Prince's thoughts returned to that fateful day back on board the *Sterling*. They had been lucky that day – if you can call seventeen dead, fifteen wounded, and a severely crippled ship lucky. The bombs from the Junkers' second attack had sailed over the heads of all on board and exploded harmlessly off to the starboard beam. The Germans had not been as accurate as they were in the first attack, and when they rose and flew away from the burning ship below, one of them was struck by fire from one of the anti-aircraft guns. It began trailing black smoke from her port engine, great plumes of it, and that sent up a roar from the crew. The two planes now grew smaller by the minute as they headed for home, possibly an airfield somewhere in France. The *Sterling* was able to crawl back to Plymouth under her own steam where her dead and wounded were removed, with weeks of repairs ahead. Prince went on to serve briefly on another destroyer, the *HMS Swift*, and then the *Holcombe* before heading here to command the *Zenobia*.

CHAPTER 8 - PEENEMÜNDE

The flight from Berlin to Peenemünde in the three-engine Junkers Ju52, the workhorse of the Wehrmacht, took a little over thirty-five minutes. These planes carried everything imaginable for the war effort. The army, navy, and air force all used this ubiquitous, if unusual looking, aircraft and today it was to ferry the three officers of Operation Surtr to the rocket research centre, located on the Baltic coast, Northern Germany. Shortly after the flight took off from Tempelhof airfield, Roth decided to engage some more with Fuchs who was sitting across from him on the low metal bench which ran the full length of the interior, normally occupied by paratroopers. He raised his voice to be heard over the noise of the aeroplane's engines.

"So, Fuchs, have you and Vogel been comrades for long?"

There was a pause for a moment before he answered.

"Four years or so, since the fall of France. But this guy here pulled my ass out of the fire, so to speak, during Manstein's counter offensive in the Rzhev salient of '43. We were part of a specially trained SS panzer corps with the new Tiger tanks." Both he and Vogel laughed as they reminisced about recent battles in their mind's eye.

"We were retreating, sorry, making a tactical withdrawal, across the Russian steppes near Kharkov using the tactic of torch and burn as we left, burning everything and anything to deny the advancing Russian army any shelter or supplies, when I was cut off from my unit. I found myself near a farmhouse, its roof already ablaze. I wasn't sure which way to go when three Russian soldiers came across the farmyard, firing at me. I took cover behind a tractor and started returning fire, but it was obvious they were about to outflank me. I had the burning building behind me, which was an inferno now, and no way out. My ammo was low, too. It looked hopeless, but then Vogel turned up." He turned to Vogel who then took up the story.

"I'd heard the gunfire, both Russian and German, from behind me so went to investigate, didn't see Major Fuchs but spotted the Russians. I took two of them out with a grenade, the last turned around and fired at me but missed. I hit him in the head with a round from my KAR 92 rifle."

"And not a moment too soon, I was about to be part of a Russian roast, the farmhouse well ablaze, as I said, my ass was about to be cooked!" The two soldiers laughed again. "What of your battles, Roth?"

"I was on board U-47 with Günther Prien during the attack at Scapa Flow. The irony wasn't lost on me that day; that was where the Imperial German navy was scuttled back in 1918 after the Great War, reducing the Reichsmarine to its much smaller size. But that was my first action, exhilarating and terrifying at the same time. Prien was a great commander, but a very arrogant man. He wasn't well liked by the crew. Perhaps his arrogance is what made him so successful. Sadly, lost in '41. He told me shortly before I moved on from his command that, "War is a killing business, and submarines are very adept at that particular art." He also said that a Luftwaffe ace is described as a hero, whereas a U-boat ace is classed as a villain."

There was no more talk before the plane landed at the airfield located next to Peenemünde itself, and then it was only a short drive to the secret rocket research and launch facility. As the car approached the checkpoint, Roth could see that the level of security here was even more intense than that in Berlin. Two anti-aircraft guns were positioned either side of the entrance and a concrete pill box was positioned over to the left-hand side of the gates. Roth could make out the barrels of two MG 32 machine guns poking out. There were also countless Luftwaffe guards in all directions. The car came to a stop. Fuchs handed over his papers to the guard and then, with a wave of the sentry's hand, they drove through the gates which were opened for them.

Roth was surprised to see a huge expanse of wasteland which stretched out before them as they drove along. He'd expected to see buildings, facilities of some sort, construction activity, military personnel, anything but the devastation and rubble he witnessed… it was quite thought provoking.

Clearly there had been buildings here of all sizes and types, but now the ground was littered with nothing but tons of rubble with patches here and there that had been cleared to make makeshift roads and paths. Single trees stood where there once were woods. Tree stumps and broken branches were scattered all around, large bomb craters too; evidence of multiple air raids. There were a few single-story structures ahead and this is where the car now headed. Vogel saw the look of disbelief on Roth's face and spoke to explain.

"Huge air raid in August '43, about five-hundred planes they say, in two waves. Apparently, General Adolf Galland's Sturmstaffel One, comprising of an elite group of fighter pilots, shot down around fifty or so Lancasters of the RAF, but enough got through to do this. Killed a couple of important scientists. Oh, and some five hundred workers, apparently. They moved the rocket construction somewhere secret as it's only a matter of time before they come back and blast the place again. Apart from the odd raid, they've not been back in any major force; perhaps they think they've stopped us?" It was a rhetorical question.

They pulled up outside an office block and the two SS officers plus Roth climbed out.

"Cigarette, Roth?" offered Vogel.

"Thanks, I will," he replied.

Roth was surprised to see the packet was an American brand: Camel. Vogel offered him the packet before passing it to Fuchs, who also took one.

As they stood there smoking, an officer of the Luftwaffe came out of the office block and marched over to them. He introduced himself.

"Hauptman Linus Meir, gentlemen, I am the adjutant here. We have received news that U-931 has left port and will arrive in approximately two to three days. If you follow me over to hanger seventeen, we can take a look at the device."

The hangar was a domed construction, covered in earth and grass to resemble a small hill from the air and was about four hundred metres away, across a concrete courtyard. The three officers had one last pull each of their Camel cigarettes and then threw them onto the ground outside the door of the hanger, stubbing them out. The inside of the windowless hanger was lit up by twenty large ceiling lights; a dozen or more moths fluttered aimlessly around them. The air smelt damp and musty, giving the illusion of the building having stood empty for a while. A wooden crate, measuring two metres by one and a half, with the words 'Camel Cigarettes' stencilled on the top stood on two trestles in the middle of the floor. Meier walked over to it followed by Fuchs, Vogel, and Roth. As Meier lifted the lid from the box and placed it on its side, he turned to the others.

"As you can see, inside the crate there is a false top with packets of cigarettes concealing the bomb underneath. This hopefully will deceive anyone from detecting what lies beneath in the crate, should you be unfortunate enough to have the crate examined. Camel Cigarettes have been a major brand in America since 1913 and are manufactured in Winston-Salem, North Carolina. The cover story is that you are delivering a consignment of cigarettes to a warehouse in Washington, so, in the unlikely event that you are stopped, this crate will blend in with the others that will be in the back of the truck that you shall be driving as you travel through the states. The drive itself is three-hundred-and-twenty miles, about nine hours or so. This is the closest that we can get you to Washington without being discovered near the coast with Captain Roth's sub. You will know where the drop-off is once you open your sealed orders, Captain. Our comrades at the drop-off will supply you with everything you will need for the journey, including food and water. This way, the only time that you may have to stop should be for gasoline, thus limiting your exposure to contact with any locals and possible discovery of who you are." He let that statement register, then Meier removed the false top before continuing.

"Here we have the device itself. In the centre is the metal box, this is made from lead to shield the radioactive material and keep yourselves from harm. The Plutonium 237 has yet to be fitted."

Roth looked at the small suitcase sized metal box before him and was amazed to think that such a compact device could cause so much devastation and death.

"Around the exterior of the box is the two-hundred kilograms of plastic explosive known as RDX. And here, in this corner, is the trigger. This has a timer on it with a delay of thirty minutes, plenty of time to get some distance between you and the bomb. You flick up this red protective cover to reveal the switch, flick this up to arm the detonator, then you push the green button – this is the timer. The black button, here on the left under this protective metal flap, is the quick switch or second trigger; it's a backup. Unfortunately, this is an instantaneous firing mechanism and means the device will detonate immediately, killing whoever has flicked the switch." Meier turned to Fuchs and Vogel. "If you two could now follow me back to the office block, there is a lot to go over for the operation, and we have an English tutor to help go over your American dialect. In the meantime, you, Hauptman Roth, have a meeting with Oberleutenant Huber who has no knowledge of any operational matters concerning Surtr, so do not say anything to him. Is that clear? He is waiting for you down by the quayside, where U-931 will dock. One of my aides will drive you over there. There is a car waiting outside for you."

After the short drive down to the dockside, Roth approached the Luftwaffe officer who was standing there, looking out to sea. The man turned around to face him, Roth's boots crunching on the gravel announcing his presence. The Oberleutenant gave Roth a traditional salute before introducing himself.

"Oberleutenant Huber, sir. I've been asked to give you these charts." He handed over four long, unmarked tubes made of cardboard.

"You are to take these with you after I have shown you the docking facilities for the arrival of the submarine. You are not to discuss any operational details with me or anyone else, but I will answer any questions I can, sir."

"Yes," replied Roth, "I've already been told not to discuss the matter."

Roth looked around. The marina was rectangular in shape, the open end facing to the south. This was a concern as they would have to pull out slowly and do a one-hundred-and-eighty degree turn to head out to sea.

Not ideal when leaving port. There were only five boats moored up as he scanned around the facility, four small civilian types and an E-boat of the Kreigsmarine all bobbing slightly on the swell from the Baltic. There was a wooden dock, measuring about eighty metres, stretching out along the right-hand side; this is where U-931 would be birthed. Roth had many doubts racing through his mind: the whole operation, the dangers of bringing his sub here, getting back out, and many more. Huber seemed to read his thoughts.

"We have successfully docked U-boats here before, Captain. The depth is over ten metres."

"Yes, everything looks in order. Not great," he admitted, "but I'll be happy to see my boat and crew again."

"I believe that should be in two days or so, Captain. Come, I will escort you back to the main building. There is an office where you can study those charts."

The three officers spent the next few days waiting for the sub to arrive by studying their parts in the plan. Fuchs and Vogel had kept to themselves for the most part. Roth had to do his homework regarding the trip out of the Baltic, through the English Channel, across the Atlantic, and onto eastern coast of America. He had gone over the charts for Pamlico Sound again and again, so he knew them like the waters around Hamburg. This patch of water would surely be even more hazardous than the Channel itself. The charts he'd been given weren't the best; the waters around the East Coast of America were sketchy at best, but rumour has it that Hardegen had used a child's atlas when he'd ventured near Manhattan, so Roth couldn't grumble, could he? He still hadn't been told the destination on American soil, though. There was obviously still an element of mistrust, he thought. He would pass on his experiences from his childhood and his upbringing in the deep South to the two SS officers as they had requested; that could only help them as they travelled through the country.

Fuchs and Vogel had been putting their part of the plan together: the landing, meeting up with the fifth columnists, driving to the target, and, ultimately, the detonation – not forgetting, their escape. This involved just simply melting into the background and heading for South America, they told Roth. They would hopefully evade capture, as a huge manhunt might begin if it's discovered that the fourth explosion was a bomb and not a sea launched missile like the others. Yesterday morning there had been another air raid on the rocket facility, this time by the American 8th Air Force. Luckily, no damage had been sustained near the docks or the building housing the bomb. Very lucky, really, considering the so-called 'precision' bombing inflicted by the Americans was very indiscriminate, just like the RAF, really. The RAF preferred blanket bombing, and the term 'blanket' was very apt; it covered a lot of ground but wasn't very precise on hitting a single target. Still, it had been extremely frightening being in the shelter for the second time in the last few days, Roth had thought. He'd thought being under a depth charge attack was excruciating, but all those thunderous explosions raining down was not something he wanted to experience again.

On the third day, after going over every tiny detail they could think of, word had come that U-931 was sailing into the harbour, so Roth, Fuchs, and Vogel had made their way down to the dock. The three of them were standing on the wooden quayside. Roth had a broad grin on his face as he saw the low outline of the sub slipping into view. It took around thirty minutes or so before the boat was tied up along the quayside and Berger stepped cautiously onto the gangplank and then the jetty. He threw Roth and the two SS officers a salute, a slight look of concern on his face as he stared at Fuchs and Vogel. Roth stepped forward and shook his exec's hand, a broad smile on his face; both men were pleased to see the other.

"Good to see you, Berger. All well with the boat and men?" he asked.

"Yes, Herr Captain. Bit of a rush after your departure. We were ordered to take on mines, four torpedoes, and given our destination. Had a few scares coming through the channel, mostly aircraft. The crew are exhausted, sir! We've hardly slept in six days, we're all tense."

Roth was about to speak when Berger stepped closer and spoke in a hushed tone, his gaze not leaving the two SS officers in their black uniforms who stood just a few feet away.

"Hoffman wasn't himself back at base, he fussed around more than normal, making sure the boat was refuelled, etc., but there was clearly something on his mind, I thought. Then, something happened just as we were about to depart." Berger had got Roth's attention. "We were moments from casting off. I'd just bid farewell to Hoffman and I was walking back towards the boat when I heard cars approaching the dock, two of them, so I stopped to see what was going on. Hoffman was heading in the direction of his office. The cars were Citroens, and I assumed they were French police as we'd seen them there before, but I was wrong, Captain.

"Three men jumped out from the first car. One of them called out to Hoffman, who stopped in his tracks. The men weren't in uniform, they wore suits, and one was also wearing a leather coat, he stood back a little as the others marched up to the captain. They grabbed him by the arms, sir, one each side, they said something, but he didn't resist. They frog marched him over to the car, he looked over at me with a blank stare as they did so, a sad smile on his face, then they pushed him inside and drove away. I think they were Gestapo, Captain. What's it all about?" enquired Berger.

Roth took in what he had just heard from his first officer. The U-boat commander was visibly shaken. He wanted to tell him about his conversation with Hoffman back in France, but dare he?

"I think Hoffman has sailed into dangerous waters. He was steering on a very dangerous course. I'll say no more; the less we all know about the matter, the better for us. I don't like knowing the security services are involved. Hopefully it's just routine, but I fear not. With luck, he's back at his desk as we speak."

Berger didn't look too convinced by what Roth was telling him, but he too had concerns now as he stood here on this Baltic peninsula. The involvement of the SS was an obvious concern, and his captain, who himself was not exuding his usual air of confidence, was hiding something about their commanding officer.

"So, what's the story with this place, why are we here?"

"Can't give you any details, yet. Get the men off, showered, and rested. There's a hot meal waiting for you all up at the mess. I'll get the sub refuelled. We leave on tomorrow's tide with some cargo and our guests here." Roth turned to Fuchs and Vogel who both stepped forward. Two crisp Nazi salutes were given and then they introduced themselves to Berger, the look of concern on his face deepening with each passing moment, more so as he shook the hands of these SS officers now standing before him.

Suddenly, the long, drawn-out wail of an air raid siren cut through the cold morning air, and a cacophony of thunder roared from the numerous anti-aircraft guns surrounding the secret rocket establishment. Roth went cold immediately, and he felt a moment of terror grip him. Could this be another bombing raid on Peenemünde? The infamous 88s, the efficient anti-aircraft guns of the Luftwaffe, fired their high explosive shells high into the sky above. The four men looked instinctively upwards; the blue sky was interspersed with sparse and wispy cumulus clouds that were now quickly being joined by the lethal puffs of inky black signs of flak. The guns were all aiming at what looked like a single aircraft. As it appeared, it was clear to those gathered around that this was only one passing aircraft and not a mass raid. None of those assembled moved towards the safety of the nearby shelter. Those on the ground at Peenemünde could just make out the distinct outline of a Spitfire, the elliptical-shaped wings giving its identity away.

Roth couldn't help but make the comparison of the shrapnel bursts surrounding the Spitfire to the depth charges dropped against his sub in the Atlantic. He felt empathy between himself and the pilot; but, at the same time, a sense of foreboding engulfed him. Was this just a coincidence that the Spitfire was here, and now? Or did the allies have some knowledge of this forthcoming endeavour that was being undertaken? The sub had arrived at the wrong time; he didn't want any photos the plane overhead would be taking to show U-931, here at Peenemünde. The less time that U-931 was docked here, the better. He had felt ill at ease ever since he'd stepped off the boat back in France and couldn't wait until he re-joined his crew and got back underway once more.

*

Later that day, the officers of U-931 and the two SS officers were all sitting around a large wooden table within the confines of a stone walled hut with a corrugated tin roof, which was to be their quarters for the night. Ten uncomfortable looking, metal framed beds awaited them there, for when they retired. At the far end of the hut was a small grate, and a fire that was lit. The trouble was that the fire was inadequate for the size of the room, and so all of those assembled were forced to keep their coats on to keep out the chill. Long lines of mould ran along the ceiling's edge because of the lack of warmth, plus there was an unpleasant odour about the place, probably due to it being damp. There was no electricity due to the recent bombing, and the room was lit by three oil powered lamps which hung from the beams holding up the roof; they barely illuminated the already dreary accommodation. All in all, it was no hotel.

Even with the awful state of the hut, the U-boat officers felt a little refreshed after having a short sleep earlier, and, together with some food, it had lightened their mood considerably even though the promised hot water for a shower was not forthcoming. Roth came in from the outside, carrying four bottles of Guntersblum wine. He closed the door with his foot and set them down.

"Here, look what I managed to find," he said with a laugh. "Someone left these around for any fool to discover." Fischer picked up one of the bottles, unscrewed the cap, and started pouring the pale coloured liquid into the six metal mugs on the table."

"Cherry wine, Captain. An excellent choice, if I may say so," remarked Vogel.

"You are a connoisseur?"

"No, Captain, he is not. He's drunk half the wines across Europe during the war and knows most of them personally," shouted Fuchs. The six men all laughed, the atmosphere a little easier, thought Roth.

"Cards, anyone?" asked Schmitt.

"We have no money, remember. You've won it all,"

Berger pronounced. Again, they all laughed.

"Well, I know you're good for it, I do accept IOUs." He dealt the cards to the places around the table. "Poker it is."

They had been playing for around thirty minutes. Schmitt so far appeared to be winning, as usual. The talk was at a minimum, but the wine was flowing freely. Vogel and Berger were sitting out this hand and stood talking off to one side.

"Where are you from, Lieutenant?" asked Berger.

"Not too far from here. Have you heard of Stralsund?"

"Yes, that's near the Polish border, isn't it?"

"There is no border, my friend, it's part of the Greater Reich now."

"Of course, my apologies," replied a hesitant Berger and although not invited to, Vogel continued.

"I was a corporal then, part of the first wave when we retaliated against the Polish invasion on September first. I was all for carrying on then, onto the Soviet Union, but that was not to be. And so, I went west in '40 into France, met up with that rouge there," he gestured towards Fuchs, "and had some great times. Lost some great comrades and pushed the British into the sea. We should have crushed them there and then, we had them by the short and curlies, hundreds of thousands around Dunkirk." Vogel was raising his voice as he recalled the day, and he drank some more. The others around the table, especially Fuchs, were glancing over to him. He continued, "Then I spent my time mostly training with the Schutzen regiments back in Germany, in preparation for Operation Barbarossa, our glorious advance into Russia.

"We were part of the battalions that attacked first, tanks and infantry together. Villages fell, towns and cities, too, and onto Moscow we marched, patriots all. We were undefeatable, we crushed all who stood in our way." He took another gulp of his wine. "And then they came; the rains, followed by the snow. The freezing bitter snows. We had little or no equipment to endure such conditions. The war was to be won before winter set in, we had been told, and so we ground to a halt. The Russians hadn't stopped us; no, it was the damn unforgiving winter. We were losing more soldiers to the frosts than to any fighting, and then they started pushing us back. Little by little, at first, but then more and more, and what was once an army of thousands became hundreds of thousands." Once more the others at the table looked over, and Roth spoke this time.

"Come, let's not talk of war this evening. Have another drink." But Vogel had had enough to drink already and rebuffed Roth's suggestion before continuing with his tirade.

"Yes. Let us drink. Drink to the men who shall drink no more! Let's drink so that we can forget their faces! Let's drink, and our troubles will disappear. Drink, drink, drink," he shouted, downing yet more wine, replenishing his empty mug once more. Fuchs stood up and walked over to his friend, placing a comforting arm around his shoulders.

"Come, Leon. Lie down, my friend," he enthused. Vogel's chin dropped onto his chest. He wasn't crying, but had become emotional, a combination of drink and melancholy making him so. Fuchs led him to a bunk in the far corner of the room where he collapsed down. His comrade and friend whispered something to him and then Vogel lay down and closed his eyes.

Berger and Fuchs both returned to the table and sat back down. Fuchs broke the silence that had developed amongst them.

"He has moments like this, more often now, and the drink seems to start him off. Nothing used to bother him.

That is until we were fighting on the Kursk salient in July '43. We were Panzer Grenadiers, called so at Hitler's bequest – his homage to Frederik the Great, apparently. We were now attached to Tiger battalion 507. Originally, we'd all worn the distinctive pink piping on our shoulder patches and had been told to change it to white piping, but we had bonded as both Tiger crews and soldier together. We wanted to keep our identity, our loyalty, our SS ethos, so we still wore the pink. The day before we had even been lucky enough to have a visit from General Guderian as he inspected the frontline troops. It was a great honour." The submariners listened, not wanting to interrupt.

"The Red Army had broken through, north of Orel, and we were pushed back, more than once. The fighting was ugly. We fought not like men but like how jackals around a carcass might fight each other. We were ruthless; we had to be to survive. We fought with guns, knives, spades, fists, whatever we had to hand. Your body was full of adrenaline every waking moment, and if you could snatch a moment's sleep your dreams were nightmares. We lost comrades, that is war, but Vogel had become especially attached to one particular tank crew with whom we had seen a lot together from the early days of our training.

"There was a massive tank battle near some woods, but, in its day, the Tiger had no equal. Ten Tigers had dispatched of forty enemy tanks without loss, their T34s no match for a well-trained company like ours. Our Tigers needed to regroup and rearm, as did we, but as we prepared to return to our headquarters a new threat appeared; it was the new Joseph Stalin tank, so many I couldn't count them all. They had similar armour to our own Tigers, but with a 12.2cm gun. The tables were turned once more. We tried to outrun them, but it was hopeless. We ran for our lives, the Tigers covering our withdrawal, but they were getting picked off one by one by the new JS-2s and then, right behind us, the Tiger I mentioned struck a mine and lost a track, stopped dead. Vogel and I watched as Rudi and Johann jumped out and tried to repair the damage. The commander, Berthold, manned the MG42 on the cupola, firing heroically at the swarms of Russians attacking. We left our own cover and ran over to help, but as we drew near, the tank took a direct hit. The turret exploded high up into the air; great tongues of flame erupted from within, and all were killed instantly – or so we believed.

"We watched as purple blue flames licked hungrily around the shattered hulk of the tank, and then we heard them: the screams. Some of the crew were alive, calling out for their mother, calling out for death to come quickly and stop the suffering. They shouted for someone to help them, but as the Russians were advancing closer through the woods it was impossible to get to them. It was certain death. The screaming from within had stopped now, so we ran, ran for our lives back to our lines, and from there we kept running all the way back to Germany."

The light-hearted mood that had brokered the start of the evening had now disappeared. The card game was no longer important. Each player laid down their cards on the table, bade each other goodnight, and found a bunk to lie down on. Roth couldn't get to sleep; he couldn't get the picture of Hoffman being led away by the Gestapo, as Berger had described it to him, out of his head. There was no way he would see his friend again.

Slowly, each man drifted off to sleep. As they did so, they thought not of Vogel's and Fuchs' horrors, but of their own.

CHAPTER 9 - PHOTO

Flight Lieutenant Raymond Hanson of the RAF Photo Reconnaissance unit, located at RAF Medmenham in Buckinghamshire, was sitting at his desk when Sergeant Hopley knocked on the office door and walked in. Hanson looked up as the non-commissioned officer spoke.

"Think you should take a look at something, sir. Just got some photos back from a run over northern Germany yesterday, and one in particular over Peenemünde looks very interesting."

Hanson rose and followed Hopley to the photographic interpretation office. The room was occupied by twenty men and women of the RAF, all seated and crouched over masses of black and white photographs. Each of them had magnifying glasses of various sizes, and some were using Vinten stereoscopic viewers which gave the illusion of a 3D image, which, in turn, helped enhance the detail. They were peering at the scenes of industrial, military, and urban landscapes taken from various heights over Germany. Many of these photos were taken by aircraft similar to the Spitfire Mk 5.

The aircraft were painted sky blue all over, which gave a better camouflage footprint at higher altitudes, and they were stripped of non-essential items to reduce weight. By having no guns or anything else that was not vital to the function of the plane, it increased speed and range. They had extra fuel tanks fitted and were equipped with five high resolution cameras. The concept was to have a very fast photo reconnaissance airframe purely for the job of getting the most highly detailed images they could. Every minute detail of the plane had been scrutinised for any improvement; even the cameras were heated to perform better. The pilots had no such heating and wore multiple layers of thick clothing to keep out the cold.

These aircraft were designed to fly fast and high; up to thirty-thousand feet. Their pilots were trained to evade any enemy aircraft, and to seek out enemy targets on the ground that might give up valuable information about the German war machine whilst taking photographs that could be studied later.

Hopley and Hanson walked over to a Women's Royal Air Force officer who was seated at a small metal desk. Hopley spoke to the seated officer, using her first name as he approached, which was not normally accepted in military circles, but an air of informality was encouraged here at Medmenham by the senior officers.

"Babs here spotted this, sir, at Peenemünde." Hanson took the magnifying glass offered to him by the thirty-two-year-old woman and stared at the twenty by fifteen inch black and white photograph on the table. Flight Officer Smith pointed with her index finger to a spot in the centre of the photo. It took a moment for the image to resonate with the Lieutenant, but it was clear to him that he was looking at a submarine moored up alongside a dock at the secret rocket establishment of Peenemünde, northern Germany. He looked up and spoke to Hopley.

"What's a bloody sub doing there? Pardon my language, Babs," apologised Hanson.

"I've heard a lot worse, sir," replied the plain looking female officer. She was wearing her hair up in a bun today and Hanson thought it made her face look thin. She looked a little tired as well, putting in too many hours probably, he mused.

"As you're aware, sir, Flight Officer Rigby discovered the marks left on the runway at Peenemünde last year, the ones we believe were from a jet or rocket-propelled aircraft, and she's become our foremost authority and leading expert on the secret base over there on the Baltic coast. Not much gets past her, sir," said Hopley.

"Yes, I'm well aware of Babs and her prowess for spotting the unusual or well hidden."

"I'm wondering, like you are, sir, what's a sub doing there? Is it dropping something off, picking something up? Or even, someone?" asked Hopley

"But why use a sub? Surely a surface vessel would suffice?" replied Hanson.

"We've seen plenty of ships there before, yes?"

"Yes, we have, Flight Lieutenant."

"But never a sub. There's got to be a reason, I don't like it. Any other related intelligence that might explain its presence?"

"Nothing, sir, just this. Since the air raid back in August and the huge one in February, we've been monitoring activity there. But the latest intelligence suggests that they've moved their production to a location that's yet undetermined. There have been no large movements of equipment or materials coming or going that we can gather. This is the most significant arrival or departure of anything bigger than a truck in the last few months."

"Right. I want a much larger photograph of the area around the sub printed immediately, then I'm taking it to my opposite number in naval intelligence, Bob Coleman. See if he can shed any light on this."

"Yes, sir, straight away."

Commander Bob Coleman's office was down the corridor from the study room and, just a few minutes later, Lieutenant Hanson walked through the open door to see the fifty-five-year-old Royal Navy veteran officer standing by the window, looking out at the airfield in front of him, a cup of tea in one hand, the saucer in the other. As Hanson walked in, he immediately smelt the strong aroma of cigar smoke; Coleman was known to puff on four or five King Edwards a day. He spoke as he walked into the room.

"Do you have a moment, sir?" The naval officer, immaculately dressed in his neatly pressed black uniform, turned to face the RAF man.

"Of course, what is it, Flight Lieutenant?"

"Need you to take a look at this, sir, see what you think of this photo we've just received; it's from Peenemünde."

With that said, Hanson placed the blown-up photograph on the Commander's desk. The Commander sat down and placed his cup and saucer on the desk before picking up his cigar from the ashtray to take a quick puff. He savoured the sweet and delicately flavoured tobacco, then blew out a cloud of blue smoke into the room. After replacing the cigar in the ashtray, he lifted the photo. He studied the image of the sub for a while before speaking.

"Looks like a Type VIIC, Raymond. When was this taken?"

"Yesterday, Bob."

The two officers were now dropping their respective titles of rank as a mark of respect to their friendship.

"No idea how long it's been there?"

"No. That's the only photo we have. Don't have any future sorties planned for there, we think they've shut rocket production down as it's too exposed and moved operations somewhere else. This was a routine fly by. Do you think this is important? I can try to get that area flown over again sooner, if it is?"

"Could be important, it's just," he paused briefly, "we had intelligence three days ago from the French resistance that a lone sub, U-931, had left port at Saint-

Nazaire after only being in dock for less than twenty-four hours. Earlier reports suggest that it had returned from patrol earlier than expected and then shipped out quickly again; unusual to say the least. I'm wondering if this is the same sub, they're both Type VIICs. What's more interesting is that the captain didn't sail with the boat! Don't know where he is, though, bit of a mystery there, unless he's been replaced. It would have had to sail through the channel to get to Peenemünde that quickly, a risky move these days. Could just be a coincidence, but if it is the same sub there must be a bloody good reason that it's gone from France to Germany in double quick time. Think we need to get bomber command over there tonight, if she's still there. I don't like where it's moored. Could be some special op, Peenemünde's no ordinary place. Can't make the connection right now between submarines and rockets, but the 'Jerries' are up to something."

"What if it's gone? We won't be any the wiser of its intentions, and if it's still there, a mass raid might even miss such a small target at night. What then?"

"I'm not sure, but it's got my hackles up; I know that much. I'll get in touch with the Admiralty and alert them of the possibility of a lone sub in the Baltic, intentions unknown. The more I think about it, the more it troubles me. They're risking a hell of a lot putting a sub there, and now it's got to get out again through the Denmark straits, and then through the channel again or the North Sea, if that's where it's headed. Thanks for bringing this to my attention, Ray. We could do with getting a sortie organised, but that won't be easy, so I'll drive up to London with the photo and the other intelligence and see what the top brass wants to do with this."

By the time Bob Coleman was striding across Ripley Courtyard in London and making his way under the archway into the entrance of the one-hundred-and-fifty-year-old yellow bricked Admiralty building known as 'Citadel' in Whitehall, the light was fading, and dusk was enveloping the capital. The drive had taken him two hours, which was quite brisk for him. Hundreds of sand-filled hessian sacks protected the front of the impressive four-story Georgian building, and standing ever watchful at the main entrance were two sentries, both standing guard with a Lee Enfield rifle with the two-foot-long bayonet fitted.

He stopped to show his credentials and repeated the process to another guard who was seated at the front desk inside. The corporal there directed him over to the stairs on the left that led to the basement level, and he walked down. The stairs were dimly lit, the metal banister cool to the touch, and there was a musty smell in the air. At the bottom of the stairs was a large green metal blast door, at least a foot thick, besides which was a small wooden desk. A Midshipman was seated behind it. Coleman knew the drill so showed his ID once again. After the sailor was satisfied with Coleman's pass, he stood and opened the door. It took a bit of effort on the sailor's part as the door was heavy. Coleman nodded to him and walked through.

Inside was a hive of activity; this was the submarine tracking room where the whereabouts of every known U-boat in the Atlantic and southern oceans were logged and tracked. Phones were ringing, tele-types constantly clicking, and people talking – information and intelligence from far and wide was gathered here by the staff, most of whom were from the Royal Naval Volunteer Reserve, and they, together with a band of civilian graduates, ran the operations. In the middle of the room was a large operations table with a detailed map of the Atlantic on it, showing the British Isles, Greenland, and the east coast of North America. Five or six Wrens were gathered around the table and were busy moving small wooden replicas of ships and U-boats across the board as they read their position from sheets of paper that they held in front of them.

Coleman was looking for Rear Admiral Sullivan, his superior and head of submarine tracking operations for the Atlantic. He spotted the black woollen uniform with the single, thick gold braid beneath the gold loop on each cuff denoting the rank of Rear Admiral as he walked into the room. Sullivan was in his early sixties, wore a thick bushy moustache, and had a pockmarked, craggy face. After the two men exchanged salutes, Coleman gave Sullivan a large brown envelope containing the photograph of the sub at Peenemünde.

"Think you should take a look at this, sir, came in this morning from a sortie yesterday," said Coleman.

"What exactly are we looking at, Bob?" he replied as he slid the twelve by ten photograph out from its sleeve.

"It's a Mark Seven sub, sir, parked up at Peenemünde, which is unusual in itself, but there are a few other titbits that may make it of interest to us."

"How so?"

"Well. We think this sub left Saint-Nazaire on March eighth without its captain after coming back from patrol early, and then turned up here. My gut says it's up to something, and I was wondering if we could spare something to track it down as it comes out of the Baltic, if indeed it is coming back out."

"Lots of buts and maybes here, Bob? Could be she's returned early in need of repairs, so they've utilised her and just dropped off some cargo or a passenger. What about a bomb run from the RAF or the Yanks?"

"We could do with looking into a sortie tonight, if possible, but she may have already sailed, sir. A naval blockade may be a better choice."

"I'm afraid that's out of the question. We just haven't got ships to spare to go running after what may be nothing. We're sinking U-boats as fast as they can launch 'em anyway. I'm not sure this one is that important, Bob. I'm sorry, but the answer's no." There was a long moment of silence before Coleman spoke once more.

"What about a quick surgical strike, sir, just a small attack force rather than a squadron of Lancasters? That's if I could get the RAF to spare us some planes?"

"Go on?" Sullivan was intrigued, but there was a note of caution in his voice.

"We need to approach the RAF, sir, see if they can set up something."

The two men stood facing each other, the buzz of activity continuing around them. After what seemed an age to Coleman, Sullivan spoke.

"Alright, you've convinced me, but I'll have a word with the RAF, give them the details. Give them a heads up, as time could be of the essence. I'm just sorry I can't give you anything at sea, it might be a wild goose chase, anyhow?"

With that, Sullivan handed back the photo and walked over to a telephone.

"Get me Wing Commander Rush at RAF Marham, tell him it's urgent." Sullivan tapped his foot as he waited to be connected on the phone; Coleman stood waiting next to him.

"This is a secure line, so you'll be able to speak directly about any op." After a couple of minutes, Sullivan spoke into the mouthpiece again.

"Hello, Dicky? It's Bob Sullivan here. Yes, fine, thanks. Listen, I need a favour and, so as to not waste any time, I'll pass you over to Commander Bob Coleman who'll fill you in, okay? Cheers." With that said, Sullivan passed Coleman the phone. He nodded to Sullivan and then spoke into the mouthpiece.

"Good evening, Wing Commander. I'll get straight to the point. We need an attack on Peenemünde, Germany, first light tomorrow. But it's got to be precise; no heavy bombing, something quick like Beaufighters, Mosquitos, or Typhoons. It's a small target, too, a U-boat, moored up. Have you got anything available?" Coleman listened for a while before speaking again.

"Thank you, and goodbye." He turned back again to Admiral Sullivan.

"All he's got are four Mosquitos, they'll depart early morning, so that they arrive in Peenemünde at dawn. I'm going to drive to Marham now and fill in the blanks with the officer commanding the attack."

"Okay, Bob, that's great. Just hope it's not a waste of time and you get the sub, whatever it's doing there!" Sullivan replied.

"Thank you, sir, I'll keep you abreast of any developments."

With that said, Coleman stood to attention, saluted the Rear Admiral, and strode purposely towards the exit.

CHAPTER 10 - MOSQUITO

Commander Coleman had driven as quickly as he dared in the light blue Humber Snipe staff car, he'd requisitioned earlier from the motor pool at Medmenham. It wasn't his preferred choice of transport, but it was the only thing available when he'd asked.

"Beggars can't be choosers, sir," he was told by the corporal in charge. Coleman was sure he spied a thin smile on the NCO's face as he handed over the keys. The three thin slivers of light emitting from each of his masked headlights were virtually useless and made driving at high speed, especially on these country roads, a risky affair. But black out restrictions dictated that the car had to have them fitted.

He was now approaching the main gate of RAF Marham in Norfolk. It was a tough three-and-a-half-hour journey from Whitehall, made all the harder by there being no road signs to help him as they'd been removed back in 1940 in anticipation of the invasion of England by the Wehrmacht – Operation Sea Lion, he believed it was called. Anything that could be done to hinder an invading army was done back then. But on this drive now he'd shook his head on more than one occasion, as he'd had to stop to study the map or ask someone for directions, and to be perfectly honest, he was feeling extremely tired. It was the best part of twelve hours since the submarine's location had been brought to his attention and he felt exhausted with the stress, the driving, and the thought processes he'd been going through.

As he finally sighted the entrance to the base, he slowed down to about five miles per hour and was fumbling in his top breast pocket for his papers whilst steering with his free hand when a burly looking RAF sergeant came quickly out of the guard house. Coleman stopped the car in front of the barrier, but before he could speak the sergeant spoke.

"Commander Coleman? I've been told to expect you, sir, and wave you through. I'll just jump into the passenger seat, and I'll show you the way, sir." With that said, he walked around the car and got in. "Straight ahead, then first left, third single story building on the right," he continued.

Coleman engaged first gear and set off. When they reached the building, the sergeant jumped out before the car could come to a full stop and walked around to Coleman's door, saluting as he opened it.

"Through that door, sir. The wing commander is in his office, you'll see the sign on the door."

"Thank you, sergeant," replied Coleman. The door to Wing Commander Rush's office was open so Coleman walked straight in.

"Evening," he said.

"Hello," came a warm reply from an immaculately attired RAF officer, his light blue uniform and insignia denoting his senior rank. He was seated behind a well-worn beech desk. He stood and walked around, extending a hand towards the naval officer. They shook hands, both with a firm grip, and Rush gestured towards a beaten-up, black leather settee set against a wall. As they sat down, the wing commander spoke again. "Right, I'll get straight to it, Bob, as I know time is of the essence. We've got four Mosquitos ready to go; Flight Lieutenant Young will lead the attack. He's an experienced officer considering he's only twenty-four, we just need you to brief him and the crews. They're on their way over here now, as the sergeant that you met at the gate will have told them you've arrived."

As he finished talking, the sound of voices and feet

treading along the wooden parquet floor came filtering through from the corridor. Both senior officers stood up as the band of eight men walked through the office door. Coleman wasn't too surprised to see that most, if not all, of the assembled throng were in their late teens or early twenties. The Flight Lieutenant at the front was probably the oldest present. As he strode in first, Coleman noted that he had a strong presence about him. Standing around six feet tall, the thing that struck Coleman was the officer's broad smile accentuated by the thin pencil line moustache favoured by RAF sorts these days. His hair was as black as coal, but strangely thin and cut short in a wispy sort of way. His build was muscular, and he was well-tanned; considering the time of year, he looked like he'd just come back from the Bahamas. A few curt nods and half-hearted salutes were thrown by the young flyers as Rush ordered them to find a seat on the floor or the available chairs and settee.

When they were settled, Rush handed the briefing over to Coleman.

"Good evening, gentlemen. I'm Commander Bob Coleman," he said. "I've got a mission for you, but, if I'm honest, when you get to the target area you may not have anything to attack." The RAF crews looked at each other and shrugged as they heard this. Coleman continued, "The thing is, chaps, we're after a sub, and it's moored at a place called Peenemünde in Germany. Can't go into any further detail except to say that we believe it's vitally important that we sink this sub. It's moored, or should I say, it *was* moored, alongside the jetty this morning." He reached into his briefcase and pulled out the enlarged photograph of the sub, plus a few more reconnaissance photos of the rocket installation in northern Germany that he'd taken to Whitehall earlier. "The U-boat is U-931. It's a Type VIIC, so one of the later designs, and it can dive quickly. So, if it's in the bay, it can disappear in the blink of an eye. Now, the place itself is heavily defended, as you'd expect. If you look at the reconnaissance photo, plus the others I've brought along, you can see the anti-aircraft positions we've marked up. I imagine this is not going to be a milk run, I'm sorry. I'll leave the finer points of the attack itself to the wing commander."

"Thank you, Bob," said Rush. "You'll leave at 0430, so your attack will coincide with the dawn at Peenemünde which is at 0610 hours, and you'll have the sun slightly at your backs when attacking from the northeast."

"You'll have to cancel that tee time you've booked, Youngy," interrupted Flight Lieutenant Lloyd, one of the other four pilots in the room. The air briefly filled with laughter and Rush let it subside before he continued.

"Now, the problem we have here is that Peenemünde is at the end of a peninsula, with the Baltic Sea all down its eastern coast. Your inbound run will be from the north, and then you'll have to swing around to attack from a north easterly direction so you have some element of surprise coming in over the treetops, and be on top of the target hopefully facing as little flak as possible on the way in. Then, when your bomb runs on the target are finished, you'll be back over the sea and away from any more flak. Now, another problem we face is that this run is close to the end of the range of the aircraft, especially as we've got to plot a course around some heavy flak areas which are on your route. Although we're avoiding central Germany, these detours will have an effect on your range. Normally you'd have approximately two hundred miles in reserve, but this will come down to a meagre eighty miles. You'll be getting home on fumes, so at most you'll have one crack at the sub. I don't anticipate you'll have a second go, but if circumstances allow, and only – and I stress, *only*, – if your fuel tanks are in the positive, you may have another bite!

"Now, you don't need me to tell you that the most important part of this mission is your safe return. If you do not see the sub at the jetty and Flight Lieutenant Young deems it possible, your secondary target is the building complex situated immediately behind the jetty, which we believe to be workshops, and then you're to get the hell out of there, right?" It was more of a command than a statement.

The assembled crew members began to talk in hushed tones amongst themselves, some with looks of concern on their faces as Rush finished talking, and then Young spoke up.

"So, you're telling us this sub is important, but you can't say why. Well, as servicemen we understand that sir, it's our duty to obey orders. They don't always make sense." This brought a smattering of laughter once again from all in the room.

"That's correct, of course, Flight Lieutenant, but that said we don't do suicide missions either. I'll go over the route in and out with you to minimise your exposure. Now, are there any questions?" Nothing was forthcoming. "Alright, dismissed." The airmen stood and filed out of the room, a few still mumbling to each other about the forthcoming sortie as they left.

CHAPTER 11 - DEPARTURE

At an altitude of two-hundred feet and going at a little over two-hundred miles per hour, the Mosquito felt comfortable as it thundered over the island peninsula of Usedom, Germany. The melodic throb of its twin Rolls-Royce Merlin engines was comforting to the crew. The Baltic Sea rushed away beneath them as they approached the target from the northeast. The terrain was quite flat here near the coastline, which was good for visibility, but not so good regarding anti-aircraft fire. Only a few sets of trees or small woods were enabling them to stay out of sight for as long as possible. Another danger was electricity pylons, or more to the point, the cables that stretched out like a spider's web from the one-hundred-and-twenty-foot-high towers, just waiting to slice the aircraft in two or send them spiralling to the ground in an instant.

Flight Lieutenant 'Youngy' Young's nerves were balanced on a knife's edge as he stared intently out of the Perspex canopy of the cabin, wrestling with the controls. Radar would have picked them up if they'd flown any higher across the sea as they'd approached from the north, but as they now swung around, so as to attack from a north easterly direction, any observer on the headland would get a bearing on them and raise the alarm at the base of Peenemünde. They hadn't flown a direct route here, as that would have taken them through the heart of Germany and all the dangers that exposed them to.

No, they'd had to take a route that both circumnavigated most of the flak and would give them an attacking vector from this direction. Still, they could see and hear you coming from miles away and get you in the crosshairs of the many types of flak guns and blast you to kingdom come. This was why Flight Lieutenant Stephen Young, Distinguished Flying Cross and Bar, was going even lower now and skimming down to tree top level on the eastern side of the island.

"Careful, Skip," said his number two, Flight Sergeant Robbie Irvine, as he studied the altimeter, "any lower and we'll be taking some tree top souvenirs back to Marham in the wheel wells." The flight lieutenant didn't respond, the concentration levels evident in his steely-eyed gaze and on his brow in the form of beads of sweat.

*

A few miles ahead of the attacking Mosquitos, Captain Ahron Roth was alone as he leaned against the rust-encrusted top rail of the U-boat's conning tower. The red primer paint was beginning to show through the grey topcoat in places; even though it was only two years old, it was already showing its age. The paint had that mottled, uneven effect where it hadn't been rubbed down properly before the new coat of paint was applied and it felt rough to the touch. Earlier, Fuchs and Vogel had helped supervise the loading of the crate containing the bomb into the forward torpedo room and then walked up the gangplank wearing their black SS uniforms – a statement of some sort, perhaps? Both carried a rucksack, and Fuchs also had a small briefcase. The lookouts had gone below on Roth's order, just a moment ago. The crew were busy scurrying around below and making ready at their stations, orders being barked out from the officers. The long, graceful slim lines of the boat now slipped away from the jetty and eased into the dark blue waters of the Baltic Sea at a sedate and cautious speed of five knots.

Roth pulled the fur lined collar of his leather jacket tighter against his neck as a light westerly sea breeze gently blew against his weathered face, the strong smell of the sea washing over him. He peered to his right at the horizon, and the first glimmers of light appeared in the distance, a thin sliver of watery red light just starting to appear to the side of the boat. As the sunlight crested the rise away to the east, he likened it to the sparkle of a gemstone caught in the light.

He adjusted the strap and shifted the weight of the 'ace' binoculars that hung around his neck; they were called 'ace' because of the twenty-one ships he had sunk in only six patrols as a U-boat commander. The steady, comforting drone of the diesel engines below and the wash of the sea against the hull were the only noises cutting through the surprisingly mild, early spring air. He licked his lips, tasting the salt on them as he did so. He couldn't wait to get out to sea and away from the confines and danger of the coast. His mind was racing with the many permutations of what had transpired in these last few days: their early return from patrol, the swift journey to Berlin, and these new orders of such a magnitude that he was still mulling over. This recent spate of new orders that hardly made any rhyme or reason from his superiors of the Kriegsmarine and its admirals had left him perplexed. He commanded a U-boat; he was supposed to attack and destroy enemy shipping, not ferry the SS around or deliver a secret bomb. But these orders had also come from the Reichsführer, and those he could not question.

He sighed long and deep, his heart heavy. At this late stage of the war, with the allies surely about to launch a second front in Western Europe at any moment, Nazi Germany's defeat was only a matter of time. In his heart he knew that the war was lost, and now this operation, which had been thrust upon him, could either be Germany's salvation or lead to its total annihilation.

His heart weighed heavy with the thought. Where

could this fool's folly take him and his crew? Perhaps a far greater penalty awaited Germany when this war was over. If the German people thought they were hard done by with the Treaty of Versailles, it was going to be nothing in comparison this time, he thought.

Roth glanced towards the stern and the wake being churned up behind the boat. From high up above, this long stream of white water stretching out in a line could give away the sub's position. The submarine's departure from here at Peenemünde was potentially the most dangerous time for the boat and crew.

The light was slowly improving by the minute, and it was evident that it was turning into a beautiful spring morning. But this, in turn, would magnify the dangers to the boat. Roth felt no comfort being here in the Baltic and not the Atlantic, but as the allies dominated the skies across most, if not all, of Europe it was difficult to be at ease anywhere. Göring's depleted Luftwaffe was conspicuous by their absence; the skies were no longer filled with the roar of Heinkel He 111 bombers and their escorts flying overhead on their way to bomb London, like he'd witnessed back in the summer of 1940. Another indication of how the mighty had fallen. It was possible to evade allied destroyers and the like for weeks in the Atlantic or the Cape, fighting them and the cruel, unforgiving sea, only to be blown up or strafed by a plane just two miles from safety. If they were spotted in the open sea, they could face an onslaught ranging from depth charges, torpedoes, heavy machine guns, and anything else the air crews could throw at them as they tried to sink him and the men under his command below.

He'd allowed his mind to wander, another momentary lack of concentration, something that was becoming more commonplace and something he must regain control of. He was brought back to the present in an instant as his subconscious and experience kicked in, all his senses suddenly tuned in as one. He looked around the sky instinctively, sensing something. Then, he heard it. The wailing and slowly increasing sound of a distant air raid siren, and then the thumping drone of an approaching aeroplane, too. No, more than one. He looked back towards the east and then the west, the most likely direction of the threat; he couldn't get a bearing on the sound as it was being masked by the tall pine trees that enveloped the shoreline.

The boat was only fifty metres from the jetty now, still relatively close to shore. He raised his binoculars and scanned the skies from left to right. It was still relatively dark, but it was light enough for the boat to stand out against the waters as the sunlight bathed the metal in its first beams of dawn. He couldn't see the planes, but that didn't matter. He didn't waste any more time, another moment's hesitation now could be the difference between life and death.

"ALARRRM, ALARRRM!" he shouted with an urgency and ferocity down through the hatch. He quickly glanced to his left and the eastern horizon as he unhooked his wide safety strap that fastened him to the boat and prevented him from being washed overboard. He caught a glimpse of approaching aircraft just above the distant tree line and immediately started to scramble down the ladder below to the base of the conning tower, his feet barely touching the rungs as he did so, and then he reached back up above his head to close the sub's hatch. The water was already cascading through the gap and drenching him with its icy grip before he could finally spin the locking wheel to seal out the Baltic.

"All hands forward!" he commanded. Below him there was an intensity of action as a rush of crew members ran forward from their off-watch stations towards the bow in an attempt to put any spare weight at the front of the boat, which would drag it down to the deep as quickly as possible.

The crew surged to the bow, pushing past the crew who were occupied with the task of steering the boat. They rushed past the bunks located on either side of the grey steel hull, past the tables, past the tangle of pipe work, valves, dials, and cables, – the veins and arteries that carried the 'blood' of the boat – all while jumping over any obstruction in their path. One or two slipped on the wet steel plates that made up the floor or tripped over themselves in their haste to get forward. Some men even dove headfirst through the circular hatches that split the boat into its watertight compartments before scrambling back to their feet. At the end of this short sprint was a mass of bodies, crushed together in the narrow confines of the forward torpedo room, maybe twenty or more sailors, all in a tangled heap.

"Down to eighty metres, no, only forty metres," Roth barked out, quickly remembering they were still in the shallow waters of the bay. "All main vents open, bow angle down to ten, stern up by fifteen! Get us down, Schmitt, quickly!"

"All main vents open, bow down to ten, stern up fifteen," shouted back Schmitt, the boat's chief engineer, and Roth's friend and rock over the last four years.

"Rudder hard to port! Both engines to maximum! I think there are four of them, Schmitt. Mosquitos, perhaps. In these calm waters and even in this twilight they'll see us from up there in these shallows and we'll stand out like a lantern down a coal mine. We're going to get a couple of presents, courtesy of the RAF, gift wrapped parcels of TNT! Why didn't our radar pick it up? The 'Tommie's' must have changed the frequency again!"

"Don't those miserable Tommies ever sleep?"

"While they are out here risking their lives to kill us, some American soldier is giving their pretty girlfriend chocolates and nylons so he can bang her senseless," shouted Otto, the navigator.

A ripple of laughter coursed through the tiny confines of the hull; always time for a little black humour, even when you were about to be bombed and possibly killed. It was escapism, a brief interlude from the grim reaper's grasp.

*

Up above the quickly submerging U-boat, Flight Lieutenant Young's balsa wood constructed 'wooden wonder' skimmed over the tops of the last of the trees at breakneck speed; he smiled to himself in satisfaction as he saw what lay to the front of the Mosquito.

The bright scarlet rising sun was lighting up a scene that, at any peace time scenario, would have conveyed a tranquil setting: a long sandy beach stretched around the headland with the waters of the Baltic lapping sedately against the shoreline. What lay before him, and the other airmen was the long, slim, low shape of a U-boat. Not exactly where they'd hoped it would be next to the jetty, but approximately half a mile ahead, not too far from the shore, but heading out to sea.

Irvine pushed the lever which opened the bomb bay doors. The mechanical grind, together with the wind's roar and vibrations that coursed through the frame of the aircraft, sharpened the minds of the two airmen. The aircraft swooped down now towards the sub but not any lower, as this height was ideal for the attack; too low and the bombs wouldn't have time to arm as they left the bomb racks. The distance to the target was now less than a quarter of a mile, due to the speed of the Mosquito. Young had it steady now at around three-hundred miles per hour, but they could both see that the outline of the sub had already begun to diminish as she started to slip beneath the waves.

Young flicked the safety catch off for the four Hispano 20mm cannons located just beneath his feet in the fuselage; he didn't bother using the Browning .303-inch machine guns located in the nose, as he knew they wouldn't penetrate the sub's hull from this range. He aimed through the gun site in front of him and pressed the trigger with his thumb. The plane recoiled from the powerful force he'd unleashed, and the rounds sped through the air, highlighted by the red tracer rounds indicating his fall of shot toward the sub. Two parallel lines of waterspouts rose up in columns on a path which quickly traced towards the sub from the front of the plane, but he could see his aim was off and so he stopped firing momentarily and eased the plane to starboard slightly before pressing the trigger again.

Irvine was lining up the sub in the bomb sites and, when it seemed that they would fly past it in the blink of an eye and miss the sub completely, he pressed the button to release the four, five-hundred-pound bombs, the plane rising immediately as the weight from the bomb racks was unleashed and they flew down at a steep angle towards the sub.

The fifty or so cannon shells had strafed near the back of the sub in less than five seconds and Young cursed for his bad aim. Hoping some had struck home, he pulled up the plane from its dive and only now did he think about any flak. They'd not heard or seen any since the start of the attack but that didn't mean they wouldn't encounter any now as he exited stage left, so to speak.

He and Robbie craned their heads to look over their shoulders to see the other three Mosquitos continuing the attack on the sub. Young noticed the final one was quite a bit behind the others for some reason, and that the sub was almost gone, the Baltic waters enveloping it in its fluid cloak of darkness; a thick, velvety cloak that would mask its presence in the briefest of moments, as if it had never been there.

*

The helmsman on board U-931 had guided the seven-hundred-ton boat down whilst other crewmen turned valves, pushed levers, and spun wheels to enable the boat to quickly dive down. The loud whistling sound of air rushing out from the ballast tanks, that were quickly filling with saltwater, was drowning out the orders from the officers as they were issued.

"Twenty metres, thirty metres," called out Schmitt as he looked at the depth gauge, the boat slipping down into the relative safety of the deep.

"Forty metres, level off," Roth ordered, brushing past him as he did so; there was barely room for two of them in the cramped space. He threw his binoculars onto the map table across from the bottom of the ladder as he stepped towards it. Unconsciously, Roth looked up, as did others in the control room, as they heard a double splash, each a second apart in the waters above them. Bombs! Then, three more. They all knew what was coming next. "Crash positions!" Roth bellowed. The command passed along from front to back and through the boat to each compartment like a baton in a fast relay race. He grabbed the table and braced himself, looking up at the depth gauge to see they had reached the desired forty metres now. Much deeper, safer water lay at least one-thousand metres ahead still. "It's not deep enough, we're done for!"

Schmitt confirmed this with his captain with a sullen nod. In each compartment the men grabbed what they could, anything solid that would help them stay upright when the shock wave hit the outside of the hull. Then, abruptly, two huge explosions, perhaps thirty metres apart in the murky depths, boomed simultaneously out around them. Five-hundred-pounds of high explosives in each detonation enveloped the boat. The hydraulic shock wave from the explosion could split the hull open, allowing tons of water to cascade inside and committing them all to a quick death. The boat was shaken in a violent rocking motion from side to side. Deafening, frightening, sickening. The hull dropped from beneath their feet suddenly and Berger, the first officer, lost his balance and crashed to the floor, his head colliding with a table's edge as he did so, immediately blacking out and lying prone on the steel floor, blood oozing from a gash in his head. No one was able to help him now; the boat was still rocking, making it difficult to come to his aid.

Suddenly, there was a jet of water bursting out from a seam on an overhead pipe above Roth's head, the gasket having given way.

"Buchwald, stop that leak!" barked Schmitt at the teenage seaman standing a few feet away from him to his left. The tall, blond-haired sailor reached for an adjustable wrench clipped to a bulkhead close by and immediately twisted the nuts on the flange that was leaking, cold water under high pressure drenching and blinding him as he worked. The boat righted itself now as the shock waves dispersed but, as it did so, two more large splashes could be heard above them as the next of the Mosquitos dropped their payload. Finally, the sub had reached deeper water, but not that much deeper.

"Left full rudder, down to eighty metres!" shouted Roth above the din. Schmitt looked at the captain, silently questioning going deeper but knowing they had no choice. It was a calculated risk; go deeper and crash into the bottom, or stay at this level and get blown to pieces. Once again, Schmitt repeated his orders to the crew in the control room. Roth knew that the skilled crew flying only sixty metres or so above the waves would estimate his course and their plan on how to evade them. The flyers would release a new wave of explosions in the area they thought the submarine would now be. The RAF crews only needed to be lucky once. Roth and his crew needed to be lucky every time. He hoped that the swerving, downward plunge would be enough to evade the explosions; it was a game of chance, a spin of the dice with a modicum of his experience thrown in.

CRASH! BOOM! Two explosions rocked them again, this time the boat swerving violently over to the port side, the captain and crew all falling over to the left, their efforts to grab onto anything to arrest their fall, futile. Once again, another pipe fractured at a joint, spraying those around with cold seawater. Three of the overhead lights shattered, too, showering the unconscious Berger, and Schmitt who was standing next to him, with glass. The boat now rolled back as it had done moments before to correct itself, throwing the sailors back from where they had been. Roth looked at the depth gauge as he steadied himself by the ladder; it was reading seventy metres.

"Level the boat!" he called out. "Steady now. Right full rudder! Hard over!" He knew that the Mosquitos, if indeed that's what they were, could carry up to four bombs each, so there was plenty more to come, if indeed there were only four attackers – there could be more. What he hoped was that the crews above him may be cautious about releasing any more if they were dropping them blind, perhaps knowing that he may have evaded the first two salvos, and that it was unlikely that any more would be successful as the sub would be too deep or not in the area they thought. A more likely course of action for the planes would be to circle around, checking for debris, oil, etc – or even for them to surface so they could attack with their machine guns or bombs.

The only small bit of comfort he could cling to was the fact that the planes hopefully had only a few minutes of fuel over the target and didn't want to engage with the heavy flak which guarded the area. He just hoped that there was only going to be one bomb run and they were now heading home.

As one, all those around Roth looked up, waiting for the next explosion. They weren't to be disappointed. Four splashes in rapid succession, but these were way off to their left; they'd miscalculated! They'd dropped the bombs on the boat's previous course. Roth's experience had paid dividends, once again.

BOOM-BOOM-BOOM-BOOM! All four explosions were in the distance, so far away the sub didn't even rock. Berger was coming around from his fall and Schmitt helped him to his feet. A tense minute ensued, but all that could be heard were the running noises of the boat and the sharp breathing of the men in the control room.

"They've gone?" asked Schmitt of Roth.

"I think so, unless they're circling, but I'm hoping they think we're sunk or damaged," Roth replied. "Get the medic in here, Berger needs attention. I want a full damage report from all sections, quickly. Get these leaks stopped in here. Any flooding, get it assessed and under control immediately. And get us back on our original course, helmsman."

"Yes, Herr Capitan," replied Markus the senior helmsman. "Coming back to course zero four five degrees."

As Schultz the medic attended to Berger, applying cotton gauze to his wound and wiping the blood from his brow, Schmitt brushed the broken glass with the back of his hand off the chart table and turned to Roth.

"Are we continuing on this course, Herr Capitan, or do we take evasive action for a while to evade any more attacks heading our way?" he asked.

"I don't think they'll have another go, but we've gotta get out of here, we have no option but to carry on." He quickly studied the sea chart of the Baltic that was, somehow, after the previous action, still laid out on the table. "We'll stay on this course for twenty minutes, then due north for twenty more and then back again."

"At this depth?"

"No, check the charts and get us deeper just in case there's a second wave of aircraft, speed four knots. Any closer to the surface and we may be spotted from the air again."

"Herr Captain, all flooding has been contained, no serious casualties or damage, I think we were lucky, sir," reported the second officer, Fischer, as he came into the control room from the engine room.

"Fine, Fischer," came the reply, a pensive look forming on the captain's face. He was considering his options. "Bauer, get some hot drinks sorted!"

"Jawohl, Herr Captain," came back the reply from the steward who was standing by the officers' quarters.

"And make sure the coffee is hot, it hides the taste that way!"

"Of course, Herr Captain."

*

Flight Lieutenant Young looked forward again and down at his fuel levels in the cockpit of his Mosquito. A quick mental calculation told him a second run would be pushing it, plus the fact that the sub had been underway when they'd attacked. This meant that if they hadn't sunk it this time, it would be lost beneath the waters and now on a different heading to the one they'd last seen it on. It was a simple enough choice; they'd have to head for home. He flicked the transmit button for the radio.

"Sierra Mike to all Potters, any goals?" He asked of the three planes behind him. What he heard back wasn't encouraging, all three said they'd dropped the bombs but didn't think they'd struck home. If only they'd been ten minutes earlier, they might have caught the sub moored up and blown it away. But, unless one of the bombs had had a lucky strike, he feared the mission was a bust and with this in mind he recalibrated the radio for another transmit, this time back to base in England. When the set was tuned in, he clicked the switch and spoke. "Matthews has hit the post. I repeat, Matthews has hit the post. Final score is four, nil. Away in the next round." With that said he turned the Mosquito in a north-westerly direction for Marham and headed home.

*

Back on the sub, the ersatz coffee was served hot by Bauer, just like the captain had ordered, but it still didn't mask the coffee's bitter taste. The four senior officers of the sub – Roth, Berger, Fischer, and Schmitt – sat at the small wooden table in the cramped mess, just off the control room, Fuchs and Vogel joining them. Any sailors who wished to get past had to ask the officer sitting at the gangway entrance to stand up to allow them to pass. Space was at a premium even in this more modern, larger type of sub.

"How's the head, Erik?" asked Roth of Berger.

"Much better, just a slight headache, Herr Capitan. I think the table got the worst of it," he replied.

"We should be able to surface in four hours or so hopefully, a little later because of our eventful departure, so long as we have no more contacts. Muller is glued to his hydrophones. I think he sleeps with those headphones on, he dreams of echo sounds pinging off British destroyers, but I wouldn't swap him, that's for sure."

"Any clues to our orders, Herr Captain?"

Both Fuchs and Vogel stole a piercing stare as Schmitt spoke. On hearing the question, Fuchs stepped forward towards the gathered huddle and addressed the four seated officers.

"All you need to know for now is that this mission is of the highest importance and shall help deliver a great victory for the Reich. Do your duties and do not ask again. Listen to your captain and follow his orders to the letter." There was an authoritative, stern tone to his voice. The atmosphere around those gathered grew tense and no one spoke for a few moments. The only sounds heard now was the sipping of the foul-tasting coffee. Berger finally broke the silence, risking the wrath of the two SS men, but he wasn't prepared to stay silent anymore.

"Our superiors shouldn't expect too much. The allies are much stronger now. This isn't 1942 anymore, they have more escorts with the convoys, better air cover, and they seem to know or anticipate our every move. I'm still convinced that some pencil pushing virgin at naval operations in Berlin is telephoning Churchill the moment we leave port, telling him where we are going.

"At least the 'Biscay Cross,' that excuse for an aircraft early warning system, isn't giving our position away anymore. That piece of garbage has cost us many good friends and comrades this last year. What next for us? Refuel, reload, and back out again. The wolf packs are now operating as one or two, not in the strength they once were. I don't want to sound defeatist, Herr Sturmbannführer, but we aren't achieving anything significant, and the odds keep getting bigger against us."

"Be careful, Berger. You are amongst friends and fellow combatants here around this table, but if someone reported your feelings you wouldn't be sailing out again, it's more likely you'd be on a butcher's hook with a Gestapo goon grinning up at you," said Vogel. But all those around the cramped table couldn't miss noting that the Obersturmführer was grinning.

"I'm prepared to die for my Führer and country, but I want my death to mean something."

"I know how you feel, just be careful, first officers are getting hard to come by now." It was Roth grinning as he said this, but at the same time he couldn't have been more serious.

*

Back at RAF Medmenham, Commander Coleman was sitting at his desk smoking another cigarette. He'd just checked his watch for the third time in a minute when the secure-line phone rang.

"Hello, Commander Coleman speaking," he said.

"Good morning, Bob, it's Wing Commander Rush here, sorry if I woke you?"

"Not at all, didn't sleep a wink, have you some news?"

"Yes, indeed I do. We received a coded radio message about twenty-five minutes ago. Bear with me, it'll make sense when I explain, but it reads as follows: Matthews has hit the post, the score was four nil, and the next round is away."

The line went quiet for a moment before Coleman broke the silence. "And that means?"

"Yes, sorry, but Flight Lieutenant Young is a Stoke City football fan and used the colloquialisms for his message. It translates as: they didn't have a direct hit, i.e., hitting the post. All four aircraft are okay, that's the four-nil bit. And, the sub was on its way, not at home or at the jetty when they attacked. Looks like they didn't sink the sub. Whatever it's up to, wherever it's going, we haven't stopped it. I'm sorry."

"Well, you did your best Wing Commander, thank

you. It's in God's hands now, wherever it's going. Good day." Coleman replaced the handset onto the cradle and sighed, pondering as he did so. Just where was she headed, and was this the start of her mission, or the end?

CHAPTER 12 - CHANNEL

"Right, listen up you lot, quiet there!" It was the forceful tone of Lieutenant Jordan's voice which broke the silence of the early evening air of March fifteenth on the foredeck of *HMS Zenobia*. He was addressing the four crewmen who had been assigned weapons training on the 'Hedgehog'. "I'm going to read from the manual here and relay to you the basics of the weapon, plus a few things I've gleaned from using it in anger before. I'll let you have some hands-on instruction from me and then I'll answer any questions you have.

"This, here, is the anti-submarine projector, to give it its proper name. You can see by looking at the empty racks here, this is where it gets its nickname from. It fires twenty-four forward-firing spigot mortars, each one weighing thirty pounds in banks of four, all launched in a few seconds, and they will complement a depth charge attack. After training and once we get up to speed, we'll be able to reload in three minutes or less, so you can see that a blanket of these will envelop the area, about one-hundred feet circumference where we believe the U-boat to be, two-hundred-and-fifty yards in front of the bow, rather than the sides and behind from where we normally attack. A depth charge, however, relies on hydrostatic shockwaves to sink the sub, that's a pressure wave to you and me. These projectiles are fitted with contact fuses and will detonate upon striking the actual hull. I'd rather be firing these than being on the receiving end, that's for sure. And, whereas with the depth charge the explosion is followed by a large plume of water rising from the water behind the ship to indicate where the explosion was, with the hedgehog you'll see a shotgun effect as the bombs hit the water in a spread-out pattern, followed by a 'crump' sound from below, if there's a strike. These Hedgehogs are estimated to be twenty-five percent effective, nearly three times more than the depth charges. Any questions?" There were none from the assembled crew, just a few stifled yawns, and so the lieutenant carried on with his lesson.

Above and slightly behind Jordan and the assembled sailors who stood around the 'Hedgehog' was Captain Prince, standing at the front of the raised bridge. He had heard enough and so turned away from looking down onto the forecastle where he'd been observing Lieutenant Jordan instructing the crew below. The crescent moon was up now and there was little cloud around, so the vision across the waves was quite clear, the last vestiges of sunlight slowly disappearing to the west. There was nowhere to get any shelter from the elements on the open bridge, and the cup of cocoa he had in his hands had cooled quite quickly. He was relieved that he had on his naval issue duffel coat as the temperature had dropped a few degrees when the sun had started to go down, but the sea spray had soaked into the coarse hair of the duffel and was giving off the distinctive and unpleasant smell of damp wool. The ship was on a southerly course, heading towards Portsmouth; the port of Ramsgate was just off to the starboard side of the ship. In times of peace, he'd have been able to see the distant twinkle of the seaside town's lights, but not this evening. No, like his ship it was in total blackout, like all the other towns and cities across Europe at the height of the greatest conflict the world had ever seen.

They had entered the fast-flowing waters of the English Channel now, a few dolphins guiding them along earlier as they swam in front of the bow, blissfully unaware of the human tragedy that went on all around them. The Corvette's brief sea trials were over. It was a case of more training now, while they still could. Soon the invasion would begin, and they would undertake their orders as tasked.

He had been very pleased with the training so far, considering that most of the crew were inexperienced, but at least his officers appeared to be well conversed in the mechanics and running of the ship. He hadn't served with any of them before, but they all seemed competent in their duties so far and, most important of all, the ship's engines were running exceptionally well after the recent overhaul. This was the four o'clock to eight watch now on the bridge, and the crew on the ship were on alert because of the threat of aircraft attack. Although now, with the diminished threat of the Luftwaffe and the envelope of darkness approaching, he felt a little easier as they approached Portsmouth. The sound of someone being sick over the side made him look down and to the portside, just to the side of the four-inch gun. He recognised one of the younger ordinary seamen losing his supper. Probably one of the newer members of the crew. He'd get his sea legs soon enough, he hoped. Today the sea was calm. Being in the middle of the Atlantic and constantly throwing up as the boat got tossed in a force three gale was no joke for anyone on board – even the 'old sea salts.'

They had met rough seas as they had steamed out from Hull and the ship being thrown about hadn't aided anyone, as it turned out. Prince was aggrieved with the sloppiness that had led to one of the wooden lifeboats coming adrift because it had not been lashed down correctly. Still, if that was all he had to worry about with an inexperienced crew aboard a relatively new ship in its early days of training, then it wasn't too bad. On a good note, the firefighting exercises on board had progressed well, plus the transition from day to night and all that entailed had been done with some aplomb. A glance at the ship's compass told him they needed a course correction and shouted to the helmsman.

"Come to starboard five degrees!"

"Aye, aye, sir," was the response, "starboard five degrees."

Upon their arrival in Portsmouth, they were to report to Flotilla command for further orders. Prince, like most of the crew, was hoping for something more than the mundane tasks they'd been told to expect. Wartime was made up of periods of absolute boredom, interspersed with moments of sheer terror, but to be waiting in the wings was even worse, he mused. With a well-trained crew and decent equipment, you stood half a chance to get through to the end, – plus with a whole lot of luck, too, of course, – and while you didn't want nonstop action you could end up climbing the walls being stuck in port. He didn't relish the thought of another engagement that led to another ship and crew being sunk, especially now that he was in direct command.

He would still have the occasional nightmare about his previous brushes with death, and yet, another part of him craved for action. He was, after all, a serving member of his majesty's Royal Navy. He drained the last drop of his cocoa, which was now lukewarm at best, and made his way to his sea cabin which was located directly below the bridge. It would be a couple of hours before they'd steam into Portsmouth harbour, so he had a little free time. The prospect of a corned beef sandwich or tinned sausages for supper wasn't making him salivate, but then he didn't fancy much as his appetite had deserted him lately. Perhaps the upcoming threat of action in the next few weeks was affecting his digestion?

In the next day or so he was hoping to spend some time down the firing range on shore and have some target practice with his Webley side arm. It had been a while since he'd fired the weapon and he needed to see if he could improve his groupings on the paper targets. He'd always enjoyed the Webley and much preferred it to the more modern automatics like the Colt Model 1911 that the Yanks used. He turned towards Lieutenant Clarke, whom he knew was still 'learning the ropes', and decided to test him, to put him on the spot.

"Can you tell me the weather situation, wind direction, the sea and swell?"

"Light rain is forecast, wind due east at a light strength with a moderate swell, Captain," replied a confident Clarke.

"Right, make sure that's reflected in the log. I'm going to my cabin. I want radar to continue sweeping the horizon for any aircraft as we lose this light, Lieutenant, and maintain the zig-zag course we're on. Let me know when we're on the approaches to the port, okay?"

"Aye, aye, sir."

Prince handed his now empty mug to the sailor nearest to him and then climbed down the steep ladder, facing forward as he did so, his hands behind him, firmly gripping the handrails as he descended to the deck. He contemplated the bit of free time he may have for the next thirty minutes or so, deciding he would be cleaning the Webley, which was in the top drawer or his desk.

*

At that very moment, whilst Prince approached his cabin on *HMS Zenobia*, the Corvette was just a few short miles to the left and slightly behind a lone submarine that was starting its own approach to the infamous English Channel.

"Boat will be entering the narrows of the 'Kanal' in fifteen minutes, Herr Captain. We'll have Calais to our south, and on our present course we will be in the middle of the two coastlines, as per your instructions, for a short while before we alter our course and start to hug the French coast as we make our way to the Atlantic," whispered Schmitt to Roth in the confines of the sub's control room.

"Good," was all Roth replied. The boat had an eerie silence running through it. It was as if the slightest of noises would echo straight to the very heart of London and the Admiralty who would then send every available ship and plane to hunt them down.

"Depth ninety metres. Speed five knots. We're battling a strong current, Captain. It doesn't get any deeper here, I'm afraid, not until we're at the end of it, nearer to the Cherbourg peninsula. This isn't so much a channel as a valley with a stream running through it, and we're like a salmon trying to jump up the falls with our tail in the air for an eagle to spot!"

"Yes, Schmitt, I know how exposed we are here, but I'm gambling that the traffic will be a little less at this time of day so we can slip through. What about surface contacts?"

"Luckily nothing so far on sonar. Horst is sweating back there like a pig outside a busy abattoir! He's listening through his headphones for a pin drop, while a brass band is playing the 1812 overture."

"You and your analogies, Schmitt. You kill me!"

"The crew are aware of our position and have been ordered to adopt silent running regimes."

"Very good, carry on."

As Schmitt turned away, Roth stole a glance at Fuchs and Vogel who were trying to keep out of the way in the cramped confines of the control room by standing huddled together near the hatch which led to the next compartment. They were still dressed in their full black SS battle dress. Fuchs had insisted they remain like that until they were about to disembark in the US. The only concession made was that their tunics had been removed for now, probably due to the overwhelming heat down here, the black shirts beneath drenched in sweat. It was clear to all on board that they wanted to impose an air of superiority over the crew.

He wondered what they were whispering about. They'd hardly said a word to anyone since the attack back at Peenemünde. He'd been struck by how frightened they were during the bombing; he supposed it was different to fighting hordes of Russian soldiers alongside your comrades, or even taking shelter from an air strike. Someone may be there to help, but being stuck down here and helpless to do anything about it was a world away. One thing for sure was that in the short time he'd known the two, he was convinced he dared not trust them – SS and all that!

He looked down at the charts laid out before him on the table. A couple of hours and they'd be out in the open sea, and he'd feel a lot safer about the next few days and the crossing to the States – where he could start to worry yet again, he surmised. Suddenly, the tension was heightened by the voice of Horst.

"Contact! Possible destroyer!" Horst's rapid, loud whispered voice came from behind Roth, the listening room being only a few metres away. Roth stepped quickly over to the eighteen-year-old Bavarian seaman sitting next to the sonar equipment, his spotty face a picture of concentration, beads of grime-infested sweat streaming down his young face, his service cap set back on his head, the headphones on both ears but with the cradle set resting on the back of his neck.

"No, not a destroyer, smaller." Horst was very young for this position on the boat, but Roth had never seen a better sonar man in the service. He trusted his word instinctively.

"How far?" questioned Roth. The concentration on Horst's face was intense, the mood on the sub now acute, strained.

"Two-thousand metres, heading straight for us!"

"Left full rudder, down to one-hundred-and-twenty metres."

"Captain, that's too close to the bottom," barked Schmitt.

"I know, but we can't stay so shallow."

"We don't know if they've spotted us?" But then, as if to contradict Schmitt's statement, the loud ping of an enemy sonar reverberated through the hull. They had been found.

*

On board the *Zenobia*, Captain Prince had entered his cabin. He strode across to his desk, unlocked the top left-hand drawer, and took out the slim, wooden presentation mahogany box which housed his Webley and placed it on top of the table. He remained standing whilst he took out the weapon and was about to break it open so he could retrieve the six rounds from the cylinder and then get his cleaning kit to commence the maintenance on his gun, when suddenly the relative silence of his cabin was broken by the sharp ringing of the alarm klaxon: the call-to-action-stations. At the same time, there was a sharp whistle that emanated from the voice tube which linked his cabin to the bridge. With the gun still in hand he spoke into the brass funnel.

"Captain here?"

"Contact, sir, a mile off the port bow, possible sub!" spoke a jittery Lieutenant Robinson who had joined Clarke on watch.

"Send a contact report with our position to the Admiralty, Lieutenant. Maintain a zig-zag course but keep an eye on their plot; I don't want to lose them. And get the battle ensign aloft. I'll be right up!"

"Aye, aye, sir." Prince spun around and immediately stormed out of his cabin, retracing his steps back towards the bridge he'd left just moments earlier. He opened an outer door which led directly back onto the main deck and made his way to the ladder, it being just a few paces to his left. The klaxon alarm was blaring loudly, penetrating through the steel plates of the hull, and everywhere sailors were rushing to their stations, pulling on helmets and life vests as they did so. The deck was already awash with men of all ages and experiences rushing to their stations. It was a crush to get past, the lower ranks giving way when they saw the captain. When he reached the base of the ladder and was about to go up, he realised he was still holding the revolver. With no place to put it down on the open deck he now found himself on, he instinctively stuffed it into the right-side pocket of his duffle coat, which he was still wearing. He'd not had a moment to remove it since coming down from the bridge just five minutes ago.

Before he strode onto the bridge, he paused to step into the small room which housed the Asdic device. As he stepped over the lip of the door well, he glanced at his watch; it was 1830 hours. Inside, he found Lieutenant Smith and the Asdic operator, seaman Parry. Smith spoke as the captain appeared.

"Parry picked it up, sir, only faintly to begin with on a bearing of two three zero degrees. It's a strong signal, now, but they've changed course bearing two seven zero, speed five knots and going deeper!"

"One of ours, by any chance?"

"No, sir, nothing in this area shows up in dispatches, it's got to be a 'Jerry', sir." There was nervous excitement in Smith's tone, which Prince needed to address.

"Alright, Lieutenant, calm down a little, please."

"Yes, sir, sorry, sir." It was fine to be nervous under the circumstances, thought Prince, but he needed his officers to be professional at all times so as not to infect the ranks with undue panic which may spread and lead to mistakes at a crucial moment.

"What do you think, Parry? U-boat?" The forty-four-year-old Asdic operator, his bald head glistening with perspiration as it was caught by the light of the single bulb of the cabin, was a veteran of the service. The captain knew he could trust him; this was a lifelong sailor who'd served in the great war at Jutland, and Prince had had a long discussion with him about his experiences just the other day. Parry replied without taking his eyes off the small round oscilloscope screen in front of him.

"Without a doubt, sir. Heard enough of these on convoy duty, sir, and they know we're here, too, I'd bet my bottom dollar on it. I'm doing sweeps, blue two-twenty degrees to two-eighty degrees. Echo bearing is now two-twenty degrees. Range thirteen-hundred yards and closing."

"Right! Keep me abreast of any course changes, Smith. I'll be on the bridge."

"Aye, aye, sir," replied Smith.

Prince left the Asdic room and stepped out onto the bridge, which was adjacent, the audible sound of the echo coming from a loudspeaker above the doorway, the ping getting louder and quicker as the ship drew nearer to its prey. The bridge now had the relevant officers and crew at their stations, a few of the lower ranks with binoculars in hand scanning the sea all around, but as the light had now all but faded it was difficult to see anything out there but blurred outlines, imagined threats, and ghosts. Suddenly, Lieutenant Jordan appeared.

"Hedgehog manned and armed, Captain, as are the

depth charges!"

"Thank you, return to your station and listen for an instantaneous echo."

"Aye, aye, sir," and with that, Jordan was gone.

"Maintain a zig-zagging course, helmsman, contact's heading is two two five degrees so don't exaggerate your turns or we'll lose him, but be prepared to come about on my command!"

"Aye, aye, sir!" replied the helmsman, who was stationed next to the captain on the bridge. Prince now addressed Robinson.

"Reduce speed to ten knots! With our zig-zagging course, I want to slowly reduce our distance in the next few minutes, without going steaming past the bugger; but be prepared to give me all we've got when I call for it. A fast attack should put them at a disadvantage. Well, Lieutenant, you wanted some action. Looks like we are back in the war after all."

"Yes, sir." With that said, Robinson turned to the voice tubes located at the front of the bridge and spoke to the engine room, passing on the captain's orders.

*

Meanwhile, below the waves and in the confines of the steel tube that was the sub, Horst snapped his fingers twice to get Roth's attention before he spoke.

"Herr Captain, it's not a destroyer but a Corvette, I believe!"

"Are you sure, Horst?" snapped back Roth. The young sonar man listened back through his headphones once more before replying.

Jawohl, Herr Capitan. Corvette!"

"Boat level at one twenty metres!" called out Berger.

Schmitt looked at the captain and spoke. "We can outrun him on the surface and in the dark, Captain, better than down here with some depth charges for company!"

"Yes, yes," was Roth's only reply. He was deep in thought, computing all the permutations in his head. The Corvette could do around sixteen knots at best, they could do maybe seventeen. The margin was too close. They couldn't go any deeper just yet, that was worrying. Maybe they could outrun them on the surface, but they were so close now that it would be suicide to surface with no distance between them. The four-inch gun on board the Corvette would make mincemeat out of them; their own eighty-eight was an excellent weapon but could not match the range of the British ship. His mind was awash with what was the right course of action. He had to decide, and now.

"What is your course of action, Captain?" The loaded question had not come from one of the sub's officers. No, it was Fuchs who had spoken. Roth turned slowly towards the direction of the SS Major and, with a piercing stare, looked at the man who indirectly was the sole reason why they were here in the English Channel, probably the most dangerous drop of water any U-boat could find in 1944. He didn't answer, but instead turned to the boat's chief, Schmitt.

"How close are they?"

"Twelve-hundred metres and closing!" replied Schmitt.

"Same course, no change?"

"They're zig-zagging, but matching our course, not closing too fast. If they speedup, they'd be on us in no time!"

"Turn to port, zero-fifty degrees for two minutes and then starboard zero-thirty for two more, see if that throws them."

"Port zero five zero degrees!"

Roth said nothing, the tension in the hot, sweaty control room was electric. He had to make a decision. It was Berger who spoke this time, with a distinct note of urgency.

"Captain, what are your orders if we can't shake them off?"

Still Roth was silent, but only for a moment. Then, he commanded his crew to action.

CHAPTER 13 - TORPEDO

Schmitt was standing next to the attack table in the control room. It was used to plot the course and speed of the target, plus how the torpedoes should be set when launched.

"Load aft torpedoes, prepare to fire! Bring the boat up to eighteen metres, they'll think we're running at periscope depth but we'll fire blind, Schmitt. Torpedo speed thirty knots, deflection ten degrees. If they're stupid enough to run down our pipe, we'll let him eat a couple of torpedoes for their trouble," ordered Roth.

"Load aft torpedoes, speed thirty, ten degrees' deflection; prepare to fire!" repeated Schmitt. Roth caught the eye of Fuchs who was giving the U-boat commander a hard stare, but he ignored him once more and turned to check on his firing charts for the attack.

*

On board *Zenobia*, Prince was getting minute by minute updates on the sub's course and distance.

"Range one-thousand-one-hundred yards and closing, sir, target is back on original bearing of two three zero!" called out Robinson.

"Give me a countdown, Lieutenant, from a thousand yards. I want to fire the Hedgehogs at two-fifty, the maximum effective distance, and then if Lieutenant Jordan's training is any good, we'll give them another salvo around one-hundred yards before we pass over their position and deploy the depth charges." He knew that Jordan's men weren't trained enough yet, and so he looked towards Seaman Thompson and said, "Run and remind Lieutenant Jordan, as soon as he hears the continuous ping he is to fire. Then he's to reload and immediately fire off a second salvo, understood?"

"Aye, aye, sir," came the reply from the sailor, who sped off in the direction of the forecastle below. Prince moved across to the ship's internal radio and selected the switch which connected him to Lieutenant Phillip Clarke, who had left the bridge upon hearing the sound of the klaxon and gone to the rear of the Corvette and his station, the depth charge racks. The receiver buzzed at the rear of the ship and the young officer dashed over to pick it up.

"Clarke here," came the response.

"Lieutenant Clarke, we're going to run right over the bugger in around a thousand yards, so when you get the signal, let them have it. Set depth to one hundred, I think they'll come back up a little to try and out fox us, clear?"

"Aye, aye, sir. We're all ready to fire, just give us the order!"

"One-thousand yards, sir, and closing, bearing still two three zero!" called out Robinson. Prince reached for the switch on the bridge that would turn up the volume on the loudspeaker, which was linked directly to the Asdic receiver. He wanted all on the ship to know how close and how fast they were chasing down their prey. All those congregated on the bridge now had an audible reminder as the series of loud acoustic 'pings' bouncing off the U-boat could be heard, the gap between each one diminishing as the ship closed in on the sub below.

"Submarine rising, sir!" shouted Smith from the back of the bridge.

"Get the four-inch gun crew ready to fire. Are they still on the same bearing?" he asked Robinson.

"Yes, sir, no change. Do you think they're surrendering, sir?" replied Robinson.

Prince pondered the possibility for a second. What was his adversary up to? Surely surrender was an option, but that could be periscope depth. Were they preparing for an attack? In the background, the Asdic's pings grew louder and closer together: *PING… PING… PING*!

"Hard to port, all ahead full!" This was no beaten sub, giving up. They were going to strike at them before *Zenobia* got close enough to fire their own weapons. How could he be in this situation again? He couldn't be on another ship lost to the enemy, could he? Would he? He'd been too eager to sink the sub; it had been presented to him on a plate and he'd let his emotions cloud his judgement. Now the fifty souls he had charge over may be killed because of his poor actions and reckless decisions. *PING… PING… PING*!

"Target changing course, Captain," shouted Horst on the sub; there was no need for silence now, just actions. "Turning to one-eighty degrees, speed sixteen knots."

Berger now took up the commentary. "I think they've twigged, Captain. Do we continue with the attack?"

Roth knew that to stop the attack would hand the initiative back to the enemy. Plus, the dark stare of Fuchs was still directed towards him.

"Yes. Change course to suit and let me know when we've matched them," called out Roth, "What's the distance?"

"Eight-hundred metres! Still turning to port!"

Roth considered his options once more.

"What are they doing, the fools? They're giving us their whole beam to fire at; that's a novice's error. We can escape and lose them while they're turning away, Schmitt."

"Yes, Captain, we'd be off on our toes before they come back around," replied the boat's chief.

But, before Roth could issue the command, Fuchs intervened once more. "Captain, as commander of this mission and sub, I'm ordering you to fire the torpedoes, *now*!" All the crew in the control room looked on in amazement at the SS major staring with a fiery rage at Roth. "*Now*, I said, *now!*"

*

On the bridge of the *Zenobia*, the sound coming from the Asdic speaker was now almost a continuous stream of uninterrupted pulses – *PING, PING, PING, PING!* – the rapid series of notes indicating that she was almost on top of the sub. Prince barked out another slight course change, this time taking the rolling boat back to starboard in an attempt to stop the sub from having a bead on him.

*

Beneath the waves, Roth knew in an instant that if he disobeyed a direct order from Fuchs, he was a dead man. With reluctance, he was about to issue an order when Horst shouted, "He's changed back to starboard!"

"Change course to match! Remove the safeties and fire immediately, we're back with him!" called out Roth. The crew in the control room all looked at their captain as one man. Removing the safeties was dangerous for all of them. The torpedoes were designed to arm themselves when they were a safe distance from the sub after launch, otherwise they could detonate close to the sub, killing them all.

In what seemed like an age, but was actually merely seconds, Berger announced, "Target back on track, Captain!"

"Aft torpedoes, fire one. Fire two!"

Berger hesitated for the briefest of moments before he obeyed his commander's order.

"Fire one, fire two!" shouted Berger as he pushed the buttons which launched the torpedoes. The whole submarine buckled and rolled slightly once, then twice in quick succession as the compressed air in the two aft tubes launched the proximity-type torpedoes towards the

Royal Navy ship.

"Torpedoes one and two launched," said Schmitt.

"Bring us back up to forty metres and a course of one two zero degrees, let's see if we can lose them at least if we miss. Time to impact?" enquired Roth.

"Less than thirty seconds, any closer and the damn things will blow us up, too!"

*

Back on-board *Zenobia*, the crew were all clinging on to anything solid as the ship turned at a steep angle back to starboard, the bow slicing through the surf at an obscene angle.

"Range to target now?" demanded Prince.

"Four-hundred yards, sir, and… *torpedoes*! Heading straight for us!" It was Lieutenant Robinson's alarmed voice which cut through the tension on the bridge. Captain Prince reacted immediately by pressing the call switch on the bulkhead which connected him to the Hedgehog station below and Lieutenant Jordan.

"Fire when ready!" he called out.

"We're not close enough, sir!" shouted Robinson again, but Prince ignored him before yelling to the helmsman.

"MID-SHIPS, MID-SHIPS!" His shouts were all but drowned out as from below the bridge the roar of a volley of mortars launched from the deck. Twenty-four bomblets arced into the air, one after the other, all-in quick succession. The first salvo of projectiles arching away into the distance and directly in front of the speeding Corvette. Prince was hoping to God that his changes of course would be enough but fearing the distance was too small, whilst, at the same time, praying to God that one of the mortars would be close enough to strike the U-boat. The distance between the two was the difference. He guessed that the submarine had virtually fired blind, a shot in the dark towards the threat on its tail, rather than directly at them, and Prince had now done the same.

"Multiple bombs striking the surface, Herr Captain!" shouted Horst. "All on our aft!" No sooner had he completed his sentence, the boat was rocked by a huge *boom* which shook them violently and flickered the lights. All were expecting another explosion to follow, but none came. U-931 hadn't been struck. One of the Hedgehog's mortars had hit another, causing an explosion, but not on the sub itself. It should have been enough to sink the sub, but miraculously it had failed to send them to the bottom. Someone, somewhere, was looking after Ahron Roth and his crew that night. Miraculous as it was, the subsequent detonation had not caused sufficient damage to sink the sub, but they did have a problem.

The shrill voice of the helmsman called out. "The steering's stuck fast, there's no response. I can't move the rudder correctly. We're going around in circles!"

Zenobia was now steaming at full tilt, trying to avoid the onrush of the double torpedo launch, when, abruptly, the sky was lit up by a colossal flash of multi coloured lights, quickly followed by a deafening explosion of noise. Then, just as suddenly, a second more ferocious explosion tore through the ship. One of the torpedoes had struck the *Zenobia* towards the stern as they had turned, the second missing wildly and running off into the distance. The secondary explosion on board was from one of the many depth charges stored on deck, and it had created an enormous hole on the port side, halfway along the beam but behind the bridge, killing half of the crew in an instant. The gaping hole caused by the torpedo strike, which was under the water line, was now allowing tons of cold seawater to surge through and envelop the insides of the ship. The force of the blasts hadn't stopped the *Zenobia*, but now she was coming to a slow crawl through the seas, driven along only by momentum, her boilers destroyed and fire raging on her superstructure as fuel oil started to catch fire and engulf the back of the ship, driven on by the breeze and on towards the bow. The ship was doomed. Only minutes remained before she would start to go under, so severe was the damage. Prince picked himself up off the floor of the bridge where the blast had knocked him down. Robinson was also getting to his feet as the captain spoke.

"Get a signal out if you can, Lieutenant. Inform them that we're listing severely and sinking fast. Pass the order to abandon ship. All hands up from below. Let the life rafts and boats go. I'll see you in Portsmouth, hopefully."

With a quick, "Aye, aye, sir," Robinson was gone to carry out his orders. Prince looked at what was left of the shattered remnants of the bridge and the stricken crew members around him. All dead. Some he had known for just a few brief days. Some he didn't know at all.

"We will have to surface, Captain, to inspect the damage," said Schmitt.

Before Roth could reply, Fuchs spoke yet again. "I suggest we do surface, Captain, and we can also have a look at our aggressor!"

"There's no need! Trust me; from the sounds alone, we know they've stopped dead and are taking in water. They're no longer a threat, probably sinking fast, too. Also, they would have alerted any neighbouring vessels to our presence. We need to fix the steering, otherwise we'll be here when their comrades turn up, which they will, very quickly! We need to get out of here!" blasted back Roth.

"Let us not waste any more time, then. Surface! Now!"

Roth was sick of this pig's arrogance and went to take a step towards Fuchs, the rage inside about to boil over, but Schmitt stood in his way and forced him to stop. Fuchs glared back at Roth with a distinct look of contempt. The silence in the control room was palpable.

"Stop engines. Surface!"

The scene which greeted the sub on the surface was one that the crew of U-931 had witnessed many times before. The ebony black sky was lit up by a fiery cauldron that had once been a ship; it was now listing to port at about a thirty-degree angle, burning from stem to stern with multiple fires raging along its superstructure. It was clear to the young men of the Kreigsmarine, who had scrambled out from below to man the forward gun and watch posts on the conning tower, that the torpedo had caused a huge blast within the confines of the ship itself. They surmised to themselves, as they ran to their posts, that perhaps they had hit the magazine store of the Corvette, or even the depth charges which were stored along the sides of the boat towards the aft. Whatever had taken place, it was clear the ship had only moments left before it slipped down below. Four more men, the ship's engineer amongst them, went to the stern to inspect the rudder damage.

The sea around the sinking ship was ablaze. Fuel oil from ruptured tanks was oozing from within and had ignited, adding to the inferno and blanketing any poor sailor who had managed to jump overboard in its deathly grasp. Bodies, too many to count, drifted aimlessly among the flotsam that stretched out around the sinking hulk.

"This inferno is like a beacon, Captain! It'll be seen for miles! We've got to fix the rudder and dive!" It was Berger, standing next to the captain, who stated the obvious. Roth gazed out at the devastation before him.

He was about to call below for Fuchs and tell him that the ship was sinking and that they should prepare to get back underway as soon as the repairs were done, if they could, when he saw a lone lifeboat appear through the billowing reams of smoke rising from the sea. It had perhaps a mere ten sailors on board. He was transfixed by this apparition before him; a handful of survivors of the attack drifting towards them. He didn't notice at first, but then, from the corner of his eye, he saw two figures dressed in black appear from his left and onto the deck of the sub.

The two men, who were walking towards the bow, were Fuchs and Vogel. The light of the raging fires illuminated them both and he could clearly see they had machine pistols within their grasp, and what their intentions were.

"*No!*" The call of despair bellowed out in the night air from Roth. It had no effect. The two SS men ignored his shout, and they looked towards the direction of the lifeboat which was quickly drawing nearer on the swell, unnervingly, like a moth to the flame. Both soldiers set their feet slightly apart on the wooden deck, raised the Schmeisser pistols to waist height, and aimed them at the oncoming boat. A sailor at the front was raising his hands in surrender as he saw the two shadowy figures only fifty feet away, realising with horror what was about to unfold.

Although the fires aboard the Corvette were raging and the death throes of the ship had a crescendo all of its own, the noises were drowned out as the chatter of machine gun fire was unleashed. A maelstrom of bullets rained down onto the small wooden boat that was bobbing between the two crafts. Wooden splinters, large and small, flew up off the craft as the rounds struck home. Cries of pain and anguish could be heard over the crackle of small arms fire as the survivors on board were struck by the swarm of nine-millimetre lead.

Roth and the few crew on the U-boat superstructure could see the SS men were smiling as they sprayed the defenceless crewmen with bullets and it sickened them all, but were helpless to stop the slaughter. As quickly as the shooting had started, it stopped. The magazines empty, the barrels smoking hot, their murdering work done, the two men gazed towards the boat, its meandering course taking it to within touching distance. They both reached into the belts around their waists and pulled out a fresh magazine, unclipping the spent ones from their guns as they did so in an automaton manner, something they'd done a thousand times in combat before. They reloaded and prepared to fire again.

As if what had transpired couldn't get any more surreal, three single loud cracks rang out, one quickly following the other, splitting the night air. Fuchs looked on in horror as Vogel staggered backwards, the force of three rounds hitting him square in the chest and sending him careering off the edge of the sub. His machine pistol fell from his hand as he spun, clattering to the deck. The SS major watched in disbelief as he watched Vogel spin around and fall headfirst off the sub and into the swell, gone beneath the waves in a flash.

Two more loud cracks rang out. Fuchs, who was still transfixed on the spot where his comrade had been just a second before, heard the whistle of one of the rounds as it sped by, dangerously close to splitting his head open. He quickly turned to look back towards the bullet riddled lifeboat. He was aghast to see a lone hand emerging from within a heap of bloodied bodies, in its grip a pistol of some sort, once more aimed towards him. He instinctively returned fire, once again spraying more rounds at what was left of the enemy crew that was piled up within the small craft before him.

Captain Prince fired off the final round from his

Webley, but it flew harmlessly into the skies above the head of the lone German. In return, the man sprayed another long burst, emptying his machine pistol again, some of the rounds striking Prince in the chest as he lay there amongst his dead and dying crew.

The final image that *Zenobia*'s captain would see from the bullet-ridden lifeboat as he lay amongst his dead crew puzzled him. What were two SS soldiers doing standing on the deck of a U-boat, here in the English Channel, and why had they chosen to murder them all as they tried to surrender?

Fuchs turned to look back at the spot once more where Vogel had gone crashing into the depths before he stormed back along the deck towards the conning tower. He glared up at Roth who was standing at the front. His face crimson red, he shouted up.

"Get this piece of crap underway and back on course immediately, on the surface, as quick as she'll go! We've wasted enough time, and I've lost a good friend because of this screw up! Get underway! You and I need to talk! *Now*!"

Fuchs climbed up the side ladder quickly, and, as he reached the top and jumped onto the bridge, he was met by Roth who grabbed him by his shirt lapels and was launching a punch when Schmitt grabbed him from behind, stopping the captain in his tracks. Berger stepped in between the two men as Fuchs reached over to launch an attack of his own.

"You murdering swine! That's not war! I'll see you'll hang for that, if it's the last thing I do!" spat Roth. The two men were held back from each other by a struggling Schmitt and Berger, but that didn't stop the tirade of abuse that was unleashed.

"That'll never happen. We'll be dead. Sunk at the bottom, all down to your incompetence. We should never have been detected. It was down to your pathetic leadership. Call yourself a commander?"

"Attacking was not the right call. But that wasn't my choice, as you're the commander; that's right, isn't it?" The irony of Roth's remark wasn't lost on Fuchs, who fell silent for a moment. He shook the grip off from Berger, his anger tempered for now, and a wary Berger released him.

"You're right, Captain, I am the commander of this mission. Get the rudder fixed and get us back underway now! I won't say it again!" The two men scowled at each other, then Roth gave the order.

"Berger, jump down there and get me a report on the damage!"

"Yes, Captain!" And with that, Berger scrambled down the ladder and raced towards the aft.

"As soon as we can, we'll resume a course of two three zero degrees, all ahead full, on the surface, Schmitt."

"And clear the tower. The Captain and I need a brief chat, in private," interjected Fuchs.

"But what about the lookouts?" enquired Schmitt. "The whole bloody Royal Navy and every plane the RAF have will be heading our way!"

"Two minutes! And then you can send as many up here as you like, but I need to talk to your Captain in private. Now, go!" With that, all the crew climbed down the internal ladder and left them alone.

"This mission will continue, we must deliver the bomb for the attack on Washington to succeed when the V1s are launched, otherwise the deception will fail. We will forget our differences, Captain, and proceed as ordered. You will send out the code word as planned, to inform Berlin we are on track. Understood?"

"We can't carry on! It's finished, done! Even if we

manage to get underway, we'll be lucky if we get out of the Channel in one piece! We should head for Saint-Nazaire and pray we don't get spotted on the way. Plus, you're forgetting that Vogel is gone! Which, I hesitate to say, was down to you both reverting to character; there's blood on your hands, and his death, too!"

Fuchs was calm and spoke softly as he looked directly into the eyes of Roth, their faces just inches apart.

"That's as may be, Captain. But we have a replacement for Vogel on board, and that's you."

Roth stood there, stunned at what Fuchs had just said, the full extent of that short sentence beginning to register with him.

"Captain! The damage to the rudder is not too serious! It's internal, we can access it from here. We can hammer it out and free the rudder, we'll be done in about ten minutes," shouted Berger from below. Fuchs and Roth were still glaring at each other as Berger called out again. "Captain?"

"I heard you! Alright! Hurry up, then, and get it fixed!" shouted back Roth. Fuchs turned away, stepped towards the ladder, and climbed down into the heart of the sub, the boat's captain following quickly behind. Once he reached the control room, he spoke out to Muller.

"Send the code word 'Surtr' to Berlin. Now."

"Jawohl, Herr Capitan," replied Muller, the radio operator.

CHAPTER 14 - MESSAGE

Around one-hundred-and-twenty miles away in London, Rear Admiral Sullivan was sitting at his desk. He was normally very fastidious about how his desk appeared, he had always been a stickler for perfection and order during his rise through the ranks, but he'd let his standards drop this last week as he'd concentrated so much on the whereabouts of U-931. What now lay in front of him was unusual, to say the least. The trays that held his documents were piled high with unrelated and unread reports, blue ink drops near the double inkwells stained the varnish, and his gold fountain pen lay next to them, the top nowhere to be seen. The telephones were sitting on the tops of reams of paperwork. He was endeavouring to catch up with the latest intelligence document concerning the naval build up on the south coast of England and possible submarine threats when there was a knock at the open door and a sailor walked in.

"Sir, this just came in," announced the junior rating as he handed the senior officer a single sheet of paper before saluting and turning away. Sullivan looked at the contact report. He'd seen hundreds of these before, but what struck him immediately was the location; ten miles off the coast of France, not far from Boulogne. He read on: *HMS Zenobia* had had contact with what they believed was a sub and was engaging, but no further reports had been received. It struck Sullivan that the ghost sub from Peenemünde may well be in the Channel by now if that had been its course. Could this be it? He called out to his liaison officer, Captain Fulton.

"Any further reports from *Zenobia*?"

"No, sir. But we have had another message come in from the *Havelock*; she's seven miles to the northeast of

Zenobia's position, and she's reported seeing a large fireball and explosion from that direction. She's heading there now at full speed."

"Anything else positioned close enough to assist the *Havelock*?"

"Only *Newark*, but she's a bit further away, about fifteen miles, she was heading towards Portsmouth."

"Right! Send a message to *Newark* to turn around and head for *Zenobia*'s last known position and inform them both that they may be hunting a sub, possibly hugging the French coast, and making for one of the French submarine bases, possibly Saint-Nazaire."

"Right away, sir."

"And I want to know if we hear anything from *Zenobia*. Immediately!"

"Yes, Admiral." With that said, Fulton charged off to carry out the orders. Sullivan picked up the receiver from the telephone on his desk, but pondered for a moment. He was contemplating calling in the RAF for a reconnaissance over the area, but a quick look at the wall clock told him it was too dark and that any sortie to hunt the sub would have a better chance at first light. Instead, he rang Bob Coleman, whom he thought should know of this latest development.

*

It had been another long day for Dorothy Gee. She was alone as she sat at the large wooden trestle table strewn with paperwork in hut four, at Bletchley Park, Buckinghamshire, the top-secret home of the British government code and cipher school. The single-story brick building was freezing, as the paraffin heater in the far corner was struggling to heat up the room. She could clearly smell the warm, oily atmosphere that the heater was emitting, but couldn't really feel any benefit of the warmth it was trying to give out. She'd been tasked with

155

putting a document together for 'the higher ups', as she liked to call them, which would outline the history behind Ultra, the codename for intelligence generated from the Enigma cypher machine and the captured codebooks acquired from the Germans. She had so far outlined in her work how it was the Polish who had, in fact, made a copy of the Enigma machine back in the thirties, and they had passed this onto British intelligence before the outbreak of war. Also, she had described in best layman terms how Enigma was really just a substitution cipher machine. That is, you switch one letter for another, for example: A becomes B, H becomes C, and so on. As an example, she had used the simple word 'CAT' to demonstrate how it might work. Once the letters had been substituted on the enigma machine, it became 'ZKG' – totally unrecognisable as the original word when it reached the second enigma machine or receiving station. But, so long as you have the original decipher key that showed which letters had become which, you could convert what appeared to be a jumble of letters back into a coherent word. The Germans would change the decipher key every day, making it virtually impossible to crack the code.

The machine itself looked like a large typewriter and consisted of a series of internal rotors which were linked electronically, which, in turn, would change the letters automatically. Recently the Germans had introduced another rotor or two to the machine which raised the possible permutation exponentially, making it even harder to crack. She had gone on to describe how submarines U-110 and U-559 had been boarded by crews from Royal Navy ships earlier in the conflict and that they had found intact Enigma machines and code books. It was careless of the German sailors who were abandoning their sinking vessels not to have destroyed them. These captured assets are invaluable in the fight against coded signals from the Germans. Indeed, the capture of these items would probably shorten the war, she wrote.

It had taken her quite a few hours to type this up from her written notes, and her thoughts were now turning to some well-earned sleep back at the dormitory. She removed her tortoiseshell-framed glasses and rubbed her eyes with thumb and forefinger in an attempt to remove the tiredness she felt. What she would do for a hot shower. She had only put on her pale green blouse and matching woollen skirt this morning as it had been quite mild outside, but now as the evening air became colder, she was regretting she hadn't brought her jacket with her. She was a pretty looking girl; blonde wavy hair, slim, aged twenty-one, extremely bright for her age and among her peers. Here was a girl highly thought of. It was only six weeks since she'd been recruited from Cambridge. She'd completed her doctorate degrees in maths, English and European history at such a tender age and had therefore come to the attention of those in charge here through her adaptive and tangential way of problem solving. She'd been recruited by one of her tutors, a conduit for talent from the pool of academia, into MI6.

She was thinking of calling it a day – best to get an early start tomorrow, she thought – and was about to stand when she heard the handle of the door turn, and then George Edwards strolled in.

"And where do you think you're going?" he said with a smile. George was an accomplished academic himself, well versed in mathematics, chemistry, and physics. Fluent in nine languages, he was quite a tall young man with wild and wavy jet-black hair, a mass of Brylcreem slicking it back on his head in an attempt to control it. He wore his usual neatly pressed light grey tank top and dark grey flannels, which Dorothy always felt made him appear older than the twenty-five he was.

"Just thought I'd grab something to eat and then turn in," she told him.

"Blimey, it's chilly in here" he said as he marched over to the heater, checking it was actually on before also ensuring that the blackout curtains were properly closed. "Good job I brought my sandwiches with me, then. We'll have to share I'm afraid. I hope you like corned beef," he said with a chuckle. "The thing is, the top brass would like you to take a look at this, it's just come in. Message originated from the Channel. Only one word. They think it could be a command of some sort. I'll give you a hand, if you like?"

Edwards blushed slightly as he spoke, and Dorothy sat back down thinking that perhaps George had a crush on her. Male and female operatives weren't supposed to work together, rules and all that, but the two of them had said that so long as no one knew, what harm could it do? Indeed, if they came up with something of importance it could only be a good thing. Besides, she would enjoy his company along with his help as they tried to decipher the message. It would be a pleasant way to end the day, she thought, as he sat down beside her and opened his sandwiches.

*

Bob Coleman was now in the officers' mess at RAF Medmenham having a well-earned beer when he was told that there was an urgent call for him in his office. It was getting near 2300 hours, and he was trying to wind down, but he took a quick gulp of the lukewarm ale before heading over to the main admin building just a stone's throw away across the yard. He recognised Sullivan's voice as soon as he spoke.

"Evening, Bob. Thought you'd like to know I may

have found your sub!"

"Where?"

"The Channel. I've gone over the timeline from when they left Peenemünde. I've plotted a course considering factors like speed, tides, weather, etc., that could possibly put her there. I plotted other possible courses and positions yesterday, but unfortunately it looks like one of our ships has come across her by accident off the coast of France.

"I was working on at least five different places she might have travelled to when something disturbing came in over the wire. It's a contact report, but I'm afraid she may have sunk the Corvette that's crossed her path. We've got two more ships on the way to check it out and hopefully intercept them. I'll keep you posted with any developments, okay?"

"Of course, sir, appreciate it. Goodnight, sir."

"You too, Bob. I'll call you in the morning with an update, as soon as I hear anything. Goodnight."

*

It had been four more long hours in hut four, and Dorothy and George had yet to make a breakthrough.

"S. U. R. T. R. You sure that's it, George, the spelling? There's nothing else attached? We seem to be going around in circles," asked Dorothy.

"It doesn't make sense to me, either. Can't think of a German word or translation for the spelling. I keep coming back to the word cert, as in certificate or a dead cert? 'Zertifikat' is the German translation for certificate. In English we would pronounce it as 'cert', not 'surtr', if that makes sense?" he replied.

"Wonder if it's an acronym for something?"

"We'll be here for weeks trying to figure that out, Dot." She liked it when he used her shortened first name. Perhaps at the weekend they could go to the dance in the village together, or maybe the pictures, she thought. She'd have to ask him; he's far too shy to make the first move.

"What about history, mythology, place names, people?" Dot asked. "They're typically used for code words. Operation Barbarossa in '41, for instance? Or Edelweiss, the mountain flower; the plan to capture the oil fields of the Caucasus in '42. Barbarossa was the nickname of Fredrick the first, the German king."

"Yes, perhaps, but Surtr doesn't ring any bells."

George stood and turned to the expansive bookcase on the wall to his left containing hundreds of the best reference books they had at Bletchley including the likes of the *Encyclopaedia Britannica* first published in 1768 and *The British Encyclopaedia* published in 1933, but he was scanning the tomes on the shelves looking for *Brockhaus*, a German encyclopaedia dating back to the eighteenth century. The edition he wanted was printed in German, and his thinking was it would be truer to any literal translation he might discover.

He brought back the large copy he'd found; clearly it had been read multiple times, judging by its battered condition. He dropped it on the table with a thump. Dorothy stared at him, knowing full well to not interrupt his train of thought for the moment. He turned the pages slowly, clearly searching for something, his colleague waiting patiently for him to speak. It was a good hour before he stirred from the book.

"Mmmmm," he mused.

"Got something?" asked Dorothy as she woke up after nodding off.

"Well, maybe. Going on the lines of deities, myths, mythology, etc., that I've been looking under, I came across Thor, the God of Thunder, and was about to dismiss him. But, in the description, I've discovered that he destroyed Surtr, a God of War, a fire giant who was turned black, charred in the battle between the two."

"Well done," said Dorothy, struggling now to keep her eyes open; it had been a long day, which had morphed into a long night.

"I don't know what else to say on the subject, really. If it is S-U-R-T-R as transmitted, and it's the same as the God, that's all we've got."

It was Dorothy who now rose and made her way over to the bookcases. She quickly found the book she was looking for: *Norse Mythology*. As she walked back to the table she leafed through the book, flicking pages along until she reached something that appeared to be of use. She sat back down, muttering to herself and paraphrased aloud to George what she had found.

"Thor, God of Thunder and Lightning, used a large hammer to crash down on the earth to project his powers. Protector of the people, associated mostly with Norse mythology, but also with the early Germanic races, particularly during the days of the Roman empire. Then it goes on to list Odin and blah, blah, blah, ah, here's something. Ragnarök, a series of battles that led to the deaths of Thor, Odin, Freyr, Loki, etc., which in turn leads to a new world. There's a reference to a poem here called Völspá."

George rose again and went back to the bookcase, this time down to the far end on the left. After pulling two or three books out but replacing them, he settled on one, standing there reading it to himself by the bookcase. Dorothy squinted in the meagre light being cast by the single bulb hanging from the ceiling, now not feeling as tired as she had earlier. George walked back to the table now and sat back down.

"Got it; the poem, that is. Surtr is a giant that brings forth fire that helps destroy the earth, leading to a new order, as you described, Dot. Surtr carried a large flaming sword and is linked to lava and volcanic fires. He rides out against the Gods, his weapon shining like the sun, and after defeating them he will burn the world to ashes, new Gods will arise to rule the world. A prophecy there, if ever there was one." He paused for a moment as something else came to him. "You mentioned that he was turned black by the fight. Surtr is also an old Norse word for Schwarz, which is German for black. Pretty nasty God this one, all told, if I'm honest. If that's the case, and the transmission is S-U-R-T-R as described, we may have a code word for a German military operation that might be linked to a new beginning that starts with fire and destruction, possibly with another link to the word black. But that's only a theory, and a very tenuous one at that. In reality, most covert operations by most armies have death, destruction, and fire in them somewhere."

"It's the new order, the new beginning slant that intrigues me, George. Sounds like maybe a rally call to rise up, to start again, if you see what I mean? The Germans are back on their heels, potentially beaten, plus the second front is on its way in France. A last hurrah, perhaps?"

"Yes, yes, I can see that. But apart from a theory on what the actual word means, and that it may or may not have originated from a U-boat in the Channel, it's not much to go on. But, we've handed over less." With that said, George gave her a wide smile, one that was reciprocated and made him blush ever so once again.

*

Back at the Admiralty, Sullivan was sitting at his desk, twirling the ends of his moustache between his fingertips when his train of thought was interrupted.

"A message from Havelock, sir. They've reached *Zenobia*'s position," said the rating, passing Sullivan the communique. It wasn't the news he'd hoped for. *Havelock* had come across multiple oil fires on the surface, a large field of debris, and only one lifeboat found so far and that with only dead aboard. As of yet, no survivors. No enemy contact in the area. The ship was proceeding in a south westerly direction in pursuit, assuming the contact was returning to base. *Newark* would search the last known position of *Zenobia* for survivors in the water when on station.

Chasing a ghost again, thought Sullivan. Possibly all the crew of the *Zenobia* lost. It troubled him, too, why the U-boat would attack. Surely it was in their own interests to evade conflict if their mission was secret? The Channel was certainly not the place to be if you were a German at this time in the war, what with the might of the allied navies to be found there. You'd try to slip through undetected, surely?

Sullivan thought back to February '42 and the failed attacks by the RAF on the cruisers *Scharnhorst* and *Gneisenau* who had sailed from Brest and had all but gone unnoticed as they made their way through the Channel in a bid to get back home to the safety of a German port. Churchill had been apoplectic with rage over the failure to sink these prime targets, and how they had managed to go undetected for almost twelve hours right on England's doorstep. It demonstrated one thing to the Kreigsmarine: that you could get through, if done properly.

Even so, to pick a fight, and a fight there of all places, seemed rash. To turn tail and dive away from your pursuer would surely have been a much smarter move. He just hoped *Havelock* would catch and destroy the buggers, and soon. But he couldn't leave them out there alone to carry out the task, he'd have to get them some help, and so he picked up the phone and asked to be put through to coastal command. He would ask for a search and destroy mission on the coordinates of the area the chasing *Havelock* was entering, then he'd call Coleman and update him on the latest events.

He'd been in touch with Eastbury Park, Middlesex, and Air Vice Marshal Christopher Smith, head of coastal command, who said he'd send two RAF Liberators to the search area and that they'd be arriving there very shortly, only an hour from now, to help seek out the sub. Now, he was calling Bob Coleman again, a bit late in the night or early in the morning now, depending on your outlook.

"Morning, Bob, just calling to update you again," said Sullivan, a hint of anger tinged with sadness in his tone after the recent unfolding events. When he'd finished, Coleman spoke.

"With the chasing destroyer *Newark* and the coastal command planes after them, now we might finally catch a break? But I agree with you, it seems incongruous as to why he chose to attack rather than run. We know Roth, – that is, if he's still at the helm – as a seasoned operator, not gung-ho at all. Surprising; his actions, that is."

"If he slips away now, we can all but forget him. He'll get back to Saint-Nazaire if that's his goal and- oh, hang on a mo', Bob." Sullivan had been interrupted mid-sentence when another sailor entered his office with a further communique. Coleman waited silently at the end of the line as Sullivan scanned the paper he held in his hand. He came back on the line shortly.

"I've had some information about a German coded signal that was intercepted from the approximate area of the sub. It's only one word, which is quite typical, honestly, informing the listeners, for example, that a way point has been reached. It's only a preliminary assessment by the codebreakers but the word itself is Surter, spelt S-U-R-T-R, and apparently it relates to a little-known German God of fire and Armageddon, if I've read the rest of this right. More analysis to follow, it says. Not as helpful as I'd have wished, but it could be something?"

"Right, sir. Hope you find the buggers, let me know if you need anything else. All the best. Give me a call later with an update if you can, bye."

Sullivan placed the receiver back in its cradle and looked at the large map of the western approaches on the wall to his left and mouthed, "Where the hell are you now, and what are you really up to?"

CHAPTER 15 - ATLANTIC

U-931 was travelling underwater at a good seven knots on a westerly heading. There hadn't been any further contact since they had dived, but Roth couldn't take the chance that there were no more pursuers after them. The rudder had been fixed in double quick time; two sailors had been armed with large hammers and had managed to beat out the crumpled metal that had been stuck against the hull, and then moved onto the steering. It had been similar damage that had led to the demise of the Bismarck back in '41, Roth had once heard, so they were lucky not to have suffered the same fate today. But, as of yet, there hadn't been much luck on this mission, what with the attacks at Peenemünde and in the Channel. They'd hardly begun the task, and yet here they were. The shooting of the British crew by Fuchs and Vogel was a death sentence for them all, that was clear. When the bullet-ridden lifeboat was discovered, all hell would break loose. They'd hunt him and his crew down to the ends of the earth. They were tarnished now as murderers.

All the factors that he was contemplating now paled into insignificance, though, as he began to realise the implications of Fuchs' comment about him taking Vogel's place. Roth's train of thought as he sat in his cabin was interrupted as the curtain was unceremoniously and quickly drawn back; it was Fuchs. He entered, drew back the curtain and sat down on the bunk. The two men stared at each other; it was Fuchs who spoke first.

"I do not like where we find ourselves, Captain. I have lost a valued friend, a comrade in arms. The mission has been compromised with that loss and, in order to proceed, I must command you to take his place. Not something that fills me with confidence if this undertaking is to succeed. Vogel and I have planned this operation from the start, we know it inside out and were both prepared to die to ensure its success. Would you be? I think not. I am assuming that we have lost our pursuers, at least for the moment?"

"We must be at our most vigilant at this moment. Your actions with Vogel have, how do I put this, not only jeopardised your mission, but put this boat and its crew at the very top of an already 'wanted' list. Every available allied sailor and airman in this part of the world is probably searching with all their might for us. The task we had was impossible as it was, but you have taken it to a new level, and your suggestion that I take Vogel's place is just ridiculous, a joke!" stated Roth, both men speaking in urgent yet low tones so as not to alert the crew to their discussion.

"As members of the SS, Vogel and I are proud to serve our country and the National Socialist movement. The actions we took were to eliminate enemies of those two institutions and a justified act of war. You yourself have sent hundreds to their deaths. Yet, you take the moral high ground because of our killing of a mere ten or so!"

"What you describe as an act of war is murder in my book. And yes, I am responsible for death and destruction on a massive scale, but it's unlikely that I will ever be hauled before a war crimes tribunal, unlike you and the rest of your Nazi thugs."

"Be careful, Roth." Fuchs didn't say anything more for a moment, but what he didn't say said more to Roth than any words ever could. Roth had to appeal to him if they had any chance of getting out of this mess alive.

"It's not too late to change course and head for Saint-Nazaire. We can call Berlin when we land and explain. You can ask for a replacement, start over?"

"As I told you before, you are Vogel's replacement. You speak the language; you know the people. You will help me blend in. I need someone to help me when we arrive in Washington to locate the bomb. Turning back isn't an option, the other submarines with the rockets are scheduled to arrive on the twenty-fifth and launch once they are in position the following day. It's all timed down to the last minute so as to give the illusion of a real atomic attack. Your intransigence and contemptible lack of enthusiasm throughout this endeavour has worried me from the day we met, Roth. If I had the opportunity, believe me, I would charge you in a heartbeat and have you shot immediately for your disloyalty."

"You're right, I do have misgivings about this fool's errand. I can see it for what it really is. It's a last grasp at holding onto the power that the SS, Himmler, and the Führer have come to know, and, dare I say it; love. Little did the German people realise back in '33 what they were letting themselves in for when they voted Hitler into power. A new order, change for the better. Yes, I believed, as did others, that he was the man to revitalise our country, to make us proud to be Germans again, and for a while, he did. But not now, not this way. We are all but defeated, and to carry on is madness means thousands more will die. When the allies launch the invasion, they will march inevitably across Europe and into the heartland of Germany, perhaps even launching their own atomic weapons. And then there's the Russians. Don't you realise that they will leave our people and buildings smashed into oblivion as they roll across Germany, just like you and the SS did as you strode over the plains eastward back in '41?"

"Have you finished? Unfortunately, we shall have to play with the cards we have been dealt, Roth. You shall help me, of that there is no question. You can turn this boat around; I cannot stop you if you so wish. But believe me when I say this, Captain; you and every one of your crew will be shot as traitors as soon as we dock in France. As I see it you have one of two choices, one of which could see you as a hero in Germany, the other a traitor. How would your father in Hamburg react to the second option? Then, there's always the question of the girl you were seeing in France – Ginette, I believe, is her name?"

Roth was about to launch himself once again at the SS major but thought better of it. The mention of Ginette and his father made him hold back. Clearly the SS had them both in their sights and would not hesitate to murder them, too, if Roth was found out to be a traitor. It did not escape him that the solidly built man would easily overpower him here in the small confines of the sub, and there was little to be gained from such an emotional attack. Instead, the two men stared at each other, the gap between the two so small and yet, at the same time, a chasm. Fuchs had stood as he said his final words. He glared at Roth, swept the curtain aside, and left.

*

It had been eight hours since the first report from *Zenobia* had come in. The Liberators sent out by coastal command had been over the area where the sub was estimated to be for a while now, but so far had reported nothing. What was most distressing to Sullivan was the news from the site of the Corvette's wreckage. The signal had stated that there was a large debris field, the hull presumed to have sunk beneath the waves. Oil fires burned on the surface and the sea was littered with dead sailors. But the worse was the news that one of *Zenobia*'s wooden lifeboats had been found drifting close by and that all on board were dead. What he couldn't come to terms with was that the boat and crewmen were riddled with bullets. It appeared to the crew of the *Newark* that the U-boat had surfaced and strafed the sailors on board with machine gun fire, killing them all.

Sullivan now felt sick to his stomach. Could this damn war get any worse, he asked himself? Why kill the survivors? They had destroyed their pursuers. Why not just get away? U-boats had left survivors of many a merchant ship to die in life rafts, hundreds of miles from any possible rescue – they couldn't take them on board, there was no room. But this? This was another level. It made him even more determined now to find and destroy Roth and his sub. He called in his adjutant and dictated a signal for *Newark* and *Havelock*. He wanted them both to continue with the search in a pattern that would lead them on a course towards Saint-Nazaire, U-931's home port. He was surmising that's where they were heading. He would also ask Coastal Command to send up further planes to do the same. If they were out there, he wanted them at the bottom of the Atlantic.

*

Seventy-five miles due south of the *Zenobia*'s sinking, a lone submarine sat quietly on the seabed. The code word 'Surtr' had been heard nearly an hour ago, and still it had not stirred. Orders dictated that U-329 was to be here at this location on March fourteenth and to carry out the remainder of her orders on the fifteenth, so all on board remained silent.

*

On board U-931, Roth approached the listening station, which was directly opposite his cabin, and spoke to Horst, who was still listening for any contacts.

"Anything?"

"No, Captain," came the reply. "Nothing to report since the last action."

Schmitt approached the captain, stood beside him, and

spoke in a hushed tone, ensuring Horst couldn't overhear him.

"What are we to do, Captain?"

"For the first time in my career, Schmitt, I don't know. We are in an impossible situation. Whichever track we take we're screwed. Go back to port now and Fuchs will have us shot as traitors. Continue with the mission, survive the war, and if any of that Corvette's crew survived, we'll be hung by the allies for murder. I'm not sure about the mission, either. Fuchs wants me to fill Vogel's shoes because of my background, but I'll admit, it scares me. This whole enterprise could have far reaching consequences for Germany and this boat. It looks like I'll have to go with him on the mission, I have no choice, but I don't like abandoning you and the crew. Plus, I fear for your safety when you land back in France. I think you might be advised to go south after you've dropped us, and head for South America."

"If we throw that SS murderer overboard and say he was killed together with Vogel, we could then go back to Nazaire with the damaged steering and say that because we had no one left to complete the mission, we returned to base. Then after the war, if there are any repercussions over the shooting, we tell the British it was the SS who did the killing."

"I would have no problem killing Fuchs myself, but all it would take is for one of the crew to talk and the game's up. Convincing them to sail south without me won't be easy, there will be opposition of course, but you will have to convince them after I have left the boat. Tell them how dangerous it would be to return because of Fuchs and Vogel killing those sailors. Fuchs can get no idea of this or he will turn the crew against us, whipping up Nazi fervour and patriotism. I can see no other way. When I have helped him with his task, I'll get away somehow and perhaps head to Carolina where I might find a friendly face to sit out the war with, if they don't give me up, that is. Where is Fuchs now?"

"I saw him lie down in his bunk earlier, perhaps to think over his actions, or not." The two stood silent for a moment. Schmitt didn't know what to think, he had a lot to mull over himself. He took Roth by the elbow in his firm grip and looked him directly in the eye.

"I think it is time for you to open the sealed orders, Captain, in your cabin, where I will join you momentarily with Berger, okay?" Roth nodded his agreement and headed for the cabin. When he got there, he spun the dial on the boat's safe until he heard it click. He opened it, reached inside, and withdrew the envelope with the embossed eagle on it. He sat down on his chair and then opened the envelope, withdrawing the single sheet of paper inside. Schmitt and Berger joined him, all three of them squeezing inside the cramped space. The comrades sat there with an air of anticipation hanging over them.

*

Fuchs had not enjoyed his pitiful sleep in the bunk he had been assigned to in the officer's section. As he lay there looking aft, he could see the captain's area; the curtain was drawn. He was hot and had a headache. It was difficult to get any quality sleep down here. During his numerous battles across Europe and Russia, he had slept in all sorts of places and could usually fall asleep on a clothesline when he was so weary from fighting. He'd drifted off easily so many times before in the backs of wagons, train carriages, slit trenches, under the bellies of tanks. But that was different. Then he knew that his fellow soldiers had his back as he slept, as he had theirs. But down here, with these strangers, and not being in control of his own destiny as he was accustomed to, was unnerving. He'd never felt so vulnerable in all his years as a soldier.

He looked further down the narrowing tunnel that was the sub's metal casing, past the crew's sleeping area, and onto the engine room. He was sure he'd dreamt about the incessant drum beat of the diesels, and that's why he was suffering with a headache now. He was still dressed in his uniform, but it was soaking with sweat and he considered changing into his civilian clothes, but then thought better of it; they would end up smelling like this badger pit he found himself in now, and he wanted to look fresh when he stepped ashore in a few days. Roth had forewarned him about the conditions on a U-boat, but he'd underestimated just how awful it would be.

To begin with, there were the smells. He'd experienced bad body odour amongst his fellow combatants many times before when lying in slit trenches or bunkers on top of each other, waiting to attack or on some peaceful rest time, his own stench mixed in with theirs. But down here it was something else, something only a gas mask could help relieve. Back at the front, they used Russian soap to wash with when they could. It helped with the body lice as it contained crushed ash in it to kill the little buggers, but it didn't have any fragrance. Indeed, it didn't smell much better than the dirty foot soldier. The food down here wasn't much better than the field rations he'd had at the front, and it led to terrible bouts of flatulence as well. Whereas a fart was something to laugh at with a bunch of similar minded soldiers, all going back to their childhoods during the barrack room banter, here it was a different matter.

There was no escape for the stench when released. They lingered for what seemed an age and any guilty sailor was taken to task if he dared to break wind in company. But they couldn't keep them in, and so they joined the aromas of rotten cabbage, sweaty sailors, and the disgusting toilet fragrance of excrement and urine which permeated through the boat even when the ship had the hatches open when sailing on the surface. Only then did small amounts of fresh air seem to filter down from outside. He was looking forward to some of that fresh air, if he got a chance to go top side. He rubbed his aching brow, his head pounding. The bloody *throb, throb, throb* of the diesel engines when they were running was another distraction in the confines of this claustrophobic tin can. But what of the mission? He couldn't find himself to have any confidence in Roth. Sure, he was a fine U-boat captain, his achievements spoke for themselves. But as a foot soldier, in very unfamiliar surroundings, even for himself? Vogel and he worked well as a team, and they would have had each other's back; but Roth? His only saving attribute was his American upbringing, which may serve them well in the days ahead. Fuchs' gaze returned back to the drawn curtain.

*

In the confines of the captain's area, the three officers had settled. Roth spoke.

"Our destination is Spencer Bay, on the Pamlico River, North Carolina. This is ironic, we are to land at a place called Germantown." Berger left them and returned with a chart of the area they were heading for. He folded it up until he found the place he was looking for. After a brief study, he spoke.

"We sail north of Cedar Island to get to the river. Any more instructions, Captain?"

"Once in the river we head for an inlet, Swanquarter Bay, where we can dock and unload the package, plus Fuchs and myself."

"I can't see anything but trouble with that union, sir," said Schmitt. "Is there any way we can get you out of this?"

"It's impossible as far as I can see. The operation calls for two men to deliver the package and, unfortunately, we lost Vogel when they decided to murder those British sailors – an act that will see us hang, as I said earlier, Jonas. I was always aware that my American heritage may be used against me some time, but I never envisaged this scenario. My background knowledge of the States should enable us to get past anyone asking questions, although I do have some doubts over my credentials. I could pass for Vogel in a dark room from twenty feet away at a push, but it doesn't fill me with confidence."

"And what of the plan, Captain? Where are you going?"

"That I can't say, my friend. The least you know, the better. Fuchs has told me he will give me all the final details when we are on shore. I know the general outline of the plan, but it is best that you do not know any more. For one, if Fuchs knew of this discussion, he may take out retribution on you both. Plus, if you were picked up by the American navy, perhaps in their waters, you could stick to the cover story about mine laying, and they couldn't interrogate you about anything else you might know."

"What about our return? Do we sail home, meet the supply sub, go on patrol in the Atlantic as normal, and then return to France? Or head south as we discussed?" This last sentence was said in barely a whisper to Roth.

"What do you mean?" asked Berger in a similar low tone. "Head south?"

Roth pulled back the curtain on his cabin, peeked out to see no one was listening to them, drew it back, and then spoke again.

"I don't think it's safe to return to Germany. I think that, because of the gravity of this operation, the Nazi top brass don't want any witnesses left to talk about this in the future. After you have dropped me off, you should head south to Argentina, you should just about have enough fuel to make it. But before you do, you should gather the crew together and tell them everything. You must convince them and get them to agree. If too many of them challenge you, it'll become a mutiny, and a divided crew is a dangerous crew."

"Most of the crew would follow you to the bottom, Captain, their loyalty beyond question, you know that. But as for Zinke and Dietz, that's another thing entirely. Both are ardent Nazis, and they would sink the boat, given the chance, if they couldn't return home."

"You may have to restrain them on board, then set them free when you land. There is something that may convince all the crew where their loyalties lie. I might be wrong, but there may be another sub with orders to sink you when we leave the river mouth, perhaps with a false belief that we are traitors to the Fatherland or some other lie. One way or the other, I believe that this boat and crew will not be allowed to return home safely. We're a liability." These last statements to Schmitt and Berger had landed like hammer blows. They both sat there, not knowing what to say next. Berger stood up.

"I will check on the steering again and then set the new course, Captain." He then saluted, turned, and left. As he did so he glanced in the direction of Fuchs' bunk twenty feet away, where he saw an arm of the officer's black uniform sticking out from the side, but no more of the big man. Presuming he was still asleep he went aft. Fuchs had watched Berger come out and had feigned sleep. He stood up, stretched, and made his way forward from the crew compartment towards the control room to find some Saridon or something similar for his headache. He would sometimes take his Methamphetamine to help with the occasional migraine he suffered from, as he found that helped, but he did not want to use any of his supply until he was on shore. As he stooped to pass through the bulkhead he thought back to how Berger, the first officer, had come out of the captain's cabin. How he had looked towards his direction before making his way towards the engine room. Fuchs stood there silently for a moment, staring at the curtain.

*

"Drink, Jonas?" asked Roth. "I have some fine Marienwerder Schnapps, here," he continued, as he reached under his bunk.

"Yes, I'd like some, please." Schmitt had the look of a very worried man. Roth poured two full glasses of the clear alcohol, the aroma of the spirit a welcome visitor, a distraction to help mask the background smells.

"Come, my friend, drink. Forget what's to come, if only for a moment."

"There is so much to think about. If we do make Argentina and find safety in La Cumbrecita, what next, after the war? We shall not be the victors; of that I have no doubt. We shall all want to return home if it's safe, but how? Plus, the British may still be looking for the crew of U-931. Our families will think we are lost, sunk. How shall they accept our return?"

"I don't have any answers for you, Jonas, but I-"

Suddenly, the curtain was swept back, revealing the imposing figure of Fuchs standing there.

"And what answers are they, Captain?"

CHAPTER 16 - CROSSING

Back at Bletchley Park, Dorothy and George were still looking for something that might throw some light on the intercepted message.

"I'm bushed, George," said Dot. "I've looked through countless encyclopaedias but can't find any more than we already have. Surtr was a German God of Fire with references to Armageddon and a new world arising from the flames. Which, if you think about it, could refer back to the rise of the Third Reich and the Nazi's new order."

"Yes. I'm inclined to agree," replied George, looking out of the window. "It's getting light, what time is it?"

"Eight-o'-bloody-clock. Think we've done all we can, here," responded his weary colleague.

"I did read something else in an old book covering European mythology that links schwarz, or black, to the god Surtr, but that's it I'm afraid. It's all down to interpretation. I'll pass on what we've got, but I'm of the opinion that the code word links to a deity with a strong link to the word black. Not much to go on, really, but I think we've gone as far as we can. It's up to someone above our paygrade to figure out what to do with it."

*

Admiral Sullivan was someone else who had not been to bed that night either. He'd been liaising with bomber command and getting signals from both the *Newark* and *Havelock*, both of whom were now chasing the elusive U-boat. He didn't feel tired at that moment, adrenaline was keeping him going. They'd had the chance to get it as it had left Germany but had missed that opportunity, and because of that eighty-five crew were dead or missing. Here, deep down in the bowels of the earth in this subterranean bomb-proof bunker, he felt claustrophobic.

Even though the streets of Whitehall in central London were above, he never felt comfortable down here in his office. It was, of course, one of the safest places to be when the bombing started, yet he always had that sense of relief wash over him when he climbed the hundred or so stairs to reach the outside world after many an hour down below. He stubbed out yet another Capstan cigarette into the ashtray on his desk. He made a mental note to get more later, if he could get out of here today. He walked over to the office door and closed it to shut out the noise from the outside office; even at this early hour there were numerous typewriters chattering away in the background. He turned off the desk lamp before picking up the phone, remembering that he'd promised Bob Coleman another update. It took a few minutes to get through on the scrambled line and, while he waited, he glanced around the walls at the posters encouraging any reader that 'careless talks cost lives', or similar doctrines. Finally, the connection was made, and Sullivan recognised the gravelly voice of his old comrade when he picked up.

"Hello, is that you, Admiral?" Bob Coleman enquired.

"Yes, Bob. Just calling to give you that update I promised. It's not good, I'm afraid. At first we thought that there were no survivors from *Zenobia*, but *Havelock* picked up a lone sailor in the water clinging to some debris and what he told them was frightening. He said he watched as the sub surfaced after the attack, and that they fired on the only lifeboat still afloat, raking the helpless crew with machine gun fire. But, then, some return shots rang out from within the boat and one of the men who fired from the sub was hit and fell overboard. The sailor wasn't sure, but he thinks that the men on the sub were dressed in SS uniforms. But what he can say for definite is the boat's number: U-931! When the *Havelock* crew checked the lifeboat, all were dead. Shot! Captain Prince among them.

"The two Liberators, which had been sent out from coastal command, have returned to base without sighting the bugger. I gave them a search area that I believed covered a possible route of escape back to a safe haven in France. They flew back and forth along that line with no luck. *Newark* continued along a similar line, again with no luck. I'm going to have to recall her as she's already out on a limb down there and will be vulnerable herself to attack from both sea and air. I don't want to lose another ship. I'm afraid we'll have to give it up. What I do propose is that we contact the French resistance and get them to keep an eye on every submarine base up and down the coast, and to report back here when they sight U-931 pulling into harbour, whether that's tomorrow, the day after, or whenever. I'm going to keep tabs on that boat from now until the end of this damned war and hunt down those responsible for their actions."

"Jesus, Admiral, I don't know what to say, that's terrible news. To sink the ship is one thing, but to murder the survivors is another. These actions don't fit Roth's profile from what I've read about him, but if it's true he does have SS on board, then perhaps that explains the trip to Peenemünde. Maybe it's some covert SS operation where they will be dropped off by the sub, somewhere in France, or wherever? Did you get any more information about the signal that was intercepted?"

"A bit vague, I'm afraid. They believe that the code word is in some way linked to a German God with links to the Nazi's and the word black; that's it. Not much to go on, probably just a jump off word for the operation, or the operation name itself. So, that's it for now. So far, we've had no luck chasing Roth down, but if we get the opportunity again, I don't intend to miss our chance. And if they don't turn up until after the war, we'll hang them then." He was about to continue when he noticed in his eye line two American army officers standing outside his door looking through the glass, obviously waiting to see him. "I'll have to call you back, Bob. Looks like I've got visitors. Bye." He hung up and beckoned the officers inside.

They opened the door and entered. Both men were immaculate in their olive drab jackets and khaki pants; all pressed to perfection and adorned with shiny brass buttons. *Impressive*, thought Sullivan. The shorter of the two was perhaps aged around forty, with an athletic build but which was starting to sag. Underneath his peaked cap was a jolly looking face accentuated with a piercing gaze from deep blue eyes. The second man, who was considerably younger than the first, was African American, tall – perhaps six feet – and thin, plus he had a natural authority about him, but a face that looked like it had lost one too many boxing matches. Both men flashed their credentials, as was customary, and the first man, a colonel, spoke.

"Good morning, Admiral. I'm Colonel Colin Lee and this is Major Miller. We're both attached to OSS. That's the Office of Strategic Services, sir."

"Yes, Colonel, I know what the acronym stands for. You're similar to our intelligence service, I believe?" Sullivan knew of MI6 but stopped short of mentioning them. "What can I do for you, gentlemen?"

There was a slight pause. Both the Americans glanced at one another before Lee continued.

"We've been monitoring what's been happening in the channel with *HMS* Zenobia this morning. I'm sorry for that loss, sir. But it's come to our attention at OSS that you've been tracking the sub that may be responsible from when it left its base in France, then onto Germany, and that, with the help of the RAF, you organised a raid at Peenemünde."

Sullivan digested what he'd just heard before speaking.

"You seem very well-informed, Colonel."

"We haven't arrived at the dance late, sir; in fact, we've had an interest in submarines and any connection to Peenemünde for a while, now. May we sit down?"

"Of course, please do."

The two men pulled out the wooden chairs in front of Sullivan's desk and then Miller took up the story.

"Back in '43 we had a number of intelligence reports about a secret rocket programme that was situated at Peenemünde, and you're probably aware that the RAF sent a large bomber force there last August: Operation Hydra. They were met with a concerted Luftwaffe response; they lost forty bombers and crew with little, or no damage sustained by the facilities there. According to our sources on the ground, the Germans have moved some of the manufacturing to secret locations across the country, and whilst we still are trying to seek these out, we are also going to launch another air raid there very soon, perhaps with the US eighth air force. Unfortunately, we've lost contact with our source at Peenemünde. It's possible that they were killed in the air raid, or their identity has been discovered and they've been shot, so we're actively pursuing other lines in an attempt to catch up, so to speak.

"We know that your security clearance allows me to continue, so I'll endeavour to clarify where we are and why we've come down here today.

"Late last year we also commenced Operation Crossbow, which was set up to gather as much information on Hitler's programme of mobile rocket launch sites. These sites consist of an angled ramp from which an unmanned plane, powered by a rocket with a range that we believe to be around two-hundred miles, can be launched at Britain. Each rocket has a warhead of about one-thousand pounds. We are in the process of trying to stop this programme before it can begin, but, during the operation, more of our agents who were monitoring the U-boat base in Wilhelmshaven, Germany, took some very interesting photographs which they managed to get back to us." Lee continued the dialogue.

"The photos showed a sub leaving port with a metal structure welded to the forward deck. At first glance we thought it was another version of their anti-ship rocket system they are developing, which, if I understand correctly, you and the Royal Navy know about?" The admiral nodded and let them continue. "On further examination, the structure turned out to be a ramp. Much smaller than the land-based one for the V1s, as we believe they are called, but definitely a ramp of some sort. There was no rocket attached when it left port, but when the sub returned a day later the structure and part of the forward deck area were damaged and twisted, leaving us to conclude that some sort of trial had taken place at sea, not all that successfully. Perhaps everything hadn't gone to plan. Once again, we lost our source. Our agent in the area was shot and killed by a sentry near the base a few weeks ago and we haven't been able to replace them. That's where you come in, Admiral."

"How so?" enquired Sullivan.

"Through our contacts with MI6, we got wind of the photo showing the sub moored up at Peenemünde and the subsequent Mosquito attack, both of which got our attention. We also knew of U-931 leaving Saint-Nazaire; we're trying to keep track of all the submarine bases. But, as they are located in France, Germany, and Norway, it's quite a task. Then, this morning, we learnt of the attack on *Zenobia* and the confirmation it was U-931. She's gone in the wind, now, we're led to believe?"

"We don't think she was sunk," said the Admiral, "but quickly left the scene, and, yes, we've lost her. We're not sure what she's up to, but I'm beginning to think that perhaps you do?"

The two Americans stole another glance towards each other.

"We believe that the German navy, together with their scientists, are developing or have already developed a submarine-launched V1. Think of the consequences. A completely mobile rocket launch system, bringing any part of the British Isles within range of attack, and virtually impossible to detect whilst submerged and getting into position."

It dawned on Sullivan what was really behind the colonel's concerns.

"If they can do it to us, can they do it to you?"

"Yes, sir, nearly every major city on the east coast of America will be within range of these missiles."

"I've seen the reconnaissance photos of the sub and she hasn't got any extra superstructure on board, so what's her involvement?"

"Like you, we're not sure, but what is of concern is that if the Germans have succeeded in developing the launch system, and then have gone on to fit it to their new submarine, the Type XXI, which has a far greater range and carrying facility, we are at an extremely dangerous moment in this war. If the Germans have developed the capability to attack America, then the plans for the upcoming invasion may have to be postponed while that threat is dealt with. You can, of course, see the gravity of any delay to the invasion? With the Russians bearing down on Berlin from the east at an alarming rate, it's imperative for the western allies to invade France and reach Berlin before Christmas. The long-term consequences of Moscow and Stalin having control over all of Germany, and perhaps even parts of France and the low countries, does not sit comfortably with either of our governments. We are convinced that U-931 is culpable in some way. Exactly why, who knows? You can see why it is of the utmost importance that Captain Roth and his boat are found."

*

On board U-931, a surprised Roth replied to Fuchs' question as he stood over the two U-boat officers.

"Jonas asked me who might be the new captain of the boat when they return, and indeed if he would be able to apply for the position. I told him he's more than qualified, but that it's up to high command." Fuchs and Roth stared at each other, each knowing the other was not satisfied with the answer.

Fuchs changed the subject. "Do you have anything for a headache?"

"There are some Neurameg on that shelf there," indicated Roth, pointing to his bookshelf. Fuchs looked to where the captain had indicated and he picked up the small red tin, opened it, and took out two tablets, throwing them to the back of his throat before picking up the bottle of Schnapps from the table and taking a long hard pull of the fiery liquid. As he did so Schmitt stood, nodded slightly, and was about to leave the two men together when Roth spoke.

"Take us to periscope depth, Jonas, and check for surface contacts. Horst says there's nothing out there but take a look, and then if it's okay we'll surface and switch to diesel. We need to make up for lost time. Put out extra lookouts and set up the Biscay cross." Schmitt nodded and left. Fuchs took the place of Schmitt next to the captain.

"So, Captain, as you will be aware even after our brief time together, as a Sturmbannführer in the SS I am strongly motivated, and I also possess drive, passion, and a determination to carry out my orders. The things I have done and seen during the last four years have all been carried out through patriotism and a fierce loyalty to the Fatherland. We are at a crossroads in this war, Captain, and if we do not act decisively now and take the fight to the Americans in their homeland instead of ours, which looks likely to happen very soon, then all will be lost. Our actions will turn the tide back in our favour, and with the Führer's leadership we shall go on and continue with the rise of the Third Reich. When given an order, I will complete it at all costs, and I assure you that this mission will continue to the end and that no one will stop me from completing everything asked of me for the Fatherland. Circumstances have transpired to throw us together and it will serve neither of us to dwell on past mistakes. If you have the time now, I will fill you in with details of the operation and your role within it. You will inform me about the places we are likely to go through on our journey north and the return journey south, which I envisage will be far more dangerous after the attack. I am presuming that we are in a position far enough from land, that at the moment, we are relatively safe from discovery?" It was a rhetorical question, but Roth answered anyway.

"I believe so. We're too far for land-based aircraft to search for us, but of course if there is an aircraft carrier nearby, they could spot us. We are well off the normal track that we would usually be on and therefore should not come across any surface vessels. Why?"

"You will find amongst the items that were brought on board with the crate a set of paint stencils, tins of grey and white paint, plus a stars and stripes flag. You are to paint out our German designation and replace it with 'SS-212' and fly the flag when we approach the American shoreline. Whilst we do not look exactly like the Gato class submarine of the US Navy that we are mimicking, to the uninitiated and in the dark of early morning we should be able to fool any civilian who may happen to see us as we slip through the coastal waters and onto our final destination, therefore not raising the alarm. When we sent the signal, back there in the Channel, it would have alerted another sub which is also engaged in this operation. She has been submerged and awaiting that signal for nearly a week, just off the coastline, and by now has limped slowly, as per her instructions, so as to give an impression of some damage and therefore a reason to report back home into the port of La Rochelle. But she is carrying the number U-931, Captain." Roth didn't respond to this latest twist; he'd learnt it was futile to discuss operational matters with Fuchs. When no reply was forthcoming, Fuchs spoke again. "From now on I would like that you and I shall only speak in English so that you may correct me on any diction that may arise."

Roth sighed deeply but still said nothing for a brief moment. He then stood, saying in English, "I'll get the map."

*

A hundred miles away, at a position northwest of U-931 in the Atlantic, the sea was quite choppy as the 'electro' boat with the designation number of U-2565 broke through the surface, a thunderous rise of bubbles heralding its appearance. She had left her secret location in the Norwegian fjord near Nese together with her two sister boats over a week ago, the modifications to her forward deck completed shortly before they left. The ramp was in place, but it had been a close-run thing to get the work done in time on all three boats. They hadn't had the luxury of any spare time to test fire the rockets from the new ramps.

The other two captains of the 'electro' boats had seen the smaller V1s being launched from the shortened styled ramp during their test flights at Peenemünde back in January, but they had not had the chance to launch one from a sub which bothered Captain Kurt Neumeyer, the leader of this special wolf pack. Fortunately, he had been able to test fire a rocket from his sub, and with great success.

He followed behind the lookouts as they scrambled up the wet ladder in the conning tower, the final trickles of sea water falling down into the control room below from the edges of the open hatch, a few of which caught Neumeyer on the shoulder, soaking his grey leather jacket. He took a long draw of breath as he reached the open part of the bridge, the sea air refreshing his lungs. They had been sitting on the bottom for nearly a week now, only rising up to just below the surface to deploy the snorkel to replenish the stale air of this radically new design of submarine.

He had served on a number of Type VIIC boats before as the first officer and was more surprised than most when he was promoted, put in charge of this brand-new boat, and then told he was going to be part of a special mission; direct orders from Hitler, according to the rumours – a great honour. He patted the rounded cool steel edge of the bridge with a sense of pride in his heart. This submarine was an engineering marvel of the highest quality, a symbol of what Nazi Germany, her scientists, and skilled workmen could achieve. God, if only we had had these incredible beasts back in '41. The battle of the Atlantic would have been won. The Americans would not dare send troops, tanks, planes, and equipment across to Europe, and the outlook of the war would indeed look so much different.

Beneath him now was a cavernous expanse compared to the cramped conditions he'd known on all his previous deployments. The disassembled rocket, fuel, warhead, and technicians were stowed safely on board, a task which just wouldn't have been possible on a smaller sub. The crew quarters were so much better, including his own. They even had a shower installed on board; no more stinking to high heaven for weeks on end. A fresher feeling crew could only perform better. The cooking facilities were much improved, the torpedo rooms operated more efficiently, torpedoes launched twice as fast, and the batteries that powered the motors could hold three times the amount of charge compared to a VIIC. Best of all, it was so quiet; it would greatly reduce the chance of being detected.

He was also impressed with the snorkel operation that allowed them to use the diesel engine to recharge the electric batteries whilst lying just under the surface of the sea, whereas before you would have had to surface completely to recharge, which would leave yourself open to attack. This advantage was enormous, especially when sailing through the Bay of Biscay. Just in the past week they had traversed through the so-called 'valley of death' completely submerged and thus not vulnerable to air attack or a surprise from the Royal Navy. Now safely out to sea and away from such attacks they could surface and make good speed across the Atlantic toward their objective: Delaware Bay. After receiving the code word 'Surtr' he had signalled the two other boats, U-2699 and U-2717, which were also submerged on the bottom and only a short distance away. He had signalled them the go order to get underway, and, with Godspeed, to be in position to carry out their joint mission.

CHAPTER 17- SEARCH

Yet another glance at the wall clock in his office didn't help Sullivan's mood. It had been four days and sleepless nights now since the sinking of *Zenobia* and there was still no news of her attacker. Neither ship nor plane had been able to spot the sub. There had been no signals intercepted, so he was assuming she'd gone radio silent, and he was getting more and more frustrated. Bob Coleman had been helping him co-ordinate the search alongside the RAF and Coastal Command, but he was now awaiting the arrival of Major Miller of the US army whom he'd met just the other day alongside Colonel Lee. Sullivan had received a phone call earlier informing him that Miller was coming over with an update.

Sullivan was behind his mahogany desk yet again. He was beginning to understand where the phrase 'part of the furniture' came from. Next to the clock on the wall was a print by Constable, *The Hay Wain.* He'd fetched it from home to give him some semblance of normality and often gazed at it and dreamt that he was in the fields somewhere, enjoying the breeze on his face, and the fresh country air. He reached for his vintage stainless steel cigarette case on the left of the desk, opened it, and gazed at the inscription inside from his late wife. It read: "Thanks for a wonderful twenty-five years, lots of love, Dawn." He took out yet another cigarette, lighting it with the matching lighter that went with the case and then got back to the swathes of paperwork on his desk, most of which he'd set aside over the last few days due to the enormity of *Zenobia*'s sinking. The tap on the door made him look up to see Miller standing outside. He waved him in.

"Good evening, sir," said the immaculately dressed

American as he entered, shutting out the sounds of ringing from numerous telephones, and from men and women orderlies talking in the outer office as he closed the door.

"Good to see you, Major," replied the admiral.

"I have an update, sir, but I don't think you're going to like it." Miller took a seat as he talked. "It's taken a day or so to come through, but we've had a report from the French resistance. Only by chance, may I say, because we hadn't been able to get in touch with them in time. Luckily, they keep a sharp watch on the comings and goings, and they've seen U-931." Sullivan hadn't been listening too intently as Miller had said at the start it wasn't encouraging news, but now his head snapped up like a dog hearing a whistle.

"Go on," he encouraged.

"La Rochelle. This morning she limped in just after dawn, very slowly; perhaps with some engine trouble; she was that slow, they said. But there's always the possibility that the sub was damaged during the engagement with *Zenobia*. But what was unusual was that the dockside had been cleared of all workers, only German personnel allowed. Our agent did see the captain of the sub on the conning tower as it entered port, he was using binoculars apparently, but noted that the captain had a ginger beard. So, we know the whereabouts of Roth but can't say if the SS men he had on board departed also. We've surmised that they may have been dropped off somewhere, perhaps on the south coast of England, and that was U-931's mission all along. We haven't dismissed the Peenemünde connection, either, so together with British intelligence and allied armed forces we are actively searching for one or more SS men, possibly now in England."

"So, what about the potential of a rocket attack on the

American coast? Is that no longer credible?"

"Whilst we believe it is clear that U-931 is no longer involved in an imminent attack of that description, we can't rule out the possibility that such an event may take place in the future. Our navy is at a heightened level of alert anyway, and is constantly looking for any threat off our coastline."

"So, you're dismissing Roth and his sub from OSS's investigations?"

"We have many other actions and operations that the Nazi's are pursuing and that are drawing our attention in the lead up to the invasion. We have to prioritise. We shall, of course, keep an eye on U-931 because of its involvement with Peenemünde, and any other unexplained visitors there."

"What's making me wonder is the secrecy around the sub's return. Why did the Germans remove all the workers from the pens? Did they unload something? Something from Peenemünde, perhaps. Where is this SS officer or men, did they land in England as you suspect, or did they depart at La Rochelle?" Sullivan could see from Lee's apathy that his mind wasn't open to persuasion. The subject was closed for any further discussion from the young black American officer.

"As I said, sir, we feel there's nothing here to pursue, at least not now." With that said, the lieutenant stood, leaned across the desk, shook the admiral's hand, saluted, and bade him farewell.

Sullivan sat there, pondering what he had just heard. There was so much to consider. The sixty-year-old, lifelong sailor was called 'the old bear' by his peers because of his tenacity. He'd never seen action during his long career, having always been in administration, and when command had placed him in the role as chief of operations covering the Atlantic it had come as a shock to quite a few, not least of all himself; he had taken on his new responsibilities with a fervour. He was admired for being a stickler for efficiency, he'd reduced bureaucracy across the service, introduced better practices for the running of a warship on a daily basis, and looked after all sailors, whatever their rank, under his command. Some of his operational ideas were judged by a few of his peers to be very radical, but what he'd introduced so far was working and getting results, which was why he'd been chosen for the role in the first place. No detail was too small for him to take note of, and he always endeavoured for improvement in both the men beneath him and the vessels they served in.

But with the situation before him now, he didn't know what course of action to take. Clearly the Americans had dismissed the events as far as they may affect them. He could not. No matter what Roth and his sub's involvement was, the slaughter of *Zenobia*'s survivors was a matter that could not be ignored, not now, not ever.

"All ahead, slow," said Roth as he pressed his forehead against the rubber eyepiece of the sub's periscope. He'd swung it round one-hundred-and-eighty degrees yet again. Nothing was to be seen on the horizon. "Anything, Horst?" he inquired of the sonar operator for the fifth time in nearly as many minutes.

"Nothing, Captain," replied Horst. Schmitt, Berger, and Fischer were at their stations in the control room and listening to their captain for any commands. Fuchs listened intently from near the bottom of the ladder which led up to the attack periscope where the captain stood. Roth was now dressed in Vogel's civilian clothes; denim trousers and a checked shirt with a denim jacket, a grey felt trilby in his duffel bag. He was ready now for the tasks that lay ahead. The boat was inching slowly along, the waters of Pamlico Sound on the eastern seaboard of the USA were behind them now. Cedar Island was off to the port side, the narrow entrance to the bay safely traversed. The entrance to the river lay ahead.

"Starboard, two degrees," ordered Roth.

"Starboard, two degrees," came back the reply from the helmsman Markus, the course correction changing the sub's direction slightly and in the direction of the river mouth. The inlet of Swanquarter Bay was not far now, but the danger levels were about to rise significantly. Roth and Schmitt had studied the charts for the bay for the last two days, carefully noting any obstacles that may hinder the boat's progress, and also every sandbank identified and marked to avoid. Schmitt was keeping an eagle eye on the sub's course, carefully plotting its way up the river with the help from his captain a few metres above him.

"Depth now thirty metres, Captain," called out Berger, "and decreasing!" As quiet a location as this appeared to be through the lens of the periscope, all Roth could make out in the early morning gloom were banks and banks of trees, only identifiable by the outline of the treetops set against the gradually brightening sky. Below that line it was as black as night, so dense was the foliage. What the high riverbanks gave regarding concealment from the shoreline was balanced out by the threat of the shallows they were traversing along now. "Twenty-five metres, twenty-two metres, twenty metres, twenty metres, still twenty metres. We have levelled off, Captain." Roth didn't answer his first officer. His eyes were glued to the eyepiece, sweat dripping down from his forehead as he concentrated on the scene before him.

U-931 crept along, hidden by the waters of the bay. The electric motors driving the boat forward, silently. The only evidence of her presence was a small trail in the water coming from the tip of the periscope as it peered from beneath the waves. But that was about to change as Berger called out the depth once again.

"Eighteen metres and decreasing, Captain, shallows ahead," continued Berger. Roth could now make out the entrance to the river itself, silhouetted in the distance. Both riverbanks were beginning to slowly appear from within the cloak of early morning mist that shrouded the water on either side and ahead of the sub. He called out another course correction. This one would take them starboard and in the direction of Swanquarter Bay and the inlet he sought. But now the depth below the sub had decreased too much and the time had come.

"Surface," ordered Roth, "but slowly, and I mean slowly." He wanted the sub to break the surface as stealthily as possible, like one of the nearby Florida alligators might break the surface as it eyed up its prey. "Slow to half speed." The sub rose majestically as it glided along. The distance between its hull and the riverbed increased, the danger of grounding reduced for the moment. Whilst Roth had been careful in not rushing these delicate manoeuvres in these shallows, he was also conscious of the time. The sub had to be alongside the jetty whilst the dark of night was still concealing them in its protective mantle. The sub was to be unloaded and away inside thirty minutes, before the first fingers of sunlight broke through the canopy of trees and perhaps revealing their presence to someone using the river.

Now only the conning tower was to be seen slipping through the surface of the river, making its own tiny bow wave as it did so. Gradually, a little at a time, the sub began to show more and more of its bulk, the newly painted 'SS-212' on either side of the tower to help with the illusion that an American submarine was sailing up the river.

"Look-outs to stations. Raise the American flag. No

hats!" ordered Berger. The five crew members who had been tasked to go up top were all dressed in their own civilian clothes; no signs of any Kreigsmarine uniform were to be seen.

"Where is the signal light?" Roth muttered to himself. "We should have seen it by now... Are we still on course? How much further?" He asked the officers below.

"We should be there, Captain, any moment, at least," replied Berger. Then Roth spotted it; one single flash and then a long sweep of the flashlight from the shore. He could see the jetty now as it too appeared out from beneath the mist that was trying to envelope it.

"Ease the boat up a little higher, Jonas, we've still got water covering the forward deck," he ordered, folding up the two stubby arms on the periscope before turning around and climbing up the ladder behind the lookouts who were ahead of him. "Stop all engines."

"Stop all engines, raise the boat to four metres," Schmitt ordered the crew in the control room, "Unloading crew to forward hatch positions, prepare to hoist the crate on shore."

The sub glided gracefully the final few metres of its journey, like an old swan coming up to the edge of a lake. After nearly four-thousand miles, ten days of sailing, and two near misses with the British, here they were by the riverbank and the jetty.

The air had that early morning dewy aroma to it; fresh, damp, but exhilarating. Roth could just make out the outline of a hoist sticking out from the back of one of the two small trucks that were parked up. Also, there were two men standing on the edge, awaiting the line to be cast over to secure the sub. As they started to tie up the boat, its forward momentum having ceased, the forward hatch was open on the deck and out sprang Fuchs, now also dressed in his civilian clothes of denim jeans, a black shirt under his corduroy jacket, and a tweed Irish flat cap. His duffel slung over his shoulder alongside his Schmeisser machine pistol which he now handed over to one of the two men on shore who placed it in the cab of the truck. Fuchs stood for a few moments talking to the other man, but Roth couldn't make out what they were saying and assumed it was an order to get the hoist in position as he jumped into action.

The hoist itself seemed to be sturdy, if yet simple in its construction. It was quite small, made from iron and painted in a dark brown-red colour. It was secured by large bolts through the floor of the second truck, which was now being reversed up to the edge of the jetty, close to where the forward hatch on the sub was located. The crane's jib and hook, together with two slings, were now swinging over the open hole below, where the crate was. The sub's crew were also working at great speed to offload this mysterious crate containing American cigarettes, of all things. None of them had an inkling of what was really inside; suffice to say it wasn't what the stencil on the wooden exterior was advertising. Time was of the essence and the longer they stayed here the more perilous it would become. In next to no time the crate was out of the sub and loaded swiftly into one of the waiting trucks, the one Fuchs had placed his gear into a few minutes before, and the one they would drive north and through the former confederate states of America.

Roth had been keeping watch through his binoculars on the river behind and in front of the U-boat as he stood at the base of the conning tower on the deck of the sub. His senses were on fire like no other time before that he could remember. The air was full of early morning bird song, the stars and stripes flag above him was fluttering around in the breeze and making that whipping sound that they make when the wind catches them just right in that certain way. He could smell the sap coming from the tall pine trees which lined the riverbank to his right, the trees themselves creaking as they swayed with the wind. He was acutely aware that any type of vessel could quite easily slip up behind them, and the game would be up if they were to be discovered unloading the crate now. He turned his attention back to see that the two men who had been tasked to offload the crate were now closing up the rear of the truck with the hoist on, the slings now safely stowed back on the floor, and they quickly jumped into the cab and began to pull away, their job done. It took off through a small gap in the trees, disappearing in an instant as it was swallowed up by the dense forest that surrounded this isolated spot.

He glanced at his watch; the time said 0630 hours, another half an hour until sunrise. It had only taken them twenty-five minutes from coming to rest to unload, and now was the time for Schmitt to get underway and safely back out to sea. Roth took another look at Fuchs who was now standing by the second truck which was a dark-coloured, high cabbed model with a low flatbed behind the cab with wooden slats along the sides. A green tarpaulin was covering the cargo beneath, ropes pulled tightly across it. The major was beckoning him to come.

There was something troubling Roth as he looked at the SS major, hurriedly waving at him. He turned his head to the side where Schmitt and Berger were standing, and then he looked back towards Fuchs. He still had his duffel bag slung over his shoulder. Indeed, Roth's own bag was lying at his own feet, ready for the journey ahead. And then it struck him. He stepped over to whisper into Schmitt's ear so the sailors on deck couldn't hear him.

"He doesn't have his briefcase, where's his briefcase?

Search the boat for a bomb. Find it and go south, my friend. Find it, and use that to convince the crew you can't go home. Good luck."

An angry Fuchs shouted from behind Roth, his temper allowing his judgement about stealth to leave him for the moment. "Come on!"

Roth quickly shook his friend's hand, picked up his duffel bag from the deck, and jumped off the sub. The lines having been cast off, it started to slip backwards and away from the shore. Roth glanced back at it as he made his way towards Fuchs, but then he stopped dead in his tracks.

The scene that lay before him made a cold shiver go through his very soul, for there, standing by the truck and slightly behind the impatient Fuchs who was glaring back toward him, were two small boys.

CHAPTER 18 - DRIVE

Fuchs was about to launch another angry tirade at Roth to get a move on, but realised that the captain was staring past him at something else – something behind him. He turned around slowly and saw the two boys. He immediately dropped his duffel bag to the ground and his right hand slid behind his back to his belt where a large knife in a sheath was attached. Everything that transpired next was over in seconds, but when Roth went over it later in his mind it seemed like an age. First, Fuchs started to walk very slowly towards the boys. They couldn't have been older than ten and one of them had a homemade fishing rod in his hand. The other boy carried a small tin bucket. Both were rooted to the spot as this giant of a man crept towards them.

"Morning, boys, out for a spot of fishin'?" said Fuchs in a very passable southern drawl. His hand silently drew the knife from its sheath behind his back. The distance between him and the boys was getting shorter as he edged closer, the two boys looking in bewilderment at the departing sub getting smaller as it pulled away, and then back to this huge man with the big friendly grin coming ever closer.

"Scoot, you hear! Git. Go on. Skedaddle!" shouted Roth at the top of his voice in English. The two boys turned tail and ran for all their worth back the way they had just come from as this second stranger shouted at them. The second of the two boys dropped his bucket onto the ground as he ran away, the dozen or so collection of worms beginning their escape as they spilled out from inside.

"What the hell?" said a raging Fuchs as he turned back to Roth. "Why did you do that? They'll run back and tell what they've seen. This place will be crawling with civilians, or worse. When they say that they saw a sub here we'll have half the Yankee army after us, you idiot!" It was clear to Roth now that Fuchs was furious with rage, the vein on his forehead sticking out, his face a fiery red; the knife was gripped firmly in his right hand as he strode in Roth's direction. He had to defuse the situation quickly, or else Fuchs' wrath might get the better of him and that knife would end Roth's life in an instant.

"Then I'd suggest we'd better get out of here, quickly," said Roth as he strode purposely past Fuchs and climbed into the passenger side of the truck. The SS major stood there for just a moment before replacing the knife in its sheath, a deep sigh escaping from him as he climbed into the driver's seat before firing up the engine. As the truck bounced down the uneven country road that led away from the river, Roth dug out the road map for the local area that had been left for him by one of the two men they'd seen earlier. Fuchs wasn't hanging about as he drove quickly down the narrow earthen track. Two lines either side of a middle grass strip where the only signs that this was a road, the tree branches encroaching here and there whipping across the windshield. Clearly this spot had been well chosen as a good place for the sub to offload its cargo; it was clearly a very isolated spot which probably didn't see much foot traffic – apart from two small boys, that is.

It took them fifteen minutes to reach the main road, and, as he neared it, Fuchs finally looked over to Roth, but only as he needed some indication of which way to turn at the oncoming T-junction.

"Right," was all that was said.

Half an hour had passed without further talk as they drove along the tarmac highway. Fuchs had slowed down the truck to a steady forty-five miles per hour so as not to draw any unwanted attention to themselves, whilst at the same time wanting to put as much distance as possible between themselves and Swanquarter Bay. Roth spoke.

"Tell me you weren't going to kill those kids back there?"

Fuchs stared straight ahead, concentrating on the road, and after a while he spoke, but without answering the question directly.

"I think you still don't fully appreciate the importance of this operation to the Reich and my commitment to it, Captain? I'd like to tell you a story from my youth and then finally you might get a measure of the man, the soldier, that you sit beside here today. I was raised by a father who thought that the best way to raise his only son was by beating him with his fists, my mother ignoring the bruises she would see on me. The one thing my father loved more than me was his dog. That dog was better fed than my mother or I, and my father would make me take it out for walks all the time. He'd had it before I was born, so that when I turned nine the dog was getting old, perhaps fourteen years.

"One day, after a severe beating from my father, I was told to take the dog for a walk. Now, as I said, the dog was old. He was half-blind and as deaf as a post, but could move when he wanted to. We were strolling down a road not far from our house, me on one side and the dog on the other, when I heard a car coming. It was going quite quickly. The dog had stopped on the other side of the road, sniffing at something, like they do. The car was getting nearer, and I whistled the dog. He could hear me whistle all right. He came bounding over to me. I timed it just so. The car smashed into him, killing him instantly, the car screeching to a halt. The front was severely damaged, blood spread across the fender. I ran to the dog and pretended to cry. Cried my eyes out.

"The driver knew our family and so took the broken body of the lifeless dog and I back home. There he apologised to my father, saying it was no one's fault and not to worry about paying for the car. Of course, my father beat the crap out of me that night, but I didn't care. I knew that I'd hurt him more so." Roth sat there and couldn't believe what he was hearing, but it was to get worse as Fuchs spoke once more. "Then, on the night I was to leave home and join the SS for training, I waited in the shadows near my father's favourite Rathaus and as he walked home. I stuck him with a butcher's knife. He bled like the pig he was, and I watched the life drain out of him before I set off for the train station and the officer training school at Bad Tolz. I wasn't too concerned with the consequences of my actions that night, if the police came calling. But I needn't have worried. My mother finally stepped up for me. She gave me an alibi for his murder. Perhaps she realised that I had done her a favour, too."

Roth just sat there, stunned into silence. The murder of the British sailors had highlighted to him that perhaps the many stories he had heard over the years about some of the atrocities attributed to the Waffen-SS were true. The depths to which Fuchs and Vogel went that day, the looks of pleasure from them as they fired their weapons on those defenceless survivors, the fact he would have slit the throats of the two boys and thrown their lifeless bodies into the river, and now this horror story from Fuchs' childhood convinced the submarine commander that here was not a soldier, but a psychopath.

If they managed to get to Washington, succeed in setting off the bomb, and managed to avoid detection and make good their escape, how long would it be before Roth would outgrow his usefulness to Fuchs as they made their way to the Mexican border? It was only a matter of time before he too would feel the cold hard steel of the major's knife, perhaps sliced across his throat, or thrust into his belly, and then left to die thousands of miles from home.

He needed to stop these dark thoughts from enveloping him for now, and so thought of Ginette again. God, how he wished he was safe in her arms right now, wherever she was. As he sat there, staring out and watching the fields flow by the truck window, he repeated in his head the French phrases that he'd been practising over and over for the last few weeks: "Qui vivra verra, petit à petit l'oiseau fait son nid." Literally, "She who lives shall see and little by little, the bird makes its nest."

It was a nod towards their future together. He had planned to say it to Ginette that last time when he had docked, only to find her spirited away by her father. In truth, it was two phrases he had combined that he felt expressed his love for her and that the future, whilst uncertain, was something they could look forward to. He would get out from this mess somehow, slip away from Fuchs when he got the chance, make his way back to Germany and then onto France and find his love. Perhaps he could return back to America with her? But that would mean that this mad man's folly would have to fail, and for that to happen Roth would have to tackle Fuchs and somehow destroy the weapon. He had to change the narrative, for the moment, at least, but how did he connect with the monster beside him? He had to convince him that he was still committed to the cause. At least that may dissuade Fuchs from disposing of him within the next few hours before they reached Washington and the bomb. Perhaps the time would allow him to come up with something?

"Is everything okay with the crate in the back?" he

asked. "I mean, is it secured down? What's the plan as we near the city? To be honest, you have only outlined the plan to me. What are the details, and what of our escape?"

"The crate is fine. Located near the front, so that anyone looking under the tarp will just see four crates of cigarettes and not look at the one crate that matters. Under your seat is a hidden shortwave radio. We are to give six hours preparation time to our comrades out at sea and transmit, in plain language that is, not in code, the operation word 'Surtr.' This will alert the three boats waiting offshore to surface, assemble the rockets, and launch them at the designated time of 0655 hours as per their instructions, so that they reach the city and explode around 0700 hours. We shall activate our timer on the bomb with its thirty minute delay to coincide with their arrival. We must, therefore, be in a position near the target tonight when we send the signal. I want to check everything is in place at the location where we shall leave the bomb. I anticipate that we will arrive in the suburbs of the city at around 1800 hours this evening. We must do reconnaissance on the area for the detonation so that in the morning we just have to act without thinking. We will only be there briefly, and then be on our way.

"We can then park up the truck in some secluded spot and try to get a few hours rest. Then, in the morning, we will drive back into the city. We will then arm the bomb, and leave again immediately," replied Fuchs. As he talked, he slipped his left hand down to the side of his seat and felt for the cold steel of the machine pistol he had placed there next to the bottom of the door earlier. In the passenger seat, Roth pondered for a moment before responding.

"Where exactly will we be parking?" The answers he received were terse and to the point.

"Near the Capitol building. Right at the heart of American democracy."

"How near? This truck isn't very inconspicuous if parked close to such a high-profile building."

"Of course not. We shall be leaving it at Union Station car park where it will blend in. That's less than a mile from the Capitol. That is also where we will find our means of escape. There will be a dark green Buick Special four-door car waiting for us, the keys placed on top of the driver's front wheel, food and water in the trunk, with money and new passports for our trip over the border and a change of clothes for us both. We will park as close to the Buick as possible, and flick the delay switch on the bomb as I described earlier, thirty minutes before zero hour, and then we'll just drive away. We should be at least ten to fifteen miles away when the bomb detonates and the V1s strike the city. No one shall be looking for us as the attack originated out at sea. The roads south should not present any danger as they shall not be looking for us, and we should have no problem crossing at Matamoros in Mexico." What Fuchs didn't say was that before they reached Mexico, he intended to be travelling alone.

"That's one of the reasons that Vogel was along, I'm guessing? We're going to have to share the driving. That'll take at least two days, and that's with hardly any stops." The mention of Vogel darkened Fuchs' mood once again; it was a while before he acknowledged Roth.

"Leon was invaluable as someone who could pass as an American for this operation and, that apart, he was my friend and brother in arms." Roth began to wonder if this course of action was the right one if he was to get Fuchs to lighten up a little and drop his guard. "The incident that we told you about in Russia, where he saved my life, was just one of the many battles we fought in together."

He stopped mid-sentence, and Roth didn't ask him to continue.

The morning's promising start to the weather had changed into quite an overcast day in North Carolina. It had been four hours since they had left the sub, but the two men had not spoken much since then apart from when Fuchs needed directions from Roth. They had shied away from the main roads as much as they could, preferring to take back roads so as to keep as low a profile as possible. They had passed the town of Rocky Mount a while back and were still heading north, on track to meet the desired arrival time in Washington by a comfortable margin. Fuchs finally spoke again.

"This truck isn't going to make it. We had a full tank when we started out, but the needle's gone past half-way down and we've still got over five hours more travelling. It's probably the weight and perhaps the age of the truck, but we're going to have to pull over and refuel. There's a jerry can in the back next to the crates, I'll pull over near those trees up ahead. The road is straight for the next mile or so; we should see anyone coming our way." Roth had been fighting the urge to fall asleep for the past half-hour, the threat of having his throat cut if he did was quite a big incentive to stay awake. He was alert now, though, and he sat up straight in the seat to emphasise the fact.

"Makes sense to stop now," he said. "Pretty deserted, here."

A few hundred metres up the road, Fuchs pulled over, the dust rising from behind the truck as he applied the brakes. Roth jumped out and looked around, but there were only the green hillsides surrounding them. There wasn't a single house to be seen in this deserted part of the countryside. He went to the back of the truck, loosened one of the ropes holding down the tarp, and then peeled it back over the crates. He hadn't seen them on the back of the low loader of the Model A pickup, as Fuchs had handled the loading back at the river, but he was impressed. To the uninitiated, all to see here were crates of Camel cigarettes, and a clipboard in the cab had the bill of sale docket to prove where they were going; a warehouse in Washington. He reached over to the jerry can that was tied with some string and held in place against one of the horizontal wooden boards that made up the side of the truck. He undid the knot and lifted the can. His heart sank. He could tell immediately from the weight that it was empty. He replaced the can and walked around to the driver's side where Fuchs had got out to stretch his legs.

"Jerry can's there, but it's empty."

"What do you mean? It can't be empty," he cursed as he swept past Roth to check for himself. He picked up the can and swore. "Jesus! Is there anything else that can go wrong on this cursed mission. Why put an empty can in the truck, the stupid morons?" He was about to launch the offending can into the nearby field when he calmed down a little and threw it into the back of the truck instead. As a way of explanation, Roth spoke.

"A misunderstanding of sorts? Perhaps they meant to fill it and forgot?" Fuchs glared at him, but just shook his head.

"Put the tarp back. We're going to have to find somewhere and buy some gasoline. I'll stay in the cab, you can deal with the garage owner when you fill up. I've got fifty dollars in my duffel bag, I'll give you two. That should more than cover it." He climbed back in the truck, slamming the door as he did so. Roth joined him after replacing the tarp, the truck's wheels spinning on the loose gravel underneath as Fuchs floored the accelerator in anger as they set off once again.

CHAPTER 19 - VIRGINIA

The Adjutant stood outside the door and paused to adjust his jacket uniform and the silver-braided lanyard that hung down from his right epaulette; he straightened both. He wanted to feel comfortable with himself before he knocked. When he had composed himself, he rapped lightly on the huge doorway and waited.

"Enter," came the call shortly after. He turned the ornate brass knob on the door and pushed it open. He strode in purposely after closing the door behind him and went up to the desk at the far side of the room, clicked his heels together smartly, and spoke.

"Reichsführer, I apologise for disturbing you, but you have a call waiting, sir. It is Grand Admiral Doenitz." The officer clicked his heels again, gave a quick curt nod of his head, turned, and left the room, closing the door behind him.

When he was alone, Himmler picked up the handset of the antique styled phone on his desk.

"Karl, how may I be of assistance?" he enquired.

"Morning, Reichsführer. I am calling to inform you that I received the unfortunate news last evening that Admiral Witzell has deemed fit to take his own life." Doenitz waited for a response, an acknowledgement of the tragedy, but as none was forthcoming he continued in an exasperated tone. "As you are aware, Witzell was the liaison for the two U-boats that you requested the use of, and I was wondering if you can clarify something for me? Firstly, the whereabouts of U-931, and, secondly, could you explain to me how U-684 left port at Bordeaux and, although there is no record of her entering the harbour at La Rochelle, how she appears to be docked in one of the pens there?"

"To your second point first, I can only suggest a clerical error of some sort, and, as for the whereabouts of U-931, I instructed Witzell that once the sub had completed the task asked of it, he was to arrange a rendezvous with a supply ship for refuelling, just south of the Canary Islands. They were then to continue on a course for its home port of Saint-Nazaire. Perhaps Captain Roth and his crew are still en route? Given time, I'm sure we shall hear from them." Doenitz still wasn't satisfied by the answers given but didn't pursue the matter, but he wasn't quite finished.

"There are two more items of concern, if I may, Reichsführer? What of the three new 'electro' boats that you also requisitioned? I'm sure that you are aware of the severity that the Kreigsmarine and especially the U-boat service finds itself in at this moment, and how imperative it is that we have every available submarine at our disposal?" The line went silent. Doenitz dared not to speak and waited. Presently, the line crackled and then Himmler spoke.

"Admiral, I am well aware of the Kreigsmarine's situation. You shall have your 'electro' boats returned shortly. You said two items?"

"I did. One of my commanders, Captain Hoffman, was arrested by the Gestapo the other day. Is that incident anything to do with the requisitioned U-boats?" Again, there was a pause.

"I know nothing of this matter with the Gestapo, good day." He hung up and then called out to his adjutant, who he knew would be standing just outside the doors. The double doors opened immediately and in strode the adjutant, stopping smartly in front of the desk. "Call Gestapo headquarters in Saint-Nazaire and find out why they arrested Captain Hoffman. When you have the information, let me know."

"Jawohl, Reichsführer, Heil Hitler." The adjutant turned and left.

*

Mile after mile had gone by with no luck in the search for a gasoline station. The state line was behind them now and they could see the snow-capped mountains of Virginia ahead. They had taken the decision to go back onto the main road just south of a town called Jarret. The fuel situation was getting critical as they continued north; they needed to find somewhere soon. Roth could see by Fuchs' twitching and fidgeting in his seat just how irritated he was becoming. Constant glances at the ever-decreasing fuel gauge, only increased his agitation. Then Roth spotted ahead what he believed may be the answer to his prayers. He nudged Fuchs in the shoulder and pointed to a spot about three-hundred metres away.

What Roth had gestured to was an insignificant set of buildings on the side of the road, perhaps a dozen at most. The truck was approaching what could only be described as a run-down collection of wooden sided single-story shacks. They looked like they hadn't seen a coat of paint in years, by the looks of things; it was probably a result of the depression era that had hit this part of the country pretty badly. But, most importantly of all, one of them had a gasoline sign swinging from the porch, the red, white, and blue of the company logo 'Esso' stamped on the metal. Fuchs eased the truck up to the single pump set out in front of the shack, making sure that the filler neck was nearest the pump. As he switched off the ignition he spoke.

"I'll stay here, don't forget the jerry can; we'll probably need to stop again to fill up. Be quick."

Roth nodded, took the dollars that Fuchs was offering him, and got out.

"Howdy. How are we today?" asked the old guy who

was dressed in dungarees and a dirty shirt that had once been white. He had come bounding out from the shack, this was presumably the owner. "Fill her up?"

"Doing just fine, thanks. Could you fill this up, too?" asked Roth as he pulled out the jerry can from the back, unscrewing the cap off the gas tank. "We've still got some ways to go yet."

"Sure thing, where ya headed?" The old man was perhaps in his seventies, guessed Roth. His dungarees were oil-stained and greasy, the knees covered over with patches of a miss-matching material. He was trying to make polite conversation to the two newcomers that had stopped for gas here in the middle of nowhere. "Don't get many strangers 'round here."

"Washington."

"Still some way to go, then." The nozzle of the pump was now in the tank, the fuel flowing. Roth could see the reflection of Fuchs' face in the large door mirror on the left side of the truck, carefully observing all that was happening behind him, the window wound down so he could listen in.

"Yea, should be there by supper, I guess?"

"Should think so, don't get too much traffic here, but I'm guessing it'll be busy once you get near Richmond. I do hear that there's a lot of army traffic up there. Mostly heading for the ports, I shouldn't wonder, loading up those big ships and setting off for England. Our boys are goin' give those Nazis a good whoopin' when the invasion gets started. Old Hitler won't know what hit him," he laughed. "If I was still twenty myself, I'd sign up tomorrow. Too old to go now, but I'd sure like to have a pop at those 'Jerries'. Fought at San Juan Hill back in '98, those were the days." He had now switched to filling up the can. Roth was conscious that he didn't want to engage too much with this friendly old guy, but at the same time was aware of not being too distant, either, which may raise suspicion. He could hear that the can was nearly full and got the money ready to pay when the sound of an approaching motorbike made him look back towards the direction they had come from. It was a cop.

"That'll be a dollar seventy-five. That's a dollar seventy-five, sir," repeated the old man. Roth wasn't listening, the cop on the bike had his full attention as it glided to a halt right behind the truck. Roth heard the man ask for his money for a third time and swung around to pay him, seeing Fuchs step out from the truck as he did so.

"Keep the change."

"No, sir, that's twenty-five cents, too much."

"No, please, keep it; I insist." The old man beamed with delight at this unexpected gift. He put the money in his pocket, turned off the pump, hung the nozzle on the side, and strode off to pocket the windfall. He wouldn't tell Maisie, his wife, of this bit of good fortune when he got back inside, she'd only waste it on something for the house. He smiled once again as he stepped on to the porch and went inside.

Roth picked up the jerry can, swung the now heavy load up onto the floor of the flat bed, and was about to tie it back up when Fuchs came to stand next to him, his right hand was already behind his back. The cop had switched off the bike, dismounted, and was walking towards them both.

"Afternoon, how we doin'?" asked the cop. Roth answered a little hesitantly.

"Err, good, good thanks."

The cop wore a black leather jacket, open at the collar. Light-coloured, thick cotton trousers and black polished knee-length leather boots made up his uniform. He'd taken off his eight-pointed service hat and had placed it on the handlebars of the Harley Davidson motor bike which was leaning on its side stand to the right. His gun belt held a Colt .38 special and Roth noticed that the cop's hand was resting on it as it swung in its holster on his right hip as he strolled over. The cop was perhaps in his forties, with thick brown hair, dark brown eyes, and a furrowed brow. He carried himself well, he had that aura of authority. Like all cops, he had an arrogance about him; just the way he walked told Roth that. The screen door of the shack creaked on dry hinges as the old man went back inside. Fuchs was standing behind Roth, ready to act if this uninvited cop got too nosey. Roth was conscious of the fact that he hadn't armed himself since he'd left the sub; he'd presumed that there must be some arms somewhere in the back of the truck and he'd been planning to ask Fuchs when he'd calmed down some more, but was now regretting that he hadn't sooner.

"Weather could be better, but we can't complain, good for March, I guess. Have you come far?"

"Winston-Salem."

"Where ya headed?"

"Got a delivery to make in DC, cigarettes. We drove up from the Camel factory. Got four crates that missed the train and the distributor up there's screaming for them." Roth's palms were sweaty, he was unsure if the cop was buying it. He could also smell Fuchs' bad breath as he stood close behind him; they both watched the cop standing facing them. The cop drew closer still, so close that he was standing toe to toe with the captain.

"I think you've come a lot further than Salem. I have to admit there's no accent that I can detect, though. You've blended right in. Should get to DC around eight, so long as you have no more unscheduled stops. Is there some sort of problem?" Both Roth and Fuchs stared at the cop, bewildered for a moment before he continued. "I've been on your tail since you left the woods back at Swanquarter Bay, after the drop off from the sub. We thought it best that you have someone watching your back as you headed off to God knows where. There's no one been tailing you, anyhow. I can't go any further, though, it might look odd if a cop from Carolina was riding through Virginia. Rest assured that we are ready to serve and obey when the time comes. You have many friends and comrades here that are ready to rise up to serve the Führer." He turned to go, but then whispered "Viel Glück. Auf Wiedersehen."

It was Fuchs who now spoke through gritted teeth.

"Pity you didn't fill up the bleeding jerry can, you moron. The truck must be leaking gas because we should have been able to get to our destination with just the jerry can as a top up. I just hope we don't have to stop again for gasoline! Idiot!" He didn't say any more but turned and got back in the truck. The cop looked a little taken aback; he wasn't expecting the German's venom. He too didn't say anything else.

He turned back to his bike, strode over, and replaced his hat before straddling the huge machine. He kick-started it into life, put it into gear, touched the peak of his cap as another gesture of acknowledgement, and did a right turn, going back in the direction he had come from just moments before.

"Did you not see him trailing us?" asked Roth as he climbed back in.

"No, not a sign. He must have held well back."

"Might have been a good idea if they'd told us what they were up to. Would have been some comfort to know that he was out there."

"No matter, come, let's get out of here." Fuchs started the truck, but before driving off he adjusted his rear-view mirror, explaining as he did so: "Just in case there's any more cops, the ones not on our side."

*

Admiral Sullivan walked across the floor of the operations room in the direction of his office. He'd been to the canteen for a bite to eat. The meal had consisted of over-boiled potatoes and something that once might have been a pork chop, but he wouldn't swear to it, the cook having grilled it beyond recognition. Still, it had been the only hot meal that he'd had in over a week. Sandwiches, tea, and biscuits were his staples over the preceding period. The office was as busy as usual: phones ringing, tele-types ticking away relaying a steady stream of information, and the steady *click, click, click* of typewriters, interrupted every so often by the return bell ringing and the ever-present sound in the background of both male and female voices talking.

Just as he was about to enter his office a female voice from behind him interrupted his train of thought.

"Excuse me, sir, but can you call Major Adams on this number, please?" said the pretty Wren who had spoken. She handed over a small piece of folded paper. She was around twenty-five, old enough to be the daughter that he and his late wife had never been able to have. He'd noticed her before, in and around the office. As per regulations she never wore makeup, and she didn't need to; she had a natural beauty about her. Her blonde hair was tied up at the back, and her cool blue eyes, together with her slim figure, would make some lucky fellow a fine wife. He realised that he was staring and so took the note from her delicate hand.

"Thank you…?" he said, searching for a name.

"Leading Wren Richardson, sir." She turned and went back to work. Sullivan went into the office and closed the door. It only took a moment or two to get through to the number he asked the operator for. He hadn't recognized the name but that wasn't unusual. The voice on the other end was quite chirpy.

"Hello, Major Adams here. MI6."

"It's Rear Admiral Sullivan here, I was asked to call you."

"Ah, yes, Admiral. Thanks for getting back to me. I've come across something that may be of interest to you. I've been liaising with our American friends at OSS and I believe that they confided in you about our interest in the V1 rockets and their possible use on submarines, plus the presumed link to U-931?"

"That's correct." Sullivan was now very intrigued.

"Well, apparently you've been searching for the submarine after the awful incident with *HMS Zenobia* and I understand that they informed you that it had docked at La Rochelle a few days ago, albeit under strict security; no dock workers allowed, I believe?"

"Yes, please go on."

"Fortunately, we didn't let the matter rest there and directed the Resistance to take a closer look. The base was locked up tighter than a drum and so they couldn't gain access to the base either in the daytime or at night. What they did do was keep a keen eye on all the comings and goings of the submarines and this is where it gets interesting. Your sub limped into port four days or so ago and, according to the French, there were five subs already docked, so that made six. No more subs have entered the harbour since then, but all six submarines have left, presumably to conduct operations in the Atlantic." Sullivan was dying for the major to get to the point. "Now, here's the rub, Admiral. Your submarine wasn't one of the six. But one of the subs that did leave was U-329, a sub that the French had never seen enter the base. Whatever sailed into the harbour may have had the look of your U-boat, but of the six moored up there, yours wasn't one of them."

Sullivan was now intrigued.

"Are the French positive about this? They haven't made a mistake? She didn't slip back out to sea, at night perhaps?"

"Every coming and going from La Rochelle over the past weeks and months has been vigorously monitored by the resistance, Admiral. We are monitoring airfields, army bases, train stations, and ports so as to gather an overall picture of the German's strengths and deployments to help the planners for the coming invasion. In my humble opinion, U-931 was never there. I'm sorry that I can't help you any further, if I can be of any assistance in the future, please don't hesitate to call."

"I will, and thanks for getting in touch. I'm not sure where we go from this point forward with this new information, but it's a step forward in our hunt for U-931. Goodbye."

"Goodbye, and good hunting."

The line went dead. Sullivan held the receiver next to his ear for a moment as he digested what he had just heard. The Wren he had spoken to a moment or two earlier was just outside sorting out a pile of mail, so he caught her eye and beckoned her in.

"Could you get me the file on U-329, please?" he asked her.

"Certainly, Admiral," she replied. Sullivan was going over in his mind the telephone conversation with Major Adams and was surprised to see Richardson return so quickly. "Here you are, sir." She handed over a thin, blue coloured transfer file to him. A few sheets of paper were inside.

"Thank you."

Inside the file was a brief description of the submarine and its crew. From the notes he could see when it was commissioned, laid down, launched, plus her known deployments so far. She had left Brest on March ninth, presumably to go out on patrol, but what was most interesting was what he was looking for: the description of its latest commander. Captain Helmet Durst, aged twenty-seven, born in Taucha, near Leipzig. Five feet eight with ginger hair.

The admiral sat there and wondered. Wondered what had transpired in the last week or so. There was so much to consider, questions and answers that required addressing. Firstly, there was the discovery, by chance, of the submarine at Peenemünde. Why was she there? Was it indeed important, or was it just a routine pick up, of sorts? He may have dismissed it as just so, if it hadn't been for what had then transpired. U-931 going through the Channel. Dangerous, without question, risky, unless you needed to get somewhere in a hurry. Then there was the unfortunate chance intervention of the *Zenobia*; surely Roth didn't want a confrontation there, of all places?

What was the interest of the American security service? He didn't think they were telling him everything, which was par for the course with them. But what was really irking him now was U-931's sudden appearance at La Rochelle. How it limped slowly into port. Was that to ensure she was seen as she entered the harbour, with a ginger haired captain visible on the conning tower? Surely that made sense, especially when you put it together with the facts that Major Adams had given him about the disappearance of one sub that entered the pens and the appearance of another that apparently was never there? The facts swirled around in his conscious mind for a few minutes, but the conclusion he came to was inescapable. The Germans had devised an elaborate plan to disguise the real whereabouts of U-931 and whatever she was up to. Wherever she was now, it could only be because her mission was vitality important to the Nazi cause, and if that was the case, at this late stage of the war, it concerned him very much.

CHAPTER 20 – RICHMOND

It was early evening now and the rain had stopped as the two Germans continued the drive towards Washington. Between the seats of Roth and Fuchs was a canvas bag that had been left there by the men who had dropped the trucks off at the jetty. Inside was food and water for the trip north, which included cheese sandwiches made from thick slices of fresh bread cut into halves and which had been wrapped up in greaseproof paper. There were also four hard-boiled eggs and two canteens of water. Also, there was a large leather wallet which contained new documents for them both, new identities for their trip up from the south and onto Washington: passports, social security cards, and driver's licences. Only the passport photo on the passport for Vogel was still a concern, but not so much as to worry Roth overly so.

They had made good time since the stop for gasoline and were now north of Richmond, Virginia. They had driven parallel to route 301 as much as they could and had then used county highways 150 and 76 to go around the city and avoid any hold ups or nosey cops. Roth checked the map again as he swallowed the last bite of one of the sandwiches. Fuchs had been content with the odd sip of water and hadn't eaten anything, preferring to concentrate on his driving. It had been so quiet between the two for so long that, when Fuchs finally did speak, it startled Roth a little.

"I'm going to pull over when I see a straight road ahead and no one around. The needle's dropped below halfway again. If we top up the gas with the jerry can now, it'll mean that we don't have to stop anywhere near our goal, which might attract some uninvited attention."

"Yes. Looks pretty quiet here," replied Roth.

About ten minutes later the opportunity to stop presented itself. This road, like most they had seen so far in their brief time in America, was arrow straight and stretched away into the distance. The landscape was very open here. Barren fields stretched away to the sides as far as you could see, no crops showing in them yet; only the multitudes of ploughed lines were evident. Hardly any trees lined either side of the highway – occasionally there was one lone one standing guard by the fence line that stretched into the distance and the horizon on both sides. There was no traffic to be seen either. Fuchs picked a spot and slowed the truck to a halt. Roth jumped out first, stretching his back as he did so. A few drops of rain were still in the wind, but the skies looked clear enough. He scanned the far ends of the road in both ways but thankfully there was nothing to see. He heard the driver's door close shut to his right as he made his way around to the back of the truck. As he got there Fuchs was on the other side and was reaching up to slacken off the ropes on the tarpaulin. When there was enough of a gap to reach underneath, Fuchs grabbed the can and pulled it out.

Roth unscrewed the filler cap on the truck, his head still turning around as he did so, checking the road again. Fuchs took the top off the jerry can and lifted it up towards the neck of the filler.

"Hold the bottom of the can, Roth, take the weight," ordered Fuchs. "There's no funnel to put the fuel in. If I pour it myself it'll slop out and miss the filler. We can't afford to lose any, we'll have to pour it in slow." Roth grasped immediately what Fuchs meant and so he went to the side of him and grabbed the bottom of the can, the strong smell of gasoline filling his nostrils as he got closer. Fuchs tipped up the can, marrying it up together with the gas tank. The precious fuel started slipping slowly out; the two men for the first time that day finally working together. A few crows were watching the scene below them from their perch on the oak tree just behind the two men. The only 'locals' for miles around began cawing to each other from the branches, it was if they were complaining that their peace and quiet was being disturbed, so deathly quiet it usually was here in this desolate part of the countryside.

Both men turned as one as the sound of a vehicle in the distance disturbed their progress. They looked at each other but continued with the task at hand. The noise of the approaching car grew; it was coming from behind them, the way they had come. Both men peered through the early evening gloom to try and make out if the car was a threat or not. It appeared to both that it was not a cop car or anything military, but just a civilian. The sound of the engine and the wheels on the gravel road grew a little louder as it neared them. The two were still pouring the gas but at the same time glancing up towards the car, hoping that it would sail on by. Just as it was about to draw level the two men looked away from the on-rushing car, the sound of it at its loudest now as it roared past. A light spray of rainwater was thrown up from the tyres as it did so, the occupants not even bothering to glance at the site at the side of the road. The noise from the car had barely diminished when, from the other direction, they heard another vehicle coming. They glanced at each other once again. The jerry can was at a higher angle now, perhaps less than half of the fuel still to go. Up the road ahead, a small truck was coming. The two men were concentrating on the refuelling. The second intruder was nearing them when the sound they didn't want to hear made both of them stare at each other; the truck was slowing down.

The can was nearly empty, and so Fuchs took over as the final drops were dribbling out. He gestured with his head to Roth, indicating that he should deal with the driver. The truck, a shiny blue Dodge half-ton pickup, pulled up behind their truck a few metres away and then reversed back slightly behind them, tail to tail. As it did so, Roth nodded and walked towards the driver's side of the Dodge. A young guy, more like a kid of about eighteen, jumped out, a youthful spring in his step, slamming the truck door as he did so. He strode purposely towards Roth as he spoke.

"Evening. Everything okay?" The kid had a broad smile on his face and bright blue sparkling eyes, just like a kid of his age should look.

"Yea, fine, thanks. Just stopped to fill her up, she's a thirsty one, is this one. That's it now, we'll be on our way, thanks for stopping, though."

"Hey, no problem neighbour. My dad would kill me if I didn't stop to help someone on the side of the road. Take care, bye." The youth turned on his heels and made his way back to his ride. In the meantime, Fuchs had pushed the empty jerry can back under the tarp and gotten back into the truck. As he watched Roth come around the back in the rear-view mirror he turned the ignition key, but the engine didn't burst into life.

Roth had jumped in just as Fuchs turned the key and sat there stunned as the major tried again. The engine was turning over but not firing up, the starter was clicking away, the mechanical *crump, crump, crump* of the cylinders raising and lowering in the block was there, but it wouldn't start. Fuchs tried once again, with no luck. Roth's eye was now caught by the fact that the blue truck he spied in his side mirror hadn't moved. *Go, go*, he wished, either for this truck to start or the other one to drive away. He couldn't take his eye from the back of the Dodge. *Go*, he wished again. But then his heart sank as the driver's door of the blue truck opened once more and the lad jumped out for a second time.

"Seems like she doesn't wanna go, eh?" he shouted. "That's what you get with a Ford. That's what my pa would say," called out the young American as he bounded up with youthful exuberance. In a flash he was by the side of Roth's open window and ordered Fuchs, who was still trying to get the damn thing to start, to pop the hood. The lad stood staring at these two strangers just sitting in the cab, waiting for them to comply. Fuchs stopped turning the ignition, reached down to his left, and pulled the catch that released the hood. It made a metallic '*pop*' as it was freed and the lad walked up to the front of the truck and raised the hood, flicking out the rod which would hold it in place. Roth jumped out to see if he could help. The lad called out now as he placed a hand on either fender and looked the engine over.

"Okay, give it a turn, mister." Fuchs did as he was asked, but still it refused to go. The lad had noticed Roth there now and continued talking, brushing his long blond hair out of his eyes as he bent over to see if he could see the problem. "Nothing obvious, think it might be the ignition." He then pulled one of the high tension leads from a spark plug, held the lead against the engine, and asked Fuchs to try again. When he turned it over, the youth was looking for a small spark to jump from the lead to the metal of the block; there was none. "Okay, hold on a minute, mister." He then unclipped the distributor cap and examined it, Roth transfixed as he did so. "Yep, thought as much. The cap's cracked, this baby ain't goin' nowhere, I'm afraid. Can't get a spark to the plugs with this broken like it is. Sorry." He raised his head from underneath the hood and wiped his now dirty hands on his blue jeans before turning to speak to Roth once more. "Guess you're wondering how a kid like me knows so much about engines, eh?" The wide grin was evident on his face once more. "My dad's a mechanic in the town, just down the road. He'll have an old distributor for this type of Ford in the garage somewhere, I'm sure. If you can wait, I'll drive into town and be back with one in an hour, hour and a half tops."

The top half of the lad suddenly arched back, a look of surprise mixed with severe pain etched across his face. A tear appeared in the corner of his right eye, his face now a mask of fear. His arms dropped down to his sides, the fingers of his hands spread wide. It was then that Fuchs' left arm appeared from behind and enveloped his neck in a firm grip, his right hand still holding the knife which was embedded deep into the lower part of the youth's back.

His legs buckled now, and he began to slide down to the ground, his eyes with a look of bewilderment in them staring straight at Roth as he crumpled downwards. Fuchs slowed his fall as took the dead weight in his strong arms, his upper body strength easing the lifeless body of the teenager on to the floor. Fuchs now stooped over and eased the knife from the body, and then wiped the blood off the blade and onto the dead boy's checked shirt. He looked at Roth; the captain had seen that look before on Fuchs' face when they had sunk the ship in the Channel. Fuchs spoke.

"Give me a hand, we need to get rid of him." Roth was stunned, why had he done it? "Give me a hand, I said. Grab his feet. Now!" Roth did as he was told, grabbing the legs as Fuchs took hold of the arms, blood seeping out from the wound in the lad's back and dripping onto the road as they hoisted him to the side. "In the ditch." The words were said with a gesture towards the sloping edge of the road that led to the drainage ditch just before the field. They carried the body over to the edge of the road. With one huge swing they threw the body into the two-metre-deep ditch, half full of muddy water. The ditches were there to take the runoff from the heavy rains that this part of the country was accustomed to; they ran all along the length of the fields which bordered the road. Before Roth had a chance to ask Fuchs why he had murdered this innocent young lad, Fuchs spoke again.

"We need his truck. We can't wait for him or his 'pop' to come back and fix it, we're getting behind schedule. It was unavoidable. Now, come on and give me a hand." With that, he moved quickly to the back of their own truck, jumped up on the back, untied the ropes once again, and threw back the tarpaulin. "We can't get all of these crates into the Dodge, there's no room, and the bomb is too heavy to move by hand, so I'll open up the fake one, remove the detonators from the RDX, and transfer the control box and plastic explosive over to it piece by piece. Now come on, move," he ordered.

Roth didn't reply. He could see the logic in why Fuchs had crept around from the driver's side after probably hearing what the young lad had said about going for the part to fix the Ford. He could see why Fuchs deemed the killing a necessity. But once again he felt sick to the stomach as he looked over to the ditch. He lumbered over to the Dodge, withdrew the pin that held the tailgate in place, and let it fall down level with the floor. He then went over to the Ford where Fuchs had been busy. The false top was off from the crate containing the bomb, the cigarettes in their boxes placed to one side for now, the detonators pulled from the explosive, and he was about to lift out the metal cased control box.

"Take the plastic and put it on the floor of the Dodge. I'll then pass you this, take care; this is the radioactive part. It's shielded with lead, as you know, and it's heavy, so don't drop it!"

Roth did as he was told, still mindful to keep taking

glances up and down the road in case a third vehicle appeared. Quickly, between the two men, they took the partially emptied fake cigarette crate and transferred it to the floor of the Dodge before replacing the control box, plastic explosive, detonators, and false top. It now looked as it had before: a crate of Camel cigarettes. Next, they threw the tarpaulin over the crate and closed up the tailgate on the Dodge. The back of the Ford just had the three remaining crates of Camel cigarettes in it now, plus the empty jerry can. Fuchs moved back to the driver's side of their truck, opened the driver's door, and reached inside to grab his duffel bag, the satchel, the holdall, and the machine pistol. He called across to Roth on the other side of the truck before turning to go back to the Dodge. "Don't forget the radio," he ordered.

Roth closed the hood first before quickly opening the door, and then removed the cushion from the seat. There, beneath it, was the compact radio transmitter, but also there was a pistol; it was an American Colt .45 automatic. He grabbed it quickly, checked Fuchs had not come back to his side of the truck, and then stuffed the gun into the waistband of his jeans near the small of his back. He reached for the transmitter and placed it on the foot well in front of the seat, and then stretched over to the middle of the cab and grabbed the holdall and his duffle bag. He scanned the cab for anything that they may have missed, but they had everything. Paranoia now took hold of him for a moment and he double checked the cab, including looking under both seats and opening the glovebox even though he knew for sure he hadn't even been in there during the trip. He made sure his jacket was now covering the weapon, picked up the radio, and turned to go back to the Dodge. He stuffed the radio and two bags in the much smaller cab and jumped in beside Fuchs who started it up immediately, put it into gear, and swung it in a large semi-circle, the tyres squealing on the dirt road. They resumed their journey north once more.

CHAPTER 21 - DELAWARE

All was silent aboard U-2565 as it lay on the bottom of the Atlantic, close to the entrance to Delaware bay. The sub had reached its launch position yesterday morning, one-hundred-and-forty miles due east from the American capital. The distance was just inside the maximum range of the V1, but with its payload weight reduced, and other weight savings made, the rocket should reach its target with ease. The commander of the boat, the vivacious Captain Neumeyer, had been amazed to see the lights of the streets and houses blazing away from the shoreline on the eastern seaboard last evening. Once the sun had disappeared over the horizon last night, he had dared to raise the sub up to periscope depth and take a quick peek. It was as if he could reach out and touch the twinkling array that was set out before him. It was over four years since Germany or her enemies had enjoyed the freedom of no blackouts at night-time, the ever-present threat of bombers a sad reality. The Americans felt safe here, thousands of miles from the horrors of war on the distant continent of Europe.

He left the control room and walked down through the sub to the officers' quarters where the rocket technicians were. He found them sitting on the edges of the bunks in there and they rose as he entered the room. He went up to the lead technician, Hubert Friebe, a greasy-haired bespectacled man of around forty. A very rotund man, thought Neumeyer, a man who clearly enjoyed his food.

"Is everything in order with the rocket?" he asked.

"It is, Captain," replied Friebe. "We have checked, double checked, and checked again, leaving nothing to chance. The electrical systems have had a thorough diagnostic performed on them, and the fuel is ready in its canister and will only be placed in the rocket once the reassembly has been completed on the ramp. The warhead will then be attached, together with the pulse jet. The guidance system is already set, so that is not a concern. We managed to get the reassembly time down to a little over twenty minutes after multiple practices, so we will be just under the time allowed for the launch."

"Excellent. We are anticipating the 'go' signal code word at midnight, and so will start a slow ascent at 0600 hours so as to be able to surface on time thirty minutes later. We shall, therefore, be at action stations from six. The moment we surface, and as soon as you are cleared to go up top after the hatches are opened, you and your men, together with the members of my crew designated to help with the rocket parts, will exit through the large forward hatch and get the rocket together for immediate launch. The sub will be aimed towards the target area when we surface, so do not concern yourself with anything except the assembly and launch. As soon as the rocket is away you must collect any loose items of equipment that you have on the foredeck and get down below immediately. Time will be of the essence. We will dive and head for home as quickly as possible, do you understand? It is imperative that we disappear as fast as we can, given our proximity to the coast."

"Yes, Captain. I have informed the others that time is of the essence once we have surfaced."

"One final point, if I may. We will, of course, be extremely vigilant from the moment we surface. If we see something on our radar or hear anything on the hydrophone and we are discovered during the assembly time, either by a surface vessel or aircraft, I will shout to you for a launch time update. If that time is in excess of five minutes, I shall cancel the launch. You and your team will go below immediately with any of your equipment, leaving the rocket at whatever stage you have reached, as I shall order a crash dive."

"May I remind you of the importance of this mission to the outcome of the war? The idea that Germany can launch missiles into the very heart of America is an act that will have the greatest impact of the war so far, and probably at the most crucial of times during this great conflict. To not proceed when we are here, at the front door of the greatest military power in the world today, may result in far greater dangers upon our return, Captain. May I also suggest, Captain, that the consequence of not launching the rockets now we are here is tantamount to an act of treason."

"Whilst I wholly agree that we find ourselves on the eve of a momentous day for the Third Reich, it must also be said that this is not a suicide mission. We both find ourselves in possession of two of the finest weapons that we could possibly hope for. Weapons, that if used properly together with the others, – that is the jet planes, tiger tanks, and the railway guns – can turn back this war in our favour. I am not willing to sacrifice this submarine, you, your technicians, and my crew in a useless act that cannot serve to achieve anything but our deaths. We shall return home and continue the fight, not become another footnote in history that is to be ignored."

CHAPTER 22 - WASHINGTON

The Dodge truck eased north along Maryland Route 5 after leaving the 301 as it neared the centre of the capital. It was nine o'clock in the evening. The sun had gone down a while ago, and the rain had tried to start up again but had petered out after only a short while. There wasn't much traffic around, and Fuchs didn't want to draw any attention to themselves and so was careful to watch their speed. They were less than an hour from the car park where they would eventually leave the truck, together with the bomb, and both men were feeling tense. Fuchs had mentioned earlier that they would be doing a recce of the station car park and would identify the escape car before finding somewhere close by to lie low. They would then park up the truck, flick the timer switch at six-fifty, and then calmly drive away. It had been a few hours since the incident with the young lad, and, once again, they had not spoken to each other. As horrible as it had been to watch, Roth had come to terms with what had transpired. He couldn't see what else Fuchs could have done. There was no way they could have waited around for the lad to go and fetch the new part to get the Ford truck going; he may have even returned with his father, which could have introduced more questions and potentially more problems.

He could understand how Fuchs' quick-thinking mind, honed on the battlefield, had weighed up the options in an instant and took the only reasonable one. The one option that removed the problem of the broken-down truck, which, in turn, would let them get back on time, and quickly. The killing of the lad was justified; Roth could see that now. He thought how 'fox', the literal meaning of Fuchs name, was so very fitting; sly, yet cunning. He decided to speak.

"What you did back there, killing the lad. I can see it was the right thing to do in this circumstance." Fuchs turned to look at Roth and then looked back at the road ahead before replying.

"It was. We had no time to wait around. If someone else stopped to help us, – perhaps a cop, a passing farmer, anyone who may stop and ask questions – if we slipped up there, the mission would in all probability fail. I reasoned that it was our only course of action. Casualties of war."

"Yes. As a submarine commander I don't see the enemies that I kill. They are hundreds, sometimes thousands of metres away. We're like the bomber pilots high above in the clouds, both detached from those we seek to destroy with our bombs and torpedoes. I've never been up close to death like that before, and to see the look on his face was unnerving."

Fuchs said nothing for a moment.

"Yes. For you, killing by the means you do gives you the luxury of not looking your victims in the face. For me, it is an everyday occurrence on the battlefield. Even through the rifle sights you are so close. Then there's the hand-to-hand combat in trenches, houses, streets, basements, fields. Killing frenzies take over. Kill or be killed, you or them. There are no politics to be thought of by simple soldiers on the battlefield, not when you are faced with a man who is determined to snuff out your life by any means possible. Gun, knife, spade, rock, fists, all are used in that moment. Superhuman strength can be mustered by even the smallest of men whilst fighting for his life as he struggles to live another precious minute. Grappling with another soldier, clawing at his eyes, grabbing for his throat, thrusting a knife at his belly, it's like dancing with the devil; most recently, a devil in a

234

Russian uniform.

"I have killed many young boys, not yet men, just like the boy today. Many face-to-face in all sorts of combat, my experience and size perhaps giving me an edge in those life-or-death struggles. I have fought for the Fatherland and Nazi Germany for five long years in the belief that what I was asked to do was right and just. This task that is before us now is no different, only in the fact that what we do tomorrow will turn the tide of war back in Germany's favour. If the same situation were to present itself again tomorrow, I would take the same course. To be a soldier is to serve, and that soldier cannot always pick the fight, but he must win that fight if he is to serve his country another day."

Roth nodded his head slightly in acknowledgement, but said nothing else.

As the Dodge drove closer toward the centre of the city, the tall historical monuments that dominated the skyline could be seen in the distance. The two Germans could now see the pointed capstone of the Washington monument, and behind that was the unmistakable dome of the Capitol building itself. There was their ultimate goal: the Union railway station near the centre of the US government. Both men scanned the side streets to their left and right as they drove along, searching for any potential threat that may arise, both subconsciously thinking about the difference to their capital that they had left behind over a week ago. There was no bomb damage to be seen here; not yet, anyway.

They weren't too far from the station now. They had left behind the sparsely populated outskirts of the city and the suburbs. Now it was becoming more like a metropolis: closely packed buildings, which were much taller, office buildings, businesses, shops, parks, and schools. They had travelled as far as they could up Route

5 and had now turned for the bridge that would take them across the Anacostia River. It was very built up here, near the river, but it struck Roth how clean it was, everything neat and tidy, a far cry from his hometown of Hamburg, or the streets of Berlin he had been so horrified to see just the other day. They crossed using the Navy Yard bridge and then turned right, crossing over the wide expanse of Pennsylvania Avenue. The White House, the home of the President, was just a short stroll down from here. It was unbelievable to think just exactly where they were at this moment in time. When they reached Massachusetts Avenue, Fuchs turned the truck left. It was a straight run now, down this broad, tree lined avenue that would lead to the station. The Capitol building was now revealing more of itself as they drew closer, no longer hidden by the occasional building that might obstruct the view.

It looked huge, even though it was still half a mile away, majestic in both its size and white sandstone structure, the cast iron dome enhancing its stately appearance. The founding fathers had chosen this sight, and, although the dome was added many years later, the choice was an inspired one. To Roth's mind, the building was impressive, its comparison to ancient Rome was not unintentional by its architects. You couldn't help but admire it. At any other time in history, this city, and others like it across Europe, would have been a place for thousands of tourists to flock to. But, after tomorrow, this city would be a place to avoid; possibly for many years to come.

The square-sided building of the Union station was in sight, and Fuchs drove the truck towards a sign that indicated the way onto the expanse that was the adjoining car park. He had no intention of stopping; it was just to get an overall layout of the place. Plus, they needed to locate the Buick Special, the car they would use for their escape. It didn't take them long to find what they were looking for. The car park had around two dozen or so cars of varying makes, colours, and sizes parked within it. Theirs could be identified by the simple fact that on the dash was a 'for sale sign' together with a fake telephone number, a number that Fuchs had memorised so he could ensure the car was the right one. Sure enough, there it was, more or less central in the car park. They drove slowly past, gave it a visual once over, and then made for the exit.

They left Union station behind and made their way back from where they had just come. They wanted to use the same route back in tomorrow morning so as not to get confused by the labyrinth of side streets that constituted the neighbourhood. Besides, on the way in they had spied a small bit of wasteland, perfect for them to park up on and be able to observe anyone who might approach. Fuchs drove onto the uneven surface of the wasteland. It looked like it had once been the site of a building that had now been demolished and was awaiting a new one to take its place. After finding a suitable spot where a partially demolished wall could conceal the truck from the road, Fuchs parked behind it, turned off the engine, and looked to Roth.

"Gauge is just above empty, but as we're so close it'll be enough to get us back to the car park. Just before midnight we shall hook up the radio to the truck battery and then send the code word 'Surtr', in plain language, and on the dot." There was a slight pause. "Do you know what the Japanese code word for Pearl Harbour was, Roth?"

"No," he replied.

"Tora. It has a literal meaning of 'lightning', which, I thought, after hearing what our code word was, was quite apt, German God of Lightning, and all that. Plus, of course, there's 'Blitzkrieg': lightning war. All very similar and fitting, isn't it? Tomorrow is a Sunday, and the attack will be at seven a.m. local time. Unfortunately, it's not the seventh, or the irony would be complete."

"I guess." Roth was a little bemused as Fuchs had suddenly become quite the thinker.

The hours between them pulling onto the wasteland and the moments before midnight had passed relatively quickly. They had sat there, not really talking, both staring out of the window and watching the streets for anyone who may approach. Fuchs had insisted on going over the details of the plan for tomorrow and their escape, but now a final look at their watches told them it was approaching midnight.

The two men exited the Dodge, careful not to let the doors slam behind them and make a noise at this late hour. Roth had grabbed the shortwave radio from beneath the seat as he had left the truck. Fuchs raised the hood and secured it in place. Roth placed the radio on the fender close to the engine bay and attached the wires that would supply the power over to the battery. He flicked the 'on' switch and the frequency dial lit up, indicating it was ready to transmit.

The sound of someone walking over broken brick ends startled the two Germans as they hunched over the radio. They both turned their heads in the direction of where the noise had come from. It was very dark here, but they could make out a silhouette of a man, backlit by the streetlights across the way. He was stumbling across the rubble that lay all around, the jagged edges of masonry making it difficult to walk properly, but then he stopped and turned his gaze in the direction of the lone truck with its hood open.

Fuchs and Roth were transfixed, staring at this lone figure out here so late at night, unsure as to what course of action to take. From where the man was it was impossible for him to see the radio, but if he approached they'd have to deal with him. He was still standing there, looking over to them, but then he turned and continued on his way. As he did so he stepped into the light of another streetlamp and now they could see he was a tramp wearing dishevelled clothing, a torn hat, and carrying a bundle of some description. He was just passing through and wasn't interested in two guys fixing their broken-down truck.

Roth turned his attention back to the radio, tuned it into the correct frequency, and looked at Fuchs who was peering in the gloom at the luminous dial of his watch. As the two fingers edged closer to become one and lined up on the number twelve, Fuchs raised his index finger towards Roth, and then, as a local church clock chimed out the time in the distance, he gave the signal to transmit.

*

It was almost five-thirty a.m. in London as Sullivan's staff car drew close to the large Portland stone clad office building that he had called home for most of the last four years. He jumped out from the back of the 1935 Triumph Vitesse, said goodbye to his driver, Anne, telling her he'd call when he required a car again, and strode over to the entrance. Most of the lower parts of the structure were invisible due to the fact that walls of sandbags, some as high as twenty-five feet, surrounded the place. The windows were either boarded up or had tape stretched across them, all in an effort to protect the building and occupants from bomb blasts. He returned the salute of the armed guard who was standing in front of the oak doors at the entrance, flashed his credentials, and walked quickly inside, glad that he could get away from the grip of the cold that he was starting to feel outside, even after his short walk from the car.

Within a few minutes, after going through more security, he was once more in his office, the familiar sounds greeting him as he walked through the busy hub therein. He hadn't gotten too far when a sailor approached him and handed him a communique marked urgent. It had come from the signals room, which was just down the hallway. He stopped walking, placed his briefcase down on the floor by his feet, and read what it said. 'Urgent, for the immediate attention of Admiral Sullivan. Message received at 0001 hours, Eastern Standard Time, this day, the twenty sixth of March, 1944. Sullivan did a quick mental calculation; the message was thirty minutes old. Message reads: 'Surtr'. NB. This message was sent in plain language and not coded.' The last line stood out to Sullivan. He picked up his briefcase and marched down the corridor to the signals room. Inside he found leading seaman Powell looking at a daily newspaper, he ignored the transgression and spoke.

"This signal, the one marked urgent for me with the word 'Surtr' on it, do we have a fix on it?" he asked.

"Just getting that information now, sir, should have it for you in a few minutes," replied the guilt-ridden Powell.

Sullivan thought for a moment before speaking again.

"As soon as it comes through, I want you to bring it to me, clear?"

"Yes, sir." With that said, Sullivan raced off to his office. He swung open the door, placed his briefcase on the desk, and picked up the phone.

"Get me Colonel Lee at OSS," he barked down the line to the operator. "Immediately!" The admiral shuffled uncomfortably on the spot as he waited to be connected. Finally, he heard a weary voice on the other line.

"Hello. Colonel Lee speaking."

"Colonel, it's Sullivan here. I think I've found a link to our missing sub."

"What, you mean U-931?"

"Yes, we've intercepted the code word 'Surtr' again, in plain language." He was about to continue when Powell entered the room and gave him a sheet of paper. "Hang on, I've got more information, bear with me for a moment." He scanned the data that he'd been handed, and, as he read what was before him, he began to frown. He sighed deeply.

"Hello? Are you still there?" enquired Lee.

"Still here, Colonel. I've just been told where the signal originated. But it's clear it hasn't originated from the sub."

"And why is that, may I ask?"

"Are you aware of the 'Huff-Duff' high frequency direction finding system, used by the allies?"

"I've heard of it, but I've not been briefed fully on the working principles as of yet, please go on."

"Imagine three sets of radio receivers at different points on the compass and they intercept a signal from an enemy source. Now, by drawing lines of interception or, as we call it, 'triangulation', – from each point, where they criss-cross is the coordinates of the source transmission. We normally use this method to locate the position of a submarine."

"Can you get to the point, please, Admiral? It's very early and I've yet to have a coffee."

"This particular signal came from a point not at sea, but somewhere on land, somewhere near Washington. Washington DC."

CHAPTER 23 - CAPITAL

The interior of the Dodge pickup cab had steamed up, and so Roth wound his window down just a little to let some fresh air in before wiping off the condensation that had formed, using the sleeve of his denim jacket. His breath was visible in the cold air of the truck. Fuchs was asleep now, as he had taken the first watch. Roth had his arms folded across his chest to try and keep out the chill of the spring morning air. Fuchs had been mumbling incoherently during what appeared to be a quite pitiful sleep, and Roth still felt weary even after his own brief respite earlier. He looked at his watch; it was 0530 hours. Less than an hour from now and they'd press the button on the bomb to start the timer. He shuddered; was it from the cold that was seeping into the cab from the outside? He looked at his watch again. With his right hand he reached into the left-sided breast pocket of the jacket and slipped out a folded envelope that he had placed there before he had left the sub yesterday. He glanced back to the still-sleeping Fuchs and then removed the letter from the envelope. It was difficult to read as only the nearby streetlights provided illumination, the sun was yet to make an appearance, but he unfolded the single sheet of crumpled paper and began to read, once more, the letter from his mother:

My dear son, I hope with all my heart that this letter finds you well and in good spirits. Your father and I are both well. Do you remember Mrs. Jagger? She lives at number seventeen. Her brother called the other day and left her some potatoes and turnips. She said that there was enough for her. Remember, she lost her husband two years ago to old age. Well, she gave us some of the vegetables.

We shall have a feast tonight as your father has managed to sneak a piece of cod from the small catch they brought in yesterday.

The next sentence had been crossed out by the censor, but Roth couldn't believe for one moment that his mother had divulged some state secret about the mundane goings on of a housewife from Hamburg as she wrote to her only son. He read on:

Coal is hard to come by, but your father chopped up the dresser the other day, so that should see us through until the warmer weather. Goebbels said on the radio that we shot down fifty bombers the other night. The soldiers here that are on the guns and searchlights near the marketplace are young, but tell us not to worry. Well, that's all for now, I must get on and peel those vegetables. Stay safe and come home soon. Love, Mamma and Pappa

He had read and re-read those lines over and over since he had received the letter, a few weeks after her death. It had been her last one. He knew that she'd been lying about the food, and possibly the wood. His father had told him later that Mrs. Jagger had moved away weeks earlier. She had gone to live with her brother in the country, as it was safer. His mother had tried to ensure that she gave the impression that both she and his father were okay, so as not to worry him. Roth knew of the food shortages back home, and of course how cities like Hamburg were being targeted by the allied bombers. The thought of how she was killed while near the same market that she had written about made him choke up. He stared out into the distance; the first slivers of dawn were slowly making an appearance over the nearby roof tops. He carefully folded the letter back up, returned it to the envelope, and placed it back where it had come from.

As he sat there trying to shut out the heavy breathing of Fuchs' tortured sleep, his thoughts turned to Ginette. In the past week or so things had moved so quickly that he had not the time or inclination to let an image of her enter his mind, for he knew that the dream of them being together was now more impossible than ever. As U-931 had sailed into Saint-Nazaire that last time, he had prayed that this was his final voyage aboard a U-boat. The war would be over soon, and he would be with her. With the war over there would be no more reasons why they should be apart. They could live together as man and wife. But now, it could never be. After tomorrow, the whole world would change. Never mind his dreams; everyone's would vanish. He looked back at Fuchs, still asleep. The time was now 0615 hours. He would wake the major in a minute or two. They would need to get going very soon.

Through the open window, Roth heard something in the distance. It sounded like a heavy truck approaching, but he dismissed it as being a threat as it was nearly dawn now and the city was waking up; there were bound to be workers going about their business at the start of the day. The sound of the oncoming truck grew louder, only he now thought it wasn't travelling alone. To Roth's ears there was surely more than one – perhaps a few. Fuchs was awake himself now, disturbed by the rumble of heavy tyres on the cobbles that made up the streets here. Those sounds, plus the roar of throaty diesel engines, was drawing nearer. Alert now, Fuchs sat up, and, with his left hand, reached down to where his machine pistol lay beside the door where he gave it a reassuring pat for his own comfort. The street, together with the wasteland they were on, was now ablaze with the glare from multiple sets of headlights from the trucks as they neared, the noise coming from the engines rising even more as six US Army four-ton 'Diamond T' heavy cargo trucks thundered past them, each one bounding along on a total of ten wheels. The army convoy was distinguishable by their olive drab colour scheme and the five-pointed white star clearly seen on the cab doors of each one as they drove by. In the rear of the six trucks, lit up by the beams of the following truck, were the faces of soldiers. Roth spoke as the sound from the last truck faded into the distance.

"Coincidence?"

Fuchs pondered the open question before answering.

"Probably. But we must be on our guard. There is only a small group of people back in Berlin who know of this phase of the operation, and I cannot believe they have betrayed us. We shall proceed as planned. Our cover story is solid, so if we are stopped or approached you shall do the talking. We should reach our target and begin the detonation sequence before making our getaway, clear?"

"Clear," said Roth, although he was no longer sure that he was.

*

It was nearing eleven a.m. in London. Why it had taken so long to assemble those present here, seated around the table in the Naval Intelligence room located deep in the bowels of the Admiralty building, Sullivan had no idea, but here they were. Sullivan was about to brief his superiors: Admiral Sir Bruce Fraser, Commander-in-Chief of the Home Fleet, and Admiral R. E. Ingersoll, Commander-in-chief of the US Atlantic Fleet. Also present were Air Marshal Leigh-Mallory, the Air Commander for the upcoming invasion, and Lieutenant

Carl Spaatz of the newly reorganised US 8th Air Force, plus Colonel Lee from OSS. There were also a few other faces that Sullivan didn't know. What he did think was that there was some serious brass present in this room. Fraser was the first to speak.

"Gentlemen, if we could all quieten down for a moment, then Rear Admiral Sullivan will begin."

Sullivan rose from his chair and began his address.

"Good morning, gentlemen. I'm aware that your respective intelligence agencies have outlined to you that we believe that there is a credible threat of a rocket attack on the eastern seaboard of the United States." There was a murmur from the high-ranking officials around the large ornate table, here in the underground bunker located deep beneath the streets of Whitehall, where they found themselves this day.

"This is what we believe has transpired during the last two weeks. On March twelfth, the Photo Intelligence Branch at Medmenham identified a submarine, U-931. It was moored at the Peenemünde rocket facility, and I authorised a sortie because of the unusual circumstances of a sub being in that location. She was attacked by four RAF Mosquitos as she left the harbour, but she then disappeared, perhaps sunk. Three days later on the fifteenth, she was sighted and was engaged by *HMS Zenobia* in the Channel. Unfortunately, *Zenobia* was torpedoed, and all but one of her crew were lost. According to the eyewitness account of the one and only surviving sailor, the lifeboat that contained other members of the crew who had survived the initial attack were shot and killed by what he believed were SS soldiers on the sub. The witness also claims that someone returned fire from the lifeboat, and one of the SS soldiers was struck and fell overboard, off the sub." Sullivan paused for a moment to let the gravity of his last statement sink in. "Once again, U-931 disappeared. The only possible link was a coded signal sent from the location of the engagement and intercepted here by naval intelligence. The message was encrypted and all it revealed was a single German word, 'Surtr', which apparently is a mythical God of Fire. We presumed that this transmission was perhaps a 'go' signal.

"Colonel Lee of OSS contacted me at this juncture, and I was informed by them of a secret submarine launch rocket programme that they were investigating, and he wanted to liaise with me about any connections with U-931. Nothing was known of the sub's whereabouts until a day or so later when she limped into La Rochelle. So now, as far as both I and American intelligence were concerned, U-931 was no longer of interest for the moment. I, of course, intended to keep a very watchful eye on the sub, its captain, and any SS involvement, in order to proceed with a war crime investigation after the war.

"It was then that MI6 contacted my office with information from the French Resistance confirming that the sub wasn't in La Rochelle at all, and that we had been the victim of an elaborate German deception, which raised a very important question. Why had they gone to such lengths to disguise the real whereabouts of U-931?

"Yet again, we had a missing sub, but no tangible evidence of a connection to anything else. Until this morning. At midnight EST last night, five o' clock for us, we intercepted a signal sent in plain language. The single word sent in that signal was again the word 'Surtr'. That signal, gentlemen, was not sent from U-931. The reason we are sure of this is that after double checking the coordinates and the triangulation calculations, we can confirm that it was sent from a location on land. After re-checking the information obtained from 'Ultra', we were able to pinpoint an area in the centre of Washington, DC." Sullivan sat down now, the officers and high-ranking civilians present all talking amongst themselves as he retook his seat. Admiral Ingersoll, who was sitting directly across from Sullivan, now spoke.

"So, what we have here, if I've come to the right conclusions from all these various sources and bits of intelligence that you've presented, is that there may be one or more U-boats close to the Eastern seaboard equipped with the capability to fire V1 rockets. May I remind you that the very existence of the V1s is still a matter for conjecture. Indeed, no such weapon has been launched in an attack on land, as of yet. But you want us to believe that this is a credible threat and that they may be targeting Washington?"

"Yes, sir, I do."

Ingersoll pondered for a moment before speaking.

"I've been in two other meetings about this matter this morning already with both OSS and MI6, plus I've had telephone conversations with the Secretary of War, Stimson, at the Pentagon, who has mobilised army units based in and around Washington. He has deployed them across the city in order to help with any civilian casualties that may arise from any attack. I've also spoken to the Commander-in-Chief of the Second Fleet based in Norfolk, Virginia." He looked at his watch. "As we speak, a large contingent of US warships, together with air support, are preparing to search the seas off the coast in question. The Canadians have also been asked to do a search and destroy mission from the north. The only caveat with this, gentlemen, is that we have an awful lot of ocean to look in for possibly one lone sub."

Fraser now spoke once more.

"With the help of RAF Coastal Command, together with ships from the Royal Navy, we too are organising a search and destroy task force around the waters of the southern British Isles in case the Germans are about to launch a similar attack on our shores. I think time is of the essence, gentlemen." With that said, Fraser approached Ingersoll to discuss a plan of action in the Atlantic. Then, a short man, probably in his mid-thirties, with wispy hair over a balding head rose from his seat and introduced himself as Professor Reginald Jones, a senior British scientist and military expert attached to MI6. He started to speak just as Admiral Ingersoll made his excuses and left the room, an urgency to his pace as he left.

"Gentlemen, this morning's events across the Atlantic have escalated an already unprecedented danger to the planned invasion. Let me explain further. As Rear Admiral Sullivan has already mentioned, OSS and MI6 contacted him with regards to U-931 and a possible link to a secret operation to launch the V1 rockets from a submarine. We didn't know what that link may be, we still don't. But I am about to divulge more information which our joint intelligence has gathered over the last year, and I'm afraid it's a far greater threat than a possible attack on Washington.

"We believe that Nazi scientists are much more advanced in this programme than we first thought, and that they have developed a system whereby they can use an upgraded Henshel Hs 293 missile in place of a V1. A regular Hs 293 has been used with deadly effect on ships like *HMS Athabaskan*, which was sunk in the Bay of Biscay last August. Now, the Hs 293 is normally dropped from an aircraft as it's designed to be an anti-ship missile, guided to its target via a radio-controlled guidance system from the host aircraft. Very effective, or at least it was until we found a way to jam its signal. We now think that the Germans have installed a new system that counteracts our jamming, have increased the range of the missile by up to around five-hundred miles, and that they are capable of carrying a warhead of one-thousand pounds of Amatol high explosive."

These last comments started a torrent of questions towards the professor, but Colonel Lee now stood to speak.

"If I can just elaborate on what the professor is indicating here, and what we at OSS know. The Germans have developed a sub-launched missile system on their new Type XXI subs. These new submarines are difficult to trace, have a far greater range than previous models, and are capable of carrying twenty-three torpedoes, or, by our estimates, fifteen Hs 293 missiles. These missiles, if we are correct, can hit a target with a high degree of accuracy. Gentlemen, what we are presented with is the scenario of these ghost submarines, loaded with these deadly missiles, firing at will at the ports along the English Channel, where thousands of troops and hundreds of ships all loaded with tanks, jeeps, ammunition, etc., are gathering to launch the invasion." He let his point sink in before he continued. "We may have to postpone Operation Overlord, the invasion of France."

CHAPTER 24 - MARBLES

Colonel Lee continued: "Over the last few months, American and British intelligence have been gathering information about these submarines and this new rocket system. What we were unable to ascertain was where these subs were being modified. At first, we had a link to the German port of Wilhelmshaven, but that didn't pan out; only so much of the work was being carried out there. Peenemünde was also under scrutiny, and when U-931 went there we thought we were onto something again. We knew that both the modified submarines and new rocket systems had to be tested, but we couldn't find out where, and the trail went cold. But then we had a stroke of luck.

"MI6 received information from the Norwegian resistance. Near a small village called Nese, a local man was riding his bicycle when he came upon a line of traffic which had stopped because a number of pigs had escaped from a farm and had blocked the road. Not important in the grand scheme of things, I hear you say, but then the local pulled up behind a civilian truck which had stopped because of the mayhem in front. You don't get much traffic in that area, so he was curious about this, especially as the truck had a full canvas canopy over it. As he was waiting for the road to clear, sat as he was on his bike and behind the truck, the canvas flap was swept back from inside and a man looked out, trying to see what the holdup was. According to the local, the man in the truck, plus at least a dozen or so more that were inside, were sailors. The significance of this is that there is no Kreigsmarine base within one-hundred-and-fifty miles of there.

"Because of this, we had a photo reconnaissance

Spitfire fly over the area and what it came back with was at first disappointing, until an eagle-eyed interpreter at Medmenham spotted something. It was a fuel bowser, parked on a track near the edge of the fjord and next to an abandoned fishery. During a further careful examination of the derelict buildings, they spotted something concealed beneath a natural overhang of the cliff wall. After enlarging the images, they identified the unmistakable outline of thick concrete walls that go to make up a submarine pen.

"Upon hearing this, we arranged for an agent to be dropped by parachute and he reported back that there were indeed modified Type XXI subs in there, six in total. He also reported that the natural topography ensured that it would be impossible for a conventional bombing raid to be launched; the overhanging rock face above the pens was a natural defence for the installation. The agent went on to report that he heard what sounded to him like the test firing of missiles or rockets further up the fjord. He couldn't confirm if the sub fired them, as he didn't have a visual. With all the evidence we have collected so far, we can now say with a certain degree of confidence that this is a base from which they will launch these submarines, and with that said I'd like to hand over to the Air Marshall."

"Thank you, Colonel," said Leigh-Mallory. "Before I came here this morning, I spoke directly with the Prime Minister and I have given him a full briefing on the situation, and he has given me a directive to destroy the pens in Norway and instruct the US 8th Air Force and Bomber Command to launch a day and night raid on Peenemünde with immediate effect." On hearing this, Spaatz just nodded and let Leigh-Mallory continue. "I have also been in direct contact with Sir Arthur Harris, as we are attacking the base in the fjord with a variation of a wonder weapon of our own." Those assembled around the table were now intrigued.

"Over the previous twelve months, we have been trying to crack open the submarine pens based in France and Germany with little or no luck. Bombers from the 'Dam busters' 617 squadron have used Barnes Wallis' Tallboy and Grand Slam bombs, both of which are twelve-thousand and twenty-two-thousand pounds respectively, but they were not able to penetrate the eight-metre-thick concrete bunkers that protect the subs. So, with Professor Wallis' help, we have devised a way where we can use his 'bouncing bomb' to destroy the pens."

At this point, Professor Jones took up the story. "After the successful raids on the dams last May, the Lancasters that returned from the mission were decommissioned and returned to normal operations. Wing Commander Gibson and the surviving crew members were also reintegrated into other squadrons, the thought being that the bomb was unlikely to be used again in such an operation. Indeed, Wallis has gone on to develop the 'Highball' bouncing bomb, which is smaller and can be launched from a Mosquito, but is only designed to sink a capital ship and does not have the capacity to destroy concrete installations like the sub pens. For this reason, I have been working alongside the professor to improve and redesign the original bomb for another use.

"This new weapon lies somewhere between the two and it is of a spherical design rather than cylindrical, so as to improve its performance. The intention being that it shall be used against the fortified submarine pens located along the coasts of France, Norway, and Germany itself. Together with the RAF we are modifying twenty Lancasters in order to carry the redesigned bomb. Unfortunately, the programme, code named 'Marbles', was only instigated in December and at present there are only three planes available to fly from their base at RAF Scampton."

"Thank you, Professor." Leigh-Mallory continued: "The plan of attack is as follows. Ten Typhoon ground attack aircraft from 198 Squadron will go in and engage with the anti-aircraft batteries identified around the submarine pens and will provide covering fire when the Lancasters are on their bomb run. Spitfires from 74 Squadron will escort the bombers over the North Sea and will set up a screen over the area to fight off any enemy fighters that may wish to attack the Lancs.

"The Lancasters will fly low across the waters of the fjord in a similar manner to when they attacked the dams in Germany, using targeting practices and height adjustments, as per operation 'Chastise', the attack on the dams. The high sides of the fjord may pose a problem as the Lancs pull away after the attack, as we always envisioned using the new bombs on bases located in seaports. Plus, according to the report from the agent that was dropped in, the hillsides and roof of the pens are heavily fortified with anti-aircraft batteries; it's going to be tough on those boys going in, and coming out. There is another difference here in that the bomb will be aimed so that it enters the opening to the pen itself as it reaches its terminal trajectory and will detonate immediately when it comes to rest. There is no hydrostatic charge fitted in this design. The one drawback of this operation is that we are literally trying to thread the eye of a needle here, the opening of each of the pens is roughly fifty feet across."

Sullivan stood once more and spoke. "When do you plan to launch this sortie, sir?"

The Air Marshall looked at his watch.

"The Lancs should be approaching the fjord

'round about now."

CHAPTER 25 - LAUNCH

Over three-thousand miles away from London, Fuchs took a long swig of water from his canteen, then poured some of it into the cup of his left hand and rubbed it over his face. Roth adjusted his position in his seat, uncomfortable from the combination of being in the same position for the last five or so hours, plus the pistol sticking into his lower back. He looked at his watch: it was 0620 hours. No more army trucks had passed by since the ones earlier. Fuchs looked over to Roth and then started up the Dodge, and they set off for Union station.

As predicted, the drive back only took five or so minutes. What they hadn't expected was the amount of traffic that was on the roads at this early hour. Commuters were on the move, as expected, but there were also more army vehicles. Truck after truck, jeeps, and staff cars; the city had become a blur of olive green everywhere they looked. It appeared to be more than just a coincidence; these troops were on the streets of the capital for a reason. Most of those seen by the two Germans were heading out from the city centre, as this part of Washington was brimming with barracks of all services of the armed forces. It was no surprise to see so many, but they were all speeding around, clearly in a hurry to get somewhere. The area that the two Germans had driven through yesterday was a hub for the armed forces stationed in the district of Columbia, but last evening it had been relatively quiet. They hadn't encountered a single army vehicle of any description; now the capital was buzzing with them.

As they crossed the Anacostia River once more, they could see Fort McNair to their left – it was one of America's oldest army forts. The surrounding area is home to many of the US naval services. Large buildings house administration centres for both navy and army. The marines also have a barracks there; this is another of the reasons why this location for the bomb had been chosen. It was to be expected to see troops in the streets here, a day-to-day occurrence. What both men wondered was why was it that so many were around now; had the plot been uncovered? Was there an exercise of some description going on just by chance? As they had no answers, they drove on.

The green Buick was still where they had seen it the previous evening. Both men scanned the area as the truck entered the car park. There were no signs of any soldiers here, in fact the car park itself was quiet, just as they had planned. With it being a Sunday morning, the first commuters driving here to catch a train hadn't arrived yet. The Dodge eased into a space, just two down from the Buick. Fuchs turned off the ignition as Roth jumped out and strode casually over to the getaway car. He stooped down as if to tie his shoelace. He was beside the front wheel, and he reached across to find the keys just where they had been told they would be. He stood, went to the driver's door, and opened it. He placed the key in the ignition and was just about to turn back to the Dodge when he stopped. He looked down to the top pocket of his jacket. Sticking out and barely visible was his mother's letter. He pushed it back down.

He was aware that Fuchs had left the Dodge and had now dropped the tailgate of the truck and was removing the tarpaulin, which would then reveal the crate containing the bomb. Roth knew that the time to act had arrived. He felt for the pistol concealed in his waistband, pulled it out, and stepped towards the truck. Fuchs was about to step up onto the floor of the Dodge when he noticed Roth, and the gun.

"Can't let you do it, Major. If that bomb goes off, the Americans will raze our homeland to the ground. All that we know will be gone. We have lost the war, and to do this will not alter that fact. You can take the car; I will drive the truck somewhere and dispose of the crate. We can both disappear, and the Americans will never know of this madness," Roth proclaimed as he pointed the automatic pistol at Fuchs' chest, just a few feet away.

Fuchs grinned and spoke. "From the moment Leon died and I had to order you to take his place, I had my doubts about your patriotism and loyalty to the Reich. You may be correct about the war being lost, and the Americans retaliating with atomic bombs of their own, but what we are doing here goes beyond all that, Roth. If it doesn't halt the invasion, doesn't bring the allies to the table to discuss terms, it doesn't matter. Your own comrades of the Kreigsmarine are risking their lives out at sea, right now. They will obey orders and launch the rockets. It is our duty to stand with them and do the same here. This act today lets the allies know that the Third Reich shall go on, whatever they do, and true patriots like me and Vogel will fight long after they have marched through Berlin and imposed more reparations and sanctions on Germany." Fuchs spoke calmly as he stepped towards Roth and the Buick, his right hand moving behind his back to his knife as he talked.

Roth had noticed the hand movement of the SS major and raised the gun to aim it squarely at the major's head, but the big German kept coming, his grin becoming wider as he neared.

"I don't want to shoot you, Fuchs! Think about what I said. Think about Germany and the consequences for its people." But it was no good, he was getting closer. Roth quickly cocked the weapon, took aim, and pulled the trigger. *Click, click.* The gun didn't fire. Roth stared down at the gun, all hope lost. Fuchs offered an explanation.

"The gas station. When you were filling up and talking to the old guy. I found the pistol under the seat when I checked the radio. Something in the back of my mind told me to remove the rounds, but leave it there for you to find. It looks like I was right to, eh, Captain?"

In an instant, Roth decided his only course of action was to attack. He leapt forward, raised the gun in his right hand above his shoulder, and, with all his might, brought it crashing down towards Fuchs' head, but Fuchs anticipated the move and blocked Roth's arm. The gun spun wildly from his grasp and flew to the ground, bouncing once or twice before coming to a rest.

Fuchs hadn't had time to draw the knife from behind his back and so smashed his right fist into the face of the onrushing captain. Roth's nose split open immediately, blood cascading out and onto his jacket. He stumbled back. Both men were amazed that he was still on his feet. Fuchs was quickest to continue, his years of battlefield experience kicking in; as far as he was concerned, this was no contest. What did concern him was that a car was pulling into the car park, a commuter. The last thing he wanted now was an inquisitive witness. He'd make this quick, before more people began to turn up. He grabbed for Roth but was momentarily distracted by the car as it now made its way over to a distant space near the station entrance. Roth took the unexpected lapse of concentration to strike again. He rushed the much larger man, his momentum pushing him back, but only as far as the open tailgate of the truck. Fuchs was taken by surprise slightly and fell backwards. The two men were now entangled together, Roth on top of Fuchs, the two of them on top of the open tailgate and the rear of the Dodge. The attack from Roth was poor in its execution, haphazard at best against this trained killer. He had his hands around Fuchs' throat and tried to strangle him, but the larger man just rolled them both over together, using his superior strength and weight, so that now he was on top and strangling Roth.

The eyes of Fuchs were looking directly into Roth's own, their faces only inches apart as he gripped tighter around the captain's throat with mandible-like hands. The U-boat captain's life was quickly ebbing away. Roth tried to stick both of his thumbs directly into the eye sockets of his attacker, but Fuchs spun his head away and then crashed his forehead back into the bloody nose of Roth to try and stun him. The blow sent Roth's head crashing backwards onto the floor of the truck, but, at the same time, Fuchs' grip around his neck loosened slightly.

Roth knew he didn't have much longer, but then he remembered the knife that Fuchs always carried. Knowing that only seconds remained now before he would lose consciousness, he reached around Fuchs' back with his right hand and searched for the weapon, located on the major's belt. Fuchs was concentrating so much on throttling the life out of the traitor lying beneath him that he didn't notice that Roth was reaching behind him. Roth found what he was searching for: the handle of the ceremonial dagger. The knife itself was already halfway out from its scabbard from when Fuchs had reached for it, moments earlier. He quickly withdrew the razor-sharp killing tool and then plunged the two-inch wide blade deep into Fuchs neck, just below his left ear. Arterial blood spurted out from the deep wound immediately. Fuchs removed his hands from around Roth's neck and stood up. He tried in vain to stem the flow of the scarlet-coloured liquid oozing from the wound. He pulled out the knife, throwing it to the ground, his left hand still trying to stop the on-rushing blood, but it was useless. With a look of finality, Fuchs stared at Roth who was now sitting upright on the tailgate, rubbing his own throbbing neck, the blood from his broken nose starting to darken on his shirt collar and jacket. Fuchs stepped forward, his goal: the bomb. Roth could see that, even though Fuchs was bleeding to death, he was going to try and get past him and arm it.

The dying SS major, with blood seeping from between the gaps in his fingers as he held his blood-soaked neck with his left hand, tried to push Roth to the side with his free right hand. He attempted to raise his leg to hoist himself up, but he didn't have enough strength remaining to lift it up. He tried once more, but it wasn't to be. He took one final look at Roth, swayed to his left, made a grab for the side of the truck, missed, and fell dead, face down in the back of the truck. The upper part of his lifeless body was now lying next to the crate whilst his legs stretched out behind him, the tips of his feet resting on the tarmac of the car park. Roth didn't have the luxury of time to consider how surreal the moment was. Here, in the Union station car park, Washington, DC, on a Sunday morning.

No more cars had come their way while the two men had been entwined in their fight to the death. One more had arrived, but that had also parked up close to the entrance, probably so as to save the driver from walking too far. Roth sat there, wondering what to do. He had to dispose of the bomb and body. He jumped up onto the floor of the truck, grabbed Fuchs' arms, and pulled the dead weight of the SS man forward so that his legs were now inside the back of the truck, his head resting against the back of the cab. He struggled to pull him, as Fuchs weighed near one-hundred kilograms, but, luckily, he summoned up the strength. It was done by a process of sheer determination and brute strength, but he had managed to do it. He now turned his attention to the crate. He slipped the loose top off and removed the false tray concealing the bomb beneath. It was of a simple enough design, as had been explained to him back in Berlin and Peenemünde. The wires leading out from the control box led directly to the detonators through a single connector block, which, in turn, were wired up in a series configuration, so as to set off the RDX.

He pulled apart the connector plug and then reached underneath the lead-lined box which contained the immense destructive power of the Plutonium. It was heavy, considering its small size. This part of the bomb was about the size and shape of a biscuit tin, and Roth placed the box on the tailgate before jumping down. After looking around once more he reached over and grabbed a corner of the tarpaulin. He wondered what the police would make of this scene that he stared at now. Here was a body with a severe knife wound, a fake crate of cigarettes, and enough plastic explosive to wipe out most of this car park, all bundled up in a stolen pick-up with Virginia plates belonging to a missing teenager. With a sweep of his arm, he threw the tarp across the body and crate, lifted up the box that contained the Plutonium, closed up the tailgate, and then turned his attention over to the Buick.

He walked over and popped the trunk, putting what remained of the bomb inside. In the trunk he found a grey canvas holdall. He pulled back the zip and looked inside to see two canteens of water, some apples, three or four road maps, and, most importantly, the new identities for him and Fuchs. He grabbed the bag, closed the trunk, and then went to the driver's side. He opened it up and threw the bag in and across to the other side. Looking around the car park once more as he sat in the Buick he turned the ignition and drove the car slowly towards the exit, but something was troubling him as he edged towards the way out. What was it? It took a moment or two, and then it struck him. He didn't know very much about bombs, but one thing he did know was that on this particular device a certain item was 'conspicuous by its absence'. There was no mechanical timer fitted. The bomb had been designed to go off the instant it was armed.

*

Out in the Atlantic, with what felt like touching distance of the coastline, all was ready aboard U-2565.

"Surface, blow all tanks," ordered Captain Neumeyer. It was just before 0630 hours. He had raised the sub to periscope depth just moments before and what he witnessed through the plane mirrors had gladdened his heart. It was fog; thick fog. The 'electro' boat broke through the surface of the Atlantic, and, together with the crew, the V1 technicians had sprung into action. They all knew that they had to get the parts of the rocket out from the sub through the forward hatch and reassemble it as quickly as possible. On deck, the sub looked a strange sight with the modified launch ramp that was fixed there. Lookouts on the conning tower tried in vain to peer through the dense fog that was surrounding them; indeed, they could only just about make out the dozen or so figures who were scrambling around below them working on the rocket. Deep down in the bowels of the sub, the sailors manning their posts on the hydrophones and radar were straining to hear any noises in their headsets which they had strapped to their ears. The only real threat at the moment was a surface vessel. The captain had told them about the thick fog on top.

Like a well-oiled machine, the technicians on the forward deck had worked frantically and the modified V1 rocket was complete, the fuel loaded, and was moments from being fired. Just then, from the port side of the sub and around two nautical miles away, the steady drone that the pulse jet engine of a V1 produced was heard, followed quickly by the loud bang that accompanied the steam powered launch up the ramp. The first rocket was on its way.

"How long to go, Friebe?" shouted Neumeyer.

"One more minute, we're just setting the guidance system," replied the preoccupied technician. As he spoke, the sound of another pulse jet starting up could be heard to the starboard side of the sub; the second rocket was about to be launched.

Suddenly, there was a bright flash of light to the right of the sub, followed instantaneously by a deafening explosion, both of which had come through the dense fog from the direction of the sub to the north of U-2565. Everyone on deck stopped for a moment and turned as one to their right. They all knew instinctively what the explosion meant. The second rocket had exploded before take-off. Suddenly the air was split open by a secondary explosion, again coming from the right.

"Fuel tank just went up," Neumeyer in the conning tower muttered to himself. His gaze wandered back to the rocket below, loaded with high explosives and fixed to a ramp on his sub. All the faces he could make out through the gloom that enveloped the deck were looking back at him, all knowing what had just happened to the second sub. He caught the gaze of Friebe and nodded for him to proceed, who then turned back to the rocket, flicking one switch on the portable control panel that he held in his hand. A thick set of cables ran from the box that then looped across to another metal box of around thirty centimetres which sat at the foot of the ramp, just below the V1. Five green lights had illuminated on the small control panel in Friebe's hands when he'd flicked the first switch. He now pushed the red fire button.

CHAPTER 26 - ESCAPE

Roth drove back out the way they had come as he knew the road and wouldn't have to stop to check the map; it would also take him back south. He didn't have a plan as to where he may dump the bomb, but he figured he'd need to dump it somewhere it would never be found; perhaps into a river? If the Plutonium was discovered and the Yanks linked it back to the Dodge and then to Germany, there may be grave consequences for all. There seemed to be even more army personnel and vehicles on the roads now, and he feared that if they were looking for him that he'd probably come across road blocks soon. Then he heard it. He wasn't sure exactly what it was, but it wasn't something he'd heard before, so it could only be one thing.

He looked left and right through the windshield, scanning the skies ahead. The sound above him was like a very fast motor bike engine with a hole in its exhaust, all in a small garage, the sound echoing off the walls from within. It sounded closer now. He was concentrating on the road ahead but transfixed on trying to see the rocket, too. The sound pitch of the missile had changed slightly now, it seemed more like a long, drawn-out buzzing.

Suddenly, the sound was joined by a much more familiar one that Roth could relate to: an air raid siren. And then there it was, ahead, about one-hundred metres up in the sky. He spotted the blue flame first, and then a pencil-like object with small stubby wings. It had come from his left and swept across his front before disappearing behind the tops of buildings. But, just as suddenly as he had heard it, now it was silent. As it was designed to do, the fuel had run out and the rocket was falling to the ground.

All he could hear now was the air raid siren, warning the unsuspecting citizens of Washington to go to the shelters. *This was an air raid, but no, it couldn't be, surely this was another drill*, they would ask.

BOOOM!

The rocket had exploded. Roth estimated it had fallen to earth about two miles from him, into a residential area named Bellevue, a place he'd seen on the map that they'd studied as they drove in yesterday. As he drove on, he could see people on the streets around pointing up to the sky. It was a beautiful sunrise this morning, but that's not what they were discussing. For those who had seen the rocket they'd taken it for an American plane that had gotten into trouble and crashed, so why were the sirens still wailing?

But now there was another coming. Roth heard it, too, but couldn't make out from where. He was still heading south and concentrating on the streets, trying to make sure he was retracing the drive in. The buzzing of the second rocket seemed to be behind him, but he had no idea where or its direction. Then it also went silent, the silence a harbinger of the destruction that was about to fall on the city once again.

BOOM!

Roth couldn't tell where the second rocket had fallen, but by sheer chance this one had exploded in the congressional cemetery, just over the Anacostia River and not too far from the Capitol building. In fact, it was located near the bridge that Roth had driven over just twenty minutes or so ago as he had left Union station. It was now only a matter of time before the final rocket was heard; it appeared to Roth that the launch of the V1s had been successful and that they had reached their intended target as planned. The fact that the black bomb had not been detonated did not trouble Roth. Perhaps it was enough for the Americans to be attacked on their own soil with rockets from an unseen enemy. Perhaps that would bring them to the negotiating table to discuss peace, to stop their plans for an invasion, and to turn the attention on the Russian threat?

*

Earlier, back on-board U-2565, Neumeyer had ordered a crash dive as soon as the technicians and crew had gone below. He didn't mind admitting to himself that, after hearing the double explosion on U-2699, he had dreaded the launch from his own sub. There was, of course, no choice. He had to give the order and pray that it was successful. The fog was lifting above, he had seen patches of blue peeking through the haze as the rocket was being assembled. That would mean aircraft. Because of the proximity to the coast, they were close to the naval bases of the US Navy and would surely now become hunted like no other. He shouted out an order.

"Engines to maximum power, take her down to eighty metres-"

He was interrupted by the sonar operator. "Multiple surface contacts! Multiple directions, Captain!"

At a little over seventeen knots, Neumeyer knew he could stay ahead of most surface vessels. What he couldn't do was outrun the whole of the US Navy.

CHAPTER 27 - FJORD

The four Merlin engines of the lead Lancaster were together pushing out over seven-thousand pounds of thrust as they neared the Norwegian coastline and Sognefjord, their target. The seven crew members on board could only communicate through their headsets, the noise generated by the Merlins being so deafening. It had taken the compact attack force of the three bombers just over two hours to get here from their base in Lincolnshire, slightly less than the time it took to get to Berlin on a bomb run, and hopefully this wouldn't be anywhere near as hazardous, although everyone on the sortie knew that this was no ordinary mission; not if all the weeks of training that they'd gone through was anything to go by. She now flew straight and level at five-hundred feet over the choppy North Sea in an effort to evade enemy radar. They had also deployed their 'Chaff', a radar countermeasure, in order to help disguise their position, but one thing for sure was that her night-time all black camouflage was definitely impracticable now as the clock neared midday on this fine morning.

"How far now, navigator?" asked Squadron Leader Craig Williams as he sat in the pilot's seat of the lead Lancaster bomber. The crews on board the other two planes were a mix of nationalities; British, South African, and Australian; but all aboard this particular one were Canadian. The name of the ship, 'Canada Kayleigh', was a tribute to the captain's sister back home in Ajax, Ontario, a small town near Toronto and not too far from Niagara Falls. Unlike their American cousins, British bombers weren't usually adorned with 'nose art', as it was called, but this crew looked upon it as a lucky charm.

"Ten minutes out, Captain. When we come around the

next headland you should be able to see the inlet for the sub pen," replied 'Sinbad', the navigator. "They're jamming our 'Oboe' radar, but it's irrelevant now, skipper, we're here!"

"Roger that." The squadron leader thought back to the pre-flight briefing they'd had this morning and the order of attack. ED915/G, piloted by Lieutenant Sammy Gordon, would go in first followed by ED817/G, flown by Pilot Officer Allan Jones, and then his own, ED817/G. The Typhoon escorts were to provide covering fire as they attacked. Each Lancaster was to fly at the extremely low and dangerous altitude of sixty feet above the waters of the fjord at two-hundred miles per hour. One small error of judgement at that height and the belly of the plane could strike the waves below, causing the plane to crash and killing all on board in an instant.

The submarine pens themselves were approximately three-hundred feet across with the opening to each bay at only around thirty-five feet wide. This was the spot where they were required to pitch the ball into, just like a good off-spinner in cricket. It'd be a one in a million shot if they hit it. The bombardier would use the same targeting device that proved so successful on the Dam Buster raid. It consisted of a 'V' shaped piece of wood – each arm of the 'V' was about eighteen inches long and had a one inch long peg located at the two tips, plus an eye piece at the bottom of the 'V' for alignment. He would look through the eyepiece, align the ends of the submarine pens with the pegs, and, when they both lined up, he would release the bomb at the designated distance of four-hundred-and-twenty-five feet from the target; a simple piece of geometry, really. One of his crew had likened it to taking a penalty in football, but from fifty yards out instead of the usual twelve, and with your eyes shut.

Williams could now see multiple aircraft swirling around ahead in the distance, contrails clearly visible as the two opposing sides danced around the sky battling each other. What looked to him like an ageing Me110 was going down, thick black and grey smoke billowing from its tail. He now swung the Lancaster one-hundred degrees around to port so he would be lined up directly facing the target. He knew that a squadron of Mark IX Spitfires were tasked to keep the Luftwaffe from getting through and attacking his small force, and it appeared that it was those he could see. Looked like 'Jerry' had sent up ageing Messerschmitt 110s which were no match for the redesigned 'Spit', but what was concerning him now were the puffs of black smoke that were starting to appear over the target; flak! Clearly the Typhoons had been unable to destroy all the flak guns protecting the pens and they were still engaged in suppressing them. Both the other Lancasters were a good mile ahead of him now and making their final approaches. The spring morning had become a clear day with bright blue skies and excellent visibility; he could see Sammy's Lancaster as it swooped in for the attack.

As he lined up his own aircraft over the fjord and directly behind the other two, more and more clouds of flak began to burst all around them, most of it concentrating on the lead plane. He struggled to fly the heavy bomber lower and lower; the wind was buffeting off the surface of the fjord and forcing him to keep adjusting the aircrafts trim. He dropped down closer to the correct height, watching his speed and listening out to the calls of his bombardier through his headset as he peered ahead and watched as the first bouncing bomb was released. He averted his eyes from the scene ahead for a moment as he concentrated on keeping the lumbering beast straight and level, but fortunately the flight engineer, Pat Hughes, who was perched on the 'dicky' seat slightly behind him, was giving a running commentary.

"Bomb away! There she goes, plane banking away to port, rising, rising, bomb on course, still on course, plane still banking, flak increasing, blimey, that was close. Christ, a bloody great burst of flak hit her nose. She's still climbing, though, the bomb still tracking towards the target. Bomb speed slowing, losing momentum now, it's not going to make it! It's short, well short, bloody distance is wrong!"

Boom! The first bomb exploded in the fjord, a hundred yards or so short of the concrete bays that housed the submarines. Williams had to think and act fast so as not to waste the two remaining bombs. He flicked the switch located at the front of his oxygen mask to transmit a message to the second bomber ahead.

"Jonesy. Delay your release by four to five seconds, the first one fell way short. Do you copy?"

"Saw that, will do, skipper," came back the reply.

'Canada Kayleigh' was hurtling down the length of the fjord now, its captain balancing the throttles to keep her at the optimum speed to release the bomb. They were only thirty seconds behind 'Jonesy,' the air buzzing all around the attacking aircraft now as hundreds of machine gun rounds were fired at them by the defenders below. Long undulating lines of tracer and bullet could be seen snaking their way upwards in paths towards the Lancasters from guns mounted on top of the pens and surrounding hillsides. They were joined by multiple rounds of flak. The air was a blanket of shrapnel, all converging on them. He'd experienced flak before, but this was intense. Clearly 'Jerry' had gone a long way to defend these pens. Williams now heard his co-pilot call out again as the second bomb was released up ahead.

"Bomb away. Jonesy pulling up hard to port, looks like he's taking some hits from the flak stations, too. Where are those bloody Typhoons? Three splashes, now four from the bomb, tracking, tracking, hit, it's hit the concrete section between the pens!"

There was a bright flash of light up ahead and his next words were drowned out by the sound of the huge explosion from the four-thousand pounder. The shock wave washed over the Lancaster now as it was less than a quarter of a mile from the target. Williams thought back to the analogy of taking a penalty; they'd hit the post with that shot and now it was their turn with the final run.

The air in front of the pens was peppered now with bursts of flak. To Williams it felt like he was driving through a hailstorm, and now the German gunners had had the two previous aircraft to get their aim sorted out; this final bomber was about to be firmly in their sights. Without warning, a flak burst exploded directly on the inboard port engine and two propeller blades sheared off, flying backwards and over the wing. The engine itself burst into flames, and, for a moment, Williams struggled to bring the stricken bomber under control whilst the flight engineer throttled back the power on the engine and pressed the internal fire extinguisher to douse the flames. The engine was out of action now, but Williams knew that the Lanc was more than capable of continuing on only three engines; they had been known to fly on one, but he certainly didn't want to try out that option if he could help it.

During many previous sorties over Germany with bomber command, he'd experienced lots of flak while over the targets; the shrapnel that hit the structure of the Lancs usually didn't cause much damage unless it was a direct hit like they'd just experienced. Planes had been known to return back from a sortie with hundreds of 'flak' holes in them and still landed safely; it was the crew on board that suffered the most from the white-hot shards of metal that showered them, often resulting in serious injury or death. Fighters with their 20mm cannon and 7.92mm machine guns could punch huge holes in the planes and send them crashing down – they were the far greater threat.

The plane rose all of a sudden, and then it banked to port as the balance of engines was thrown out in favour of the starboard side. Williams used his experience to get the plane back on track. He trimmed the throttles, and, with sheer strength, wrestled with the control column as the twenty-seven ton beast tried to swerve away. They had to get back down to the required level, the bombardier was shouting out that he was close to releasing the bomb.

"Steady, steady. Starboard slightly. Starboard. Steady, hold it there, hold it," the bombardier called out.

Machine gun rounds began raining down on the Lancaster, the Perspex window above William's evidence to it as a dozen holes suddenly appeared there. Tiny fragments of the Perspex canopy rained down on them. The rounds themselves had safely exited above their heads and out through the thin metal skin of the bomber.

"Bomb away," came the call from just below where the bombardier was perched in the nose. Williams pushed the three remaining engine throttles forward to the max and began a sharp turn to port and upwards.

The fire to his left on the wing and engine had abated for now, but he watched as more lines of tracer arced its way up from the ground below and whistled past his window yet again. He couldn't watch how the bomb had fared and so this time was relying on his tail gunner to give them an update. The roar of the three remaining Merlins could not drown out the thunderous explosion that erupted from down below the climbing aircraft. Williams' headset was suddenly filled with a shriek of joy from the rear gunner.

"Bull's eye, right down the middle, we got it, skipper! The whole bloody things gone up like a roman candle, huge explosion came out through the front, too!"

Williams and the other pilots had been told to climb away extremely quickly after releasing the bombs at the briefing, as it was expected that, if successful, the bomb would reach the far end of the pen, and, when detonated, it would create a funnel effect inside, compressing the explosion and enhancing the effects of the Torpex by a factor of three and ultimately destroying the complex completely.

The Spitfire escort had successfully seen off the eight or so enemy fighters that had tried in vain to defend the complex below, and so were now lining up and getting on station at three-thousand feet above and behind the retreating Lancasters. The Typhoons had also broken off their engagement, the task of attacking the flak positions no longer a priority. Williams was reaching to flick the transmit button on his facemask again when the distinctive Australian accent of Jonesy came through the headset.

"Got three dead here, skip. We took a beating as we pulled up. Flak burst hit the cockpit. Killed Taffy, took half his head off. He's lying here now. I'm covered in his blood and brains, and I've been hit in the right arm, can't move it much." Williams could tell by the tone in his voice that Jonesy was emotional as he sat there next to his dead flight engineer and friend. "Mitchell and Gannon bought it, too, in the rear, whole bloody planes riddled with holes back there apparently, somethings not right with the starboard trim. Baker says he can see the ailerons shot to pieces. She's a pig to fly now, but we'll make it." It sounded like he was fighting back tears as he finished off.

Williams called back. He was horrified to learn of the casualties but had to reassure his comrade at the same time.

"Okay, Jonesy, I hear you. It's clear that you need help in the cockpit. Get Baker to leave his position and give you a hand. Ask him to lay Taffy down on the floor behind the seats and tell him to sit next to you. He can take the weight of the aircraft when you come into land, that'll help with your arm. You can still fly it, right?"

The twenty-two year old Jonesy took a moment or two to reply. He was now struggling to stem the flow of the tears and to make himself heard from the shattered remains of the Lancaster's cockpit. The wind was howling around inside as it rushed through the shattered Perspex remnants of the cowling.

"I can do it, sir, with Baker's help. We'll get back. Over and out."

The line went dead. Williams didn't reply, unsure as to just what to say. He checked his altimeter. They had reached eight thousand feet as he made for home. All of the Lancs had taken a beating, his own aircraft was full of holes of different sizes and in a multitude of places, but beside a few minor injuries sustained from the heavy flak, his crew were unscathed. The loss of only three men, considering how dangerous the mission was, would, in some quarters, be seen as a good result, to them it was a success. But he knew that the eighteen airmen who were heading back to Scampton with him now wouldn't see it that way.

CHAPTER 28 - DISPOSAL

Roth had been driving for over two hours now but had been unable to find a quiet location to dump the bomb. Each time he thought he'd found somewhere he dismissed it as unsuitable for a multitude of reasons. He was still on Route 5 heading south, and at the back of his mind was: should he ditch the car? He was aware that if anyone had seen him leave the Union station car park and made a connection to the Dodge that it may become a problem.

Then he spotted what might be useful. The road had been more or less empty now, seeing as he was a good distance from the capital, and up ahead was a bridge, and a river ran beneath the road he was on. He slowed down and eased the truck off the road and up to a gate. The road was lined all along on both sides with a barbed wire fence, and this gate would give him access to the river below. He pushed open the gate, looked around for anyone, and then carefully backed the car down the gentle incline that was the riverbank.

The river itself wasn't fast flowing but it did appear deep, which suited his cause. He backed up as close as he dared, applied the handbrake, and switched off the engine. After opening the trunk, he was about to pick up the bomb when he stopped; he realised his shirt was awash with blood. Blood that had sprayed there from the stricken Fuchs, plus some of his own from his bloody nose. He took off his jacket and then, without undoing the buttons, he pulled the bloodied shirt off and over his head before reaching into his duffel bag on the front seat and grabbing a fresh shirt.

He went down to the water's edge, squatted down, and grabbed handfuls of the ice-cold water. He began to scrub the blood from his face and hands before pulling on the clean shirt. Now he felt a little refreshed, and so he went back to the car and removed the bomb from the trunk. He closed the trunk and walked towards the river once more. He'd come halfway across the world, had nearly been killed three times, and for what? He was separated from his boat, his men, and now his country. He gazed at the box he held in his two hands, shook his head in dismay, and, with arms outstretched, he turned his upper body and was about to launch it as far as he could into the river – but he didn't. All it would have taken would be to throw it now and with a splash it would be gone, sunk without trace to the bottom, but something held him back from doing so.

He knew that this way was the simplest of solutions to his problem, but what was inside the box was still deadly to anyone who may come into contact with it. The radioactive Plutonium poison that would eventually leak out would contaminate all the river's wildlife, and probably the drinking water, for miles downstream. This was not the way to dispose of the bomb. Roth looked down at the metal box he held in his hands, so innocent looking yet deadly beyond comprehension. He stood there by the river for another couple of minutes, thinking, before retracing his steps back to the car.

As he stood next to the open car door, he glanced back to where the box would have disappeared into the cold waters below. He thought about how easy it would have been to get rid of the problem there. He'd done the right thing by not disposing of it in the river, plus the much bigger issue of stopping Fuchs from detonating it in the first place.

A black bomb, detonated in the American capital? Then, American atomic bombs falling on Germany in retaliation? Atomic bombs used in warfare by any nation was a future he didn't want to accept. But now what was really troubling him was just how far away were Germany from dropping one of their own?

Thirty minutes later, Roth could see the outlying buildings of a moderately-sized town up ahead. There were only one or two folks around that he could see as he drove at a leisurely pace down the main street. It was still too early for most folks to be up on a Sunday morning. Roth exited the town and began to speed up a little more. He'd been driving for around another thirty minutes now and there were fewer and fewer buildings to be seen as he drove further from the city and deeper into the countryside. The prospect of being discovered now was slim, but he could feel another panic attack rising from within. He hadn't experienced any in all these last seven days or so, but his paranoia was getting the best of him; where could he leave the bomb?

But then his prayers were finally answered. The road ahead was about to cross over another bridge and yet another river, only this time the bridge was under construction. In fact, it was being reinforced with brand new concrete pillars to shore it up. He slowed the Buick down and pulled off the road before parking up by the front of the bridge and near a temporary wooden fence that had a 'keep out' construction sign nailed to it.

Because it was a Sunday, there were no workmen here today: perfect. He quickly opened the trunk and removed the bomb before closing the lid back down. He could see the opening down below where a new concrete pillar was due to be poured, so he carefully scrambled down the banking that led to the river's edge and walked up to the hole. At the bottom of the three-metre opening he could see a bed of gravel and hundreds of loose stones, each one measuring around fifty millimetres or so, along with the reinforced steel cage that would strengthen the concrete once it was poured in. He stepped down carefully now and eased himself into the hole along with the box, placing it down next to his feet and onto the gravel. He bent down and scraped back the gravel with his bare hands to reveal a hole for the box, about thirty centimetres deep. After placing the box in the hole, he pushed back some of the ballast over the top of the box. Satisfied that it was well hidden, he climbed back out and walked over to the car.

Ten minutes later and back on the open road he spotted a dilapidated and isolated barn up ahead. Its blue paint was bleached almost white on its southern side, and on another many of the wooden sidings that made up its construction had fallen off and were missing. It appeared deserted, so he slowly parked the car off the road and behind it. He was still having doubts over his action of placing the bomb in the hole for the bridge pillar. He reasoned with himself that it would be covered in concrete within a day or so, buried for one-hundred or more years, hopefully, before another bridge eventually took its place. It would be safe from discovery and encased in concrete. It would be of no harm to anyone, right?

He sat there and contemplated what to do next. It didn't make any sense to go through with the plan to get to the Mexican border. Besides, if he did make it to Argentina without Fuchs, questions would be asked as to why he was alone, and about why the bomb hadn't gone off as planned in Washington. No, his best chance now was to head back to Carolina, a place he knew, and to try to get to a port. He couldn't go anywhere near the town where he'd been raised in case he was recognized. No, he'd make for Wilmington. It was a large seaport with lots of merchant shipping leaving there, for many locations. If he acted the part well enough, together with his new fake identity papers, passport, and a plausible story of a sailor who was looking for a working passage on a ship, he could hopefully get aboard a ship heading for Europe, maybe to a neutral country like Spain from where he could get back to France. Back to France, and perhaps Ginette.

It would take Roth a good few hours to drive down to the Carolina coast, but he still couldn't shake off the paranoia that was once more trying to get a hold of him. Perhaps the Buick had been spotted back in Washington, in the town, or even near the bridge. Should he ditch it? Something else was troubling him; it was concerning Fuchs and the bomb.

When Fuchs had dismantled the bomb and swapped it all over from the first truck to the second, surely he couldn't have missed the fact that there was no timing device fitted. Yet, with that in mind, he would still have carried out the detonation with the full knowledge that he would be killed instantly, Roth alongside him. The SS major would have pressed the switch, sacrificing himself for the mission, the Reich, and the Fatherland.

Finally, Roth came to a decision. He grabbed what he needed from the duffel, threw those few items into the holdall, stuffed the money that Fuchs had given him earlier into his jean pockets, and made sure he had a canteen of water, too. And then, he started walking away.

EPILOGUE

Fred Dunne reached for one of the three stacks of newspapers which had been tossed up against his newspaper stand on the corner of East 42nd Street and Park Avenue; a prime location for him to catch commuters on their way into Grand Central Station just across the road. It would be a while or so before the sun appeared over the skyscrapers towering above him on this chilly start to Saturday the twenty-fifth of March, 1944.

He glanced at his watch; it had just gone six a.m. The morning rush would get under way soon. He picked up the first bundle, tossed it onto the open countertop of his newspaper stand, and cut the string of the bundle with his pen knife. He took off the top copy of the *New York Times* and glanced at the headlines. It said that the allies had made more advances in Italy, and the Russians were advancing towards Berlin. A large map of the area around Rome stood out, too, but he could see nothing yet about the second front he'd heard was coming. He was about to put the paper back when he heard a voice from behind.

"I'll take that, please."

He turned around to see a tall guy dressed in a dark suit, matching grey overcoat, and a trilby hat. His right hand was outstretched. Behind him there was another man, similarly dressed with a small brown leather suitcase on the sidewalk beside him. He wasn't as tall as his companion, but he too had a presence about him. *Perhaps military*, thought Fred, *off on leave?* A wisp of blonde hair was peeking out from beneath his hat, the wind off the East River blowing it across his eyes. The first guy struck Fred as quite imposing as he towered over his own small stature. The stranger was over six feet, easy, and nearly as wide. Although he was giving Fred a wide smile from a chiselled jawline, it came across as forced and for a moment he felt uneasy.

"Yea, sure thing, fella," replied Fred, passing it to him. He was about to say something else, banal chatter about the war or the Yankees, but he didn't.

The guy passed him a fresh dollar bill for the three cent newspaper, telling him to keep the change, his Chicago accent very distinct. He turned and walked over to his companion. Fred stared at the money in his hand, wondered what didn't add up about these guys, but then a regular customer broke his concentration as he picked up another copy from the pile and left three cents on the counter.

"Morning, Freddy," he said as he strode away.

Fred didn't acknowledge the greeting; his attention was on the two strangers who had now walked a short distance from the newsstand. They were talking to each other, but too far away for him to hear what they were saying.

The first guy gave the newspaper to his companion and spoke.

"Let's go over the plan."

"I walk in slowly and find a bench near the entrance to the platforms, sit down, and slide the suitcase under the bench, flicking the switch as I do so. I've then got fifteen minutes before the timer activates the pump to disperse the agent. I start to read my paper, trying to look like just another commuter, but at the same time scan the area to see if anyone is watching me for any reason. And, when I feel the time is right, I walk away, hopefully within five minutes. I will then join you by the entrance," he replied.

"Good, I'll see you presently." And, with that, the second guy picked up the suitcase, tucked the paper under his arm, and walked towards the entrance, his companion beside him.

Ten minutes later Fred was serving a customer across the street from the station when his eye was caught by the two men he'd seen earlier, who were coming back out, which struck him as odd, for some reason. If he'd thought for a moment more, he'd have realised that there was no longer a suitcase.

It was still there, where it had been left, emitting the odourless and invisible mist from within from the exact moment the switch had been thrown, as designed.

The two men strolled casually along, heading in the direction of Penn Street station, just a twenty-minutes' walk away. The tickets for the train ride to Florida had already been purchased.

"It will be a relief to get back home, Obersturmführer," whispered the smaller man, "but I don't fully understand what our actions can achieve here?"

"Yes, we will soon be on our way. Away from this Dante's inferno. Within a week there will be an epidemic that will start to spread across the continent, as it did with the Spanish Flu outbreak back in 1918. Back then it originated in army camps in the Midwest and was eventually brought to Europe by soldiers sent over to fight on the western front. But, our strain is not Spanish Flu. This is a strain of the plague, made twice as infectious and deadlier than the first by our scientists. And, if I remember correctly from history, it was a fleet of ships that brought the original strain across the Black Sea from Asia to Europe in the 1300's, hence the name 'Black Plague'. Now with Germany's own strike on American soil, just like our Japanese allies attack at Pearl Harbour, we too will also become synonymous in history, my friend.

"It's hard to imagine that a few short weeks ago we stood together, side by side with the Reichsführer in the

283

laboratory, overseeing the work of Professor Klein. Himmler's vision to orchestrate this attack on America will make him a paragon of the highest standard within the history of the Third Reich. In just a few days we shall be on board a U-boat taking us back home. I just hope that U-931 is a more comfortable boat than the one that brought us here."

*

The diesel fuel was almost gone on the submarine, no life left in the batteries, and the shoreline was tantalisingly close, huge white capped rollers were crashing in from the Atlantic. The boat was drifting slightly to port as the tide wrestled with it. Schmitt had ordered the life rafts to be brought out onto the deck; they would be needed soon for when they had to abandon the boat and make for shore. The hidden suitcase of explosives in the torpedo room had long since been dealt with.

Once the last of the crew were safely off, Schmitt would activate the timed detonators on the scuttling explosives below. As he stood on the conning tower, he gazed up to the heavens. The skies were clear, and it looked like a fine start to this new day. The sun was just beginning to rise, and he could already feel its warmth on his back as he looked to the tops of the Argentinian hills on the horizon to his west.

About The Author

Ian Thomas Gwilliams, originally from Liverpool, England, has been married to his wife Jane for thirty-nine years and they have two grown up children. Ian's a retired blue-collar worker and served an apprenticeship at Rolls-Royce Motors Crewe, where he was lucky to be involved in building bespoke motor cars for the British Royal family and also armoured limousines for foreign dignitaries. After twenty years of service, he then went to live and work in Canada for a short while before returning to England and starting a career in the aerospace industry, before finally retiring in 2019.

Ian's hobbies include golf, lots of reading, walking, cycling, and model making, plus a fascination with all things concerning World War II historical facts. His favourite authors include Damien Lewis, Stephen E. Ambrose, and James Holland. His influences for writing also include classic WWII films like *The Longest Day*, *A Bridge Too Far* and *Saving Private Ryan*, plus the *Band of Brothers* TV series. After visiting the battlefields and cemeteries of the D-Day landings in Normandy and following the route of The Battle of the Bulge through Belgium, Ian was inspired to write his debut novel, *U-boat 931, Attack on America*, which was completed during the lockdown periods of the covid pandemic. All the facts, weapons, and timeline contained within the story were painstakingly researched and the actions described could have actually taken place during the period of the conflict. The narrative is a good old-fashioned action and adventure tale, full of heroes and villains.

Follow me on Twitter: @gwilliams_ian

Coming soon: *U-Boat 931, Attack on Germany*.

www.blossomspringpublishing.com

Printed in Great Britain
by Amazon